HEAD HU

Michel Crespy is professor of sociology at the University of Montpellier. *Head Hunters* won the Grand Prix de littérature policière on its publication in France.

Michel Crespy

HEAD HUNTERS

TRANSLATED FROM THE FRENCH BY
John Brownjohn

VINTAGE

Published by Vintage 2003

2 4 6 8 10 9 7 5 3 1

Copyright © Michel Crespy 2000 and © Éditions Denoël 2000
English tranlation copyright © John Brownjohn 2002

First published by
Éditions Denoël in 2000

First published in Great Britain in 2002 by
The Harvill Press

Vintage
Random House, 20 Vauxhall Bridge Road,
London SW1V 2SA

Random House Australia (Pty) Limited
20 Alfred Street, Milsons Point, Sydney
New South Wales 2061, Australia

Random House New Zealand Limited
18 Poland Road, Glenfield,
Auckland 10, New Zealand

Random House (Pty) Limited
Endulini, 5A Jubilee Road, Parktown 2193,
South Africa

The Random House Group Limited Reg. No. 954009
www.randomhouse.co.uk

A CIP catalogue record for this book
is available from the British Library

ISBN 0 099 44978 1

Printed and bound in Denmark by
Nørhaven Paperback, Viborg

HEAD HUNTERS

The fir trees slope gently down to the lake. Sky and water meet somewhere on the horizon, each as flat and grey as the other, with soft green foliage languishing between them like an eiderdown. Eiderdown . . . Must be the influence of those associative techniques they used so often during the preliminary tests. I could drop, I'm so sleepy.

They'll be back before long. The great, empty silence of these wild surroundings will be punctured by degrees. First by the subdued hum of engines on the lake. Then, perhaps, by the rhythmical throb of a helicopter's rotor blades. And finally, when they come ashore, by voices: distant to begin with, then nearer and accompanied by the tramp of feet. Seven or eight centuries ago, when a deer took refuge in the depths of these woods to escape the huntsmen, chest heaving with every laboured breath, it must have felt fear, keenly alert to the slightest sound. My sole emotion is glum indifference.

I have nothing in common with that deer save the hounds at my heels and my own stupidity – my crass stupidity, I have to admit. They conned me. It was all my fault, I didn't have the sense to flee before the hunt began. They knew from the outset how the whole thing would end. They brought us to this pass willy-nilly. We had no way out. When I pointed the gun at Charriac I gave him no time to explain that it was all a misunderstanding. I find it immensely comforting to reflect that he departed this life without an opportunity to repent of his many sins, the first and gravest of them being that he was what he was. The certainty that he'll pay for those sins would give me exquisite satisfaction. If there were a God, on the other hand, things would never have gone this far.

Nothing yet. Not a sound. It doesn't matter much what I do now, not any more. I find it hard to contemplate the future, dwell too much on the immediate past. If they'd left the door open, even a crack, would I have seized the chance? I should have thought of that earlier. It was all strictly logical. An insufficiently in-depth analysis of future developments, that's my tragedy. Charriac had a point.

In the beginning, though, only the devil himself would have spotted the trap. We were lured into it in a thoroughly innocuous way, some of us by small ads in professional journals, others via government offices, most by phone calls at home.

I myself received a call from one of those secretaries whose drawling, air-hostessy voices proclaim their membership of some big Parisian firm. She wanted to know if I was still "available", and if I might be prevailed on to consider a potential proposition. She might as well have asked some explorer lost in the desert if he would be interested in a map and a water bottle, I thought with a smile. If so, she went on, could I give her my e-mail address? E-mails are a love of mine. I prefer them to communicating by word of mouth. You have time to reread them, to scrutinize every word, to weigh shades of meaning and study the phrasing of a reply. When talking on the phone you involuntarily transmit undesirable elements of communication – intonations, inflections, accents, tones of voice – which indiscreetly convey information about the speaker: age, background, social class, state of mind. E-mails confine themselves to pure meaning. They're devoid of parasitical adjuncts, devoid of anything you haven't expressly wanted to say. In an e-mail you aren't what you are; you're what you want to be and show yourself to be. If nothing but e-mails had passed between us, I wouldn't now be fighting off cold and sleep under the bristly branches of an impassive fir tree.

I'd insisted on keeping up my Internet subscription in defiance of my wife, who pleaded with me to make economies. Oh, not a Web site complete with family photos and the name of my dog, just an address, cold and professional. That was how, one hour later, I received a message whose every word I still recall. I wish I could forget it today, but important matters automatically imprint themselves on your cerebral hard disk, and it's impossible to reformat it. Impossible, that's to say, except in the drastic way they're planning to reformat mine this morning.

We have been instructed by a number of European companies to recruit senior executive personnel. Your profile may well be of interest to us. Would you get in touch?

De Wavre International

There followed the usual trilogy: phone, fax, e-mail address. No polite form of words, neither at the beginning nor at the end, just an e-mail as it should be. De Wavre was a name from the north of France, from Flanders or Belgium. It sounded like an iron and steel firm converted into a service industry with the aid of EU loans.

I had been on stand-by for two months. No, why should I go on using their civilized euphemisms when they're looking for me with lethal intent? I wasn't on stand-by, serenely waiting for the next flight with an airline ticket in my pocket. I was unemployed – I'd been slung out on my neck. My company's share price had not been rising fast enough to suit certain US pension fund managers, so the top brass had decided to downsize. I didn't hold it against them: someone had to go, them or us, and I would certainly have done the same thing.

Two months' unpaid leave seems trivial when you've accumulated

4

a big enough cushion, but no cushion can withstand the prospect of several years without pay. That's the main problem with inactivity: you don't know when it will end. Or *if* it will end. You start by calling one or two people who made you offers, or merely hinted at openings, in the days when you still had a job. But now, oddly enough, they've suddenly lost all interest in you. At first, being ignorant of your tribulations, they accept your calls. Then word gets around and you can't negotiate the secretarial roadblock. That's when you realize you've got the plague. You used to be a hotly contested property in great demand – one that people were always striving to poach. Now, just because you've ceased to belong to anyone, you've become a person to be *helped*. This is an age in which freedom is on everyone's lips, but which, when you announce that you're free, spurns you like a dead fly in a bowl of soup.

You reject the first job offer with amused disdain. What, half my previous salary, you can't be serious! You don't get a second, worse luck. The phone stops ringing and you start to look around. No longer waiting for the next flight on stand-by in a comfortable departure lounge, you wonder how to sneak on to the runway and secrete yourself in a baggage hold. Air Cameroun or Air Sri-Lanka, anything would do. You read the small ads and realize how unsuited you are to any job at all: air-conditioning technician, pastry-cook, roofer, experienced shoe salesman. You get together with government employment advisers who avoid your eye and explain that the economic climate is difficult, that the market is sluggish, that you're overqualified, too old, too pricey.

However, they say as they see you out, all smiles, they're not worried about you. You have a reputation, a network of connections. Just think, most people don't even have those. You're a victim of "frictional" unemployment, the kind of person who lands another job in no time. You aren't an over-50 or a youngster with no professional experience. *They* are ab-so-lute-ly impossible to place.

Your wife consoles you, too. She consults a fortune-teller who sees new and highly remunerative opportunities on the horizon – not forgetting to pocket a little of your future wealth right away. You feel like a cancer sufferer who has been optimistically informed that no new metastases can be detected – at present.

And then, one fine morning, De Wavre International shows up. You've never heard of them, but there are many things you've never heard of that now form part of your daily round. You gauge your response precisely, taking care not to summon up the image of a gazelle being eyed by a lion, and obtain an interview with a very well-dressed woman who would be genuinely pretty if she removed her heavy horn-rimmed glasses.

"Well," she says, "we're a headhunting agency, but our concept is somewhat different. It entails a reversal of input and output. Instead of responding to a request, we ruthlessly select the very best and undertake to offer them to firms with development projects in the pipeline."

"Like a model agency, you mean?"

She smiled. Her lips widened, but her teeth remained invisible.

"I'd prefer to compare us to an impresario or a talent scout for a football club. We guarantee the people on our books. If they were no good, it would mean *we* were no good. We can't afford that, and the bosses know it. We approach them, not the other way round, and we offer them nothing but the crème de la crème. We pick out a nugget and put it on the market. Those who survive our screening process are a hundred per cent reliable. Above all, we know exactly where to place them and in what capacity. I don't say we'll sell you – no, but we'll see if you have what it takes to be saleable. That's the challenge. If you pass muster, we'll place you within months. If not, thank you and goodbye."

"And who pays you?"

"The firm in question. You pay nothing, not a cent. The firm finances the transfer in return for a full guarantee. We take care of everything else, inclusive of food and accommodation during the tests. Our bet is that out of 15 or 20 preselected candidates we'll find four or five we can sell – four or five who'll repay us handsomely. But watch out: you'll be put through the mill, and it won't necessarily be much fun. At worst, you'll know exactly what you're worth. For free."

I asked where the test was held and what form it took.

"Well, to start with there's a questionnaire to complete. It's quite long, because we want as many details as possible. These days everyone knows how to word a job application and draft a flattering CV. That isn't what we're after. We insist on total candour. Deliberate lies are the only grounds for disqualification. If you conceal something – anything – and we spot it, all bets are off: we stop right there. We get our experts to handle this preliminary screening process. It eliminates roughly half the original applicants. If you pass, there's a minor medical examination and an interview. The one-third of applicants that remain are invited to attend a one-week seminar. And that's it."

"In the end, if I've understood you correctly, all that's left is a third of a third. Ten per cent or so."

She gave me another of her robotic smiles.

"I congratulate you on your mental arithmetic. Yes, more or less."

"So the crème de la crème amount to ten per cent of the total?"

"No, less than that. We don't pick up everyone lying around in the job market, far from it. We keep our ears to the ground. When collective or even individual redundancies crop up, we make inquiries. Firms sometimes fire good people, either because they can't afford them, or, more often, because the boss himself is useless.

Or they engage in wholesale downsizing and discard the baby with the bathwater. We retain, let's say, one in every ten of the files we examine. We're pretty well-informed about you, that's why we've made you this proposal."

From one angle this was reassuring – indeed, rather flattering. I was already among the ten per cent of "good people" and had a chance of being in the one per cent. How could I resist?

I didn't resist. The risks seemed non-existent (ironical to recall that this morning!) and it promised to be an amusing experience. At worst I was dealing with a bunch of charlatans – pretentious, over-paid, sucker-impressing "experts" – and could pull out at a moment's notice. To set my mind at rest I asked if De Wavre could produce some references, or if this was an entirely novel concept – one way of insinuating that they might be amateurs embarking on a scheme whose results were far from guaranteed. The woman smiled for the third time.

"That's quite in order. Prudent of you, too. It's a point in your favour, and I won't forget to mention it. My notes on this prelimi-nary interview will also go down in your file, of course. You see? I'm being absolutely straight with you. One moment . . ."

Opening a drawer in her desk, she took out a thick folder and handed it to me. It contained enthusiastic letters of appreciation from some of the biggest French and European companies signed by people in very senior positions. Several of them – those who wouldn't accept my phone calls – I knew by name. I looked at the little letters in the top left corner that served to record the mailing details. Not everyone knows this, but they're an excellent guide to the seniority of your correspondent. For instance, "AD/BG 99/124" signifies that the letter has been dictated by someone whose initials are AD and typed by someone whose initials are BG, and that it is the 124th such communication mailed in 1999. If the initials of the signatory are also AD, he dictated it himself. If the initials are, let's say, JH, it means that the letter has been drafted by a relatively junior associate, a subordinate entrusted with an unimportant formality, and that the person responsible has confined himself to signing it – usually without reading or even seeing it – with the aid of a signature machine operated by his secretary. In this case all the initials matched, so De Wavre dealt on equal terms with the masters of the country, the most powerful bosses in post-industrial society. It was just possible that the whole thing was a hoax, of course, but if so I couldn't see the point of it. All they required of me was to tell them everything about myself, and I had no money anyone could have designs on.

We fixed another appointment for the following week. I jotted this down in my diary in the woman's presence. If I'd simply made a mental note of it, she would have inferred – rightly so – that I had nothing better to do. To make a good impression, an unemployed person (sorry, a senior executive on stand-by) should have a diary so full that he needs to check it to see if he has time to consider an offer of employment. I had already begun to watch my step! A job interview resembles a lover's first assignation. Not too much after-shave and no ostentatious wad of banknotes when settling the bill, just a gold card and some half-truths and half-lies leading up to the punchline: "How about a nightcap at my place?" – *not*: "Let's go to bed together." Similarly: "Your particulars will be carefully examined." – *not*: "I'm going to throw back my head and roar with laughter when you've gone." That's what is known as civilization.

Right now, with my back propped against a fir tree and a rifle across my thighs, I'm coming to regret the fact.

The forms I had to complete were handed me by an extremely nice young man. I had seldom seen a face so open, smiling and dynamic, so intelligent and eager to please. All we exchanged were a few commonplace remarks, but they sufficed to modify my state of mind. I had gone back to De Wavre's feeling tense and wary. Now, seated alone at a table, I had suddenly become optimistic and determined to cooperate. If they selected all their staff in the image of that young man, their methods must be most effective.

The questionnaire was extraordinarily long and detailed, as predicted. It scanned the whole of my life in the traditional, chronological order. No indiscreet questions, no subjective impressions or moral judgements: facts, just facts. I had first to give an account of the professional careers and domestic circumstances of my parents and even my grandparents, then supply some information about my brothers and sisters. By dissecting my family background I suppose they were trying to gain an indirect idea of the problems I might have encountered: the relative ease or difficulty with which I had identified with my father, the events in childhood that might have left a mark on me and would sooner or later affect the decisions I made.

Next, they turned to my education. Where, why, with whom, and a list of the people I had known. This part of the questionnaire must have been specially aimed at graduates of the prestigious Grandes Écoles, who were known to be recruited on the strength of their address books. There was no point in employing an alumnus of the École Nationale d'Administration, or college for senior civil servants, unless he consorted with other so-called *énarques* and could, by means of a few well-placed phone calls, swiftly resolve an awkward situation and blaze a trail through the government jungle. Only one or two questions seemed a trifle odd: I was asked, for example, what historical events had made a lasting impression on me and why. I mentioned D-Day and the first moon landing, neither of which struck me as particularly compromising.

I then had to present an account of my professional career, giving details of any references, and briefly describe the firms I had worked for, their strengths and shortcomings. Industrial espionage was only a collateral bonus stemming from these questions. My interrogators wanted to assess the factors I considered important when assessing myself.

By this time, all the empathy generated by the young man's welcome had evaporated: I studied every question, wondering why it had been put there and what it was expected to yield. Faithful to my undertaking, I never misrepresented the truth, but it is common knowledge that several different truths can exist concurrently. I didn't ask myself what would be the right answer in general, but which would be the best of the answers I could provide without betraying what I was.

Although I had been given no deadline, I guessed that the time factor wasn't unimportant. Slow-wittedness is one of the things abhorred by all employers. My mind works fast, fortunately, so I had no worries on that score.

Two-thirds of the way through my paperwork the young man

reappeared and offered me some coffee. I declined with a smile. It could have been a friendly gesture on his part, or another test. Nobody likes to pay someone 200 francs an hour and see him spend that hour discussing football beside a percolator. That was the moment when I started to topple over into paranoia. I got the feeling that nothing here was free or devoid of some specific purpose – that every word, every gesture, was a trap in itself, a riddle to be solved. In normal life there are separate spheres: remarks of which some are anodyne and others crucial, times to relax and times to re-enter the fray, the stage and the wings. With De Wavre, everything might have some hidden meaning. Possibly. Or possibly not. When a Pavlovian dog ceases to distinguish between a rewarding square and a punishing circle, it goes mad. That was what they were turning me into.

But I was desperately in need of a job. I couldn't let myself be eliminated for answering white instead of black when they showed me grey.

I tried to cool it once the young man had gone. I was what I was. If they liked it, so much the better; if not, too bad. De Wavre weren't the only fish in the sea. If I failed, I would get another chance elsewhere. I realized at the same time that this wasn't true: all employers looked for the same thing, and if De Wavre slammed the door in my face no one else would open another. It would simply be easier and quicker this way. Our whole social structure is founded on the same principle: you stake your future on a single day – three or four days at most. On that day, a handful of people who know nothing about you get ten minutes to form an idea of your abilities and character. De Wavre took much longer. That should have reassured me. On the other hand, the longer you take the deeper you dig, and the deeper you dig the more you unearth. I shook myself. Come on, I had nothing to hide. On the contrary, I was good and I would show them so. I set to work again.

The next section concerned my working habits, the facilities I required and knew how to use (Internet, spreadsheets, word-processing), and the qualities I expected in a secretary or assistant. After that came my way of life: how many hours a night I slept, if I engaged in sports, if I was a smoker (a disqualification for US firms), and – of course – my hobbies. I've never fathomed why people insist on mentioning these in their CVs, as if an employee fond of figure skating were more likely to appeal than a basketball fan. Only a few leisure activities are revealing, for instance golf, which is indicative of social category, or stamp collecting, which denotes a finicky and unadventurous temperament. The rest don't matter. Fanatical trekkers through the mountains may be tough and persevering, but their craze may render them useless for six months a year. De Wavre prudently inquired how many hours a week I devoted to my hobbies – not enough, in my opinion.

Thereafter the questionnaire turned to my lifestyle. It wanted to know the make of my car and my computer, and if my home was mortgaged – in other words, more or less what a bank manager would normally ask. This section presented me with no problems. They simply wanted to be able to gauge my salary by reconstructing my family budget – to discover if I had any expensive tastes or crushing debts that might prompt me to do something rash and regrettable.

There followed some questions about my wife and children: age, education, any known physical or mental disabilities, any ongoing medical treatment. That was all. Not a word about my sexual habits, of course. The questionnaire was subsequently processed by computer, I suppose, and the data protection act is something of a stickler on that point.

Last of all came a catch-all section: what languages I spoke, what countries I had visited, my favourite places, six items clearly lifted from the Marcel Proust questionnaire (the things that scared me, the attitudes I hated most, etc.), and a volley of multiple choice questions relating to situations in everyday life. Vaguely based on psychological profiling tests too hackneyed to merit copying, this section was as woolly, subjective and devoid of rigour as all the others had been precise. I carefully reread these final puerilities, which resembled one of those ridiculous silly-season quizzes published by newspapers and filled in by holiday-makers lazing on the beach. I had no need to distort my answers; every time I amused myself by completing one of those things, my total score put me in the average category: neither irascible nor apathetic, neither philandering nor faithful, neither emotional nor phlegmatic. I stopped doing them the day I idly borrowed one of my wife's magazines and discovered to my amazement, on turning the page, that I was neither clitoral nor vaginal but a little of each.

The whole exercise terminated in a blank page reserved for any comments the candidate might care to add. This was a crude trap, and I took care to steer clear of it. Second thoughts are no more appreciated by headhunters than interminable justifications of a blunder already committed. Firms expect you to do things, not explain why you failed to do them.

I was especially careful with my handwriting, of course. Although in-depth graphology is less and less often used these days, some of its basic elements, for instance exaggerated descenders and letters sloping in opposite directions, are too well-known to be ignored.

In other respects, the paper was a cross between an exceptionally detailed CV, a consumers association questionnaire, and a private eye's report, seasoned with fragments of projective tests and hypothetical scenarios. In short, nothing very original. The secret of the sauce, as ever, had to consist in balancing the various ingredients.

I was just rereading my copy, more to preserve a recollection of it than to correct it, when the nice young man reappeared. He congratulated me on having finished – it would, he said, enable him to go to lunch early – and fixed the time of my medical examination that afternoon.

I lunched at a local snack bar. Salad and mineral water only. I wasn't expecting a blood test – they hadn't asked me to turn up on an empty stomach – but one never knew.

The doctor was an another of De Wavre's in-house employees based on the premises. This was rather a good thing. You were usually sent to a laboratory, which charged you, or to an industrial practice.

A young man with rimless glasses and strawberry marks, the medic was neither cordial nor chilly, just professional. He kept me for a good hour. While he was examining me, I worked out some little sums in my head. Assuming he examined five candidates a day and devoted the rest of his time to writing reports, that made roughly a hundred a month. If De Wavre eliminated half of these, they must retain 50 for their famous seminars. Four seminars a month would yield ten to fifteen successful candidates. Their organization must employ a staff of eight or ten: the receptionist, the doctor, the enthusiastic young man, a computer expert, an office manager, at least two course organizers, and one or two others hidden somewhere in the beast's maw.

Allowing for average salaries and social security contributions, that put the wage bill at 200,000 francs or 30,000 euros a month. Add in corporate costs, rent, consumables, taxes, and – of course – some kind of profit margin, and you could double that figure. The seminars themselves must be quite expensive: accommodation for fifteen-odd people, even at a modest hotel, a few technical aids, two days' evaluation for five days' work. At a rough guess, tightening all the screws and setting the ratios at their minimum, the annual turnover had to amount to at least 1,000,000 euros. And all in order to turn out 150 to 200 individuals of whom, say, half or two-thirds were placed. That priced each scalp at around 10,000 euros or, say, two months' salary. Not unreasonable. A firm that had in any case to pay thirteen months' salary would certainly be prepared to shell out fifteen in the first year provided it could be sure of getting a worthwhile employee who would need no training. It was a nice little earner.

While I was mentally scanning his employers, the doctor examined me from head to toe. Having weighed and measured me, he palpated my entire body, including muscles whose existence had hitherto escaped my notice. I had to blow up balloons, pedal an exercise bike both before and after the test, have my blood pressure checked, my temperature taken, my chest sounded. I had to show him my teeth, my throat, and every accessible part of my anatomy, anus included – a neat way, army fashion, of ascertaining my sexual proclivities.

He then authorized me to get dressed and gave me another questionnaire to complete. Hygienic habits, dietary habits, medical history. The most important point, it seemed, was backache. Firms detest the back pains that afflict one Frenchman in six, especially at my age. Their origin is obscure, you can't cure them, and the dynamic executive for whom you've just paid a fortune shuffles pathetically along the corridors, wretched and useless, too preoccupied with futile operations and ineffective physiotherapy to do any work. Coming out from behind his desk, the doctor proceeded to carry out an experimental check: he thumped me in the small of the back, alert to the slightest grunt or grimace. I preserved a stoical silence. I had never really suffered from back pain.

Satisfied, he resumed his seat.

"Do you have any medical knowledge?" he asked.

"Not really, no. It isn't my line, exactly."

"First aid?"

"No. I know the recovery position, but that's about all."

"You're wrong, it can be useful. Cast your eye over this."

He handed me another list of imaginary scenarios. What to do if a colleague collapses on the fitted carpet (dial Emergency); if a secretary has a fit of hysterics; if a client starts projectile vomiting. (God Almighty, could such things happen?)

Last of all came a childish trap. Did I know what diseases the following forms of medication or chemicals were used to treat? This inquiry into my medical knowledge was obviously a covert way of finding out if I somehow had been in contact, even indirectly, with cancer, AIDS, STD, osteo-arthritis, Alzheimer's, et cetera. A negative response to all the questions would have denoted the deliberate dissimulation they were so afraid of; an affirmative would have implied the medical knowledge I'd just disclaimed. I decided to play it straight.

The doctor didn't even glance at the sheets I handed him. Clearly, they were also processed by computer. He got up. Then, as if on second thoughts, he handed me a slip of paper.

"There are one or two tests we can't perform on the premises. Could you drop in at that laboratory tomorrow morning? On an empty stomach, if you don't mind. We foot the bill, of course."

I waited until I was outside before looking at the slip of paper. Blood test, chest X-ray, Doppler test, abdominal scan – the works. They left nothing to chance. At least I would have had a complete physical check-up free of charge.

The receptionist called me the following week to fix a date for my oral. I gathered that I had successfully passed the foregoing tests – a very comforting thought. We settled on Friday, or in three days' time, and she asked me to set aside the entire morning.

I turned up feeling quite enthusiastic. My morale had become eroded of late, and the knowledge that they hadn't found me too bad – so far, at least – had restored it. At the stage I'd now reached, a third of my competitors were no longer in the running. I started to picture the finishing line: a delighted employer waving a cheque – the month's advance I needed so badly. It would have seemed improbable two weeks ago, but now, thanks to De Wavre International, the sunlight seemed brighter, the streets more lively, people more affable, and my breathing easier. Bad news makes you feel that the sky is about to fall in – that you're going to die tomorrow. Good news, and you feel invincible, immortal. Such was the new frame of mind in which I pushed open the heavy oak door that led to the inner sanctum.

The setting was carefully gauged this time. I haven't mentioned De Wavre's offices until now: functional and thoroughly ordinary, their décor so neutral that no adjective would have been insipid enough to describe them adequately.

But this office was different. I had been to see so many directors of human resources in recent months, I'd classified them for fun: those who stack mountains of files on the edge of the desk to show you aren't the only pebble on the beach; those who, on the contrary, leave their desktops bare to convey that they've nothing available; those who build themselves a rampart of family photos to emphasize the H in human resources; and those who adorn their walls with posters indicative of the firm's "philosophy" (youthfully up-to-the-minute or classically respectable).

The décor I encountered here was straight out of the 1930s: a wooden roll-top filing cabinet such as you'd find only in an antique shop, two worn leather armchairs, shelves bearing a few old knick-knacks and a random assortment of books, some slightly faded curtains, and a small seascape in a rather dusty frame. The kind of room whose occupant does not confine himself to number-crunching but lives at peace with the world – a kindly scholar of the type you see in black-and-white movies, or a sympathetic, fatherly psychiatrist.

On the Louis Quinze desk were a dark green blotter with dog-eared corners, a small scratch pad, and a black pen quite unlike the Montblancs people leave lying around with discreet ostentation. Not a sign of a computer, personal organizer, or laptop – none of the obligatory, turn-of-the-century gadgets. And behind the desk sat a woman with a triangular face and wide, watchful eyes.

She greeted me with an air of relief, as if she'd been waiting for me, and me alone, for hours. Having given me the kind of little, nose-wrinkling smile a woman reserves for her special friends, she waved me into an armchair.

"We're not going to try to outsmart each other," she began by saying.

No, of course not – nothing like that, not between us. After all, her tone conveyed, we're accomplices. Her voice was warm.

"Your results to date are quite satisfactory, I'd sooner tell you that right away. We haven't detected anything, well . . . disappointing. We should be able to proceed quite quickly. I'd simply like to clear up one or two points of detail. Let's see . . ."

She opened a drawer and produced a sheet of paper, only one, making no attempt to conceal it. In any case, the few words it bore were indecipherable from where I was sitting. She barely glanced at them.

"We got the results of your medical examinations yesterday. They seem quite satisfactory. Disgustingly normal, in fact – I wish mine were as good. However, you don't do much in the way of sport, I gather . . ."

It wasn't a question, so she didn't get a reply.

"You're quite a rarity, you know," she went on, undiscouraged. "At your age there's usually a minor defect somewhere: cholesterol, sugar, blood pressure a trifle higher than it should be."

"But you don't eliminate people on those grounds, do you?" I retorted. I had to cooperate with her efforts to involve me in her game, if only a little.

She fanned the air with her long, slender, carefully manicured fingers.

"No, of course not. Once every seven or eight times, though, a problem comes to light. You know, one of those chronic ailments that poison a person's life. It's the same with football clubs. They don't like to employ a star and see him immobilized instead of performing on the pitch. You know what we're particularly interested in?"

"No."

"Gamma GTs."

"I don't know what they are."

She raised her eyebrows.

"Happy the man who doesn't! They indicate an excessive consumption of alcohol. A liver condition. It isn't cirrhosis, certainly not – or not yet. It's just a sign that someone drinks a little too much, and it rules him out. On one occasion we identified AIDS. The person was unaware of it."

"And that entitles you to eliminate someone? You mean you haven't had the gays breathing down your neck?"

She shrugged her shoulders.

"No, why should we? We don't employ anyone. At this stage, we're simply taking soundings. There's no contract, nothing signed, no promises. Have *you* signed anything?"

I suddenly realized she was right: no signature, no commitment on either side. Legally speaking, it was a free, voluntary assessment.

"Do you let people have their results?"

"Of the medical examinations? Yes, of course. It's their body, after all. They've a right to know. Yours are waiting for you at reception."

"What about the other tests?"

"Ah no, they're part of our system. It's patented. If you managed to get hold of them we could have you prosecuted for industrial espionage, or whatever the lawyers call it. May I ask you one or two questions?"

Having ascertained that she meant me no harm, and that others had bigger problems than I did, I should have been relaxed enough to get down to brass tacks. I prepared myself for some additional questions about my family or the precise reasons for my redundancy, but she took me by surprise.

"Are you scared of flying?"

I was silent for a moment.

"Er, no, not really . . . But I always tense up a little when we come in to land. Is that bad?"

She started to laugh. It was a rather hollow, strangely throaty laugh, coming from such a slight woman.

"No, no, it's just a bet. One of our analysts always draws Sherlock Holmesian conclusions from these examinations. You know: the man in question has lived in India and favours his left leg. We tease him about it. He thought you must be scared of flying, I didn't. There's a bottle of Bordeaux at stake. So you tense up when you land ... He's lost, hasn't he? Everyone feels that way. It's logical: that's when 50 per cent of accidents occur. But you've no real objection to flying, I take it?"

"Absolutely none."

She smiled like a cream-fed cat.

"So he's lost. How many times have you flown this year?"

"Not many, but last year six – no, seven times."

"He's lost, he's lost," she repeated girlishly. "I'm delighted. But let's be serious. You've stopped smoking, haven't you? Since when?"

"Around ten years ago."

"When, exactly?"

"I don't recall. In August, I think. During the summer holidays."

"If you can't remember the exact date, you're cured. All unreconstructed smokers can tell you, 'I gave it up on the 24th of November 1982.' They've forgotten the date of their wedding and their children's birthdays, but that they do remember. Did you smoke a lot?"

"Twenty a day."

"What method did you use? Patches?"

"No, nothing. I gave up, that's all."

"Bravo. A true hero. Did you know you're a hero? An extremely rare specimen?"

I advanced with care, avoiding the traps. We might have been shooting the breeze like two old friends, but this was a job interview. What confronted me was not a feather-brained creature but a dangerous predator intent on lulling me to sleep before pouncing.

"I don't feel like a rare specimen," I said cautiously.

"What could give you that feeling?"

"I don't know. Performing some feat no one else could have pulled off."

"What, for instance?"

"Succeeding at something I hadn't thought myself capable of."

"And you've never been given a chance to do that, right?"

I smiled to myself. This was it.

"Yes, of course I have. I salvaged a failing business no one would have paid a cent for. It's all in your files."

"And how many jobs did you save?"

Trap.

"I don't like the expression 'saving jobs'. It isn't a question of hauling people out of the water when they're drowning. The secret is to stabilize a business so it continues to be useful and profitable. The jobs come by themselves. Simply try to save jobs and you'll sink the whole ship."

I wasn't too displeased with my balanced response: humanitarian but primarily economic. My interviewer's eyes gave nothing away.

"Interesting," she said. "So you're not opposed in principle to downsizing?"

"That depends. If the object is to squeeze another one per cent at the risk of jeopardizing future profitability, it doesn't strike me as very smart. But if it's to slim down a business whose ill-considered operating costs are threatening its survival, well, that I understand."

"Very creditable. Still, that's what they did to you, isn't it?"

She had unsheathed her scalpel and was starting to cut into the flesh with merciless precision.

"Yes, in a way."

"And you don't hold it against them?"

"I blame myself for not having seen it coming soon enough. There's always a tendency to regard oneself as indispensable. You know why? Because one *is* indispensable – to oneself."

She leant back in her chair and gazed at the ceiling.

"Very neat," she said. "I hadn't thought of that. Mind if I borrow it?"

"Feel free. It's not under copyright."

She gave me an amiable smile, suddenly friendly again. Bullfighters adopt this procedure, it seems: they perform a few passes, then give the beast a short breather.

But only a short one. She returned to the centre of the arena.

"And the firm you turned around – did they also show their gratitude by firing you?"

"No, I quit. I'd had a good season, so I was worth more – they couldn't afford me. You used the football club analogy yourself."

She dodged the horn that threatened her with another smile.

"Good. You catch on fast – or you caught on a long time ago. Tell me about your most recent redundancy. How did you react?"

"Why do you think I'm sitting here right now?"

"Unemployment must be rather disheartening."

"You've never sampled it?"

"Not to date."

One could almost hear the clash of blade on blade.

"Well," I said, "it does call for a little courage. It also depends on your mental resources. 'If you can see your life's work destroyed and set about rebuilding it without a murmur, you'll be a man, my son' – or words to that effect. Kipling. My parents hung it up in my nursery when I was little. The whole poem. On vellum. Framed."

She raised her hands, palms uppermost.

"Ah," she sighed, "Victorian England. Genuine he-men. How ever did they manage to lose India?"

"They didn't have a hope. A few thousand of them to five hundred million? You should never fight a war you're bound to lose."

"Machiavelli?" she hazarded.

"No, some Chinese guy, I think – I don't remember his name. But anyone could have said it."

"So you don't like fighting unless you're the stronger?"

"Not exactly. Only if I've a fair chance of ending up the stronger."

She propped her elbows on the desk and stared at me, half serious, half amused.

"Help me. There must be some chink, some flaw in your armour. Where is it?"

"The flaw is, there isn't a flaw."

She rose.

"You may be right, it probably is a flaw. We'll call you to fix the date of the seminar."

It was hard to disguise my satisfaction, but I didn't lower my guard all the same. I wouldn't be safe until I was outside in the street. Plenty of people had invited a final, lethal thrust by lowering their guard too soon.

She looked me straight in the eye.

"You've taken in what I just said?"

"Yes, I think so. You mean I haven't failed the examination."

"The match. A match against me."

"That's the way I took it."

"So I see. I'll tell you a story. One day, when I was in personnel selection, a young man turned up in my office. This was down south in the Midi. The youngster wasn't too prepossessing. It was hot, and he was wearing a short-sleeved shirt. I suddenly spotted a scar on his arm and asked him what it was. He told me he was a *razeteur*. You know what that is?"

"No."

"They hold corridas in the Midi, but without killing the bulls. They drape lengths of string over their horns, and the *razeteurs* have to remove them with a kind of hook. They get gored occasionally."

"Must be unpleasant."

"Pretty unpleasant. They can even get killed. This young man had acquired his gash from a bull. I asked him if he'd abandoned the sport after his accident, but he said no, not at all, he still went in for it. I hired him on the spot. If he had enough pride to go back and face the kind of animal that had put him in hospital, I reckoned it ought to be possible to make something of him."

"And?"

"And nothing. That's it. That's what they'll be doing to you on the seminar, gashing you to see how you react. I'm telling you this because you know it already. I could have asked you another 50 questions and we'd both have been wasting our time. You're too well prepared. Down there it'll be another story. They use live ammunition."

"Sounds as if you hope I'll fall flat on my face."

"Far from it, you mustn't think that. I'd only like to know, for curiosity's sake, what goes on inside that armour of yours. But don't take that as an invitation to dinner. Maybe there's nothing there at all."

Not very nice of her, but it was her final shaft. I left the building with my head held high.

When I got home my wife asked how things had gone. "All right, I guess," I told her. That was the reply Anna had heard most often in the last two months – or possibly since the start of our marriage. I've never expected much help from anyone, and the best way of banishing another's temptation to help has always been to reply "All right, I guess" to every question, whatever its purpose. Kipling again. Riesman, the American sociologist, once wrote a book detailing our transition from an "inner-determined" society composed of men requiring no aids to self-construction to an "other-determined" society composed of men who are wholly dependent on others. I am a steadfast member of the former category.

I know this hurts Anna – no, that's an overstatement: she feels piqued by it. She thinks I don't ask her to console me because she isn't important enough to me. She's quite wrong – in fact it's the other way round. I don't ask because I love her, because I'm afraid of losing her, because I'm loath to display my weaknesses. It's the educational system prevailing in the 'sixties, the one I went through, that has set the fashion: if you're strong you win and are rewarded; if you're weak you lose and are penalized. Anna married me not because I sobbed on her bosom, but because I was going places and she had a positive image of me. I want to retain that – retain them both, the image and Anna. I've known too many types who lost their jobs and their wives in quick succession because their character changed and they no longer gave them what they wanted. There's psychological satisfaction, reciprocal but temporary, in exchanging the role of a wife for that of a consoling mother. But women soon tire of it. You can't reconstruct the whole of the architecture on which a couple is founded, not lastingly. "May the Force be with you." On the threshold of the third millennium, that's still the best-known phrase from one of the best-known movies ever made. We haven't made much progress since the great anthropomorphic apes walked the earth.

It's the same in business. It isn't necessarily the most intelligent type that wins, but the most ruthless – the one that wants something more than the rest.

Anna says she wants to share everything with me. She took me on for worse as well as for better, she says – she remembers that perfectly well. If I retain a secret garden, she won't be able to love the whole of me. I'm sure she believes this with absolute sincerity. I'm equally sure she's wrong. She won't stop loving me if I'm eliminated from the running; she'll love me in a different way. She'll love someone else, a different me. That's too great a risk to take.

But Anna has been a model wife. When I announced that I was out of work she didn't instantly conclude, like many of her women friends in the same situation, that our income would dry up – discounting the unemployment bureau's survival kit. Her first thought wasn't for herself. She spent a long time exonerating me – a pointless exercise, since I didn't feel guilty in the least – and remotivating me, which was equally futile. I asked her, rather curtly, to stop giving me psychological first aid, and we dropped the subject. In the past two months she has asked me from time to time how

I'm getting on, to which my invariable response has been that I'm following up some leads. She's worried, I can tell. About me. A few weeks from now, when the unpaid bills start piling up, she'll start worrying about herself and the children. That's when things will get serious: when she feels that our children are at risk because of me.

In fact, our two daughters aren't in much danger. The elder girl, who's brilliant, is completing a course in business studies after passing her *baccalauréat* with distinction. She'll be inundated with offers when she goes on the job market at the end of the year. The younger girl presents bigger problems. She's vaguely endeavouring to study art history, which strikes me as rather unpromising. I see her only once a week, and then she accuses me of stifling her. Perhaps we made her like that despite ourselves, her mother, her sister, and I, and she feels she has to break free. It's been going on too long, though. You'd think my unemployment would have endeared me to her: no longer the one who succeeds at everything, like her elder sister, I've become the one who's in the process of ruining everything, like her. But not at all. She was tactful enough to tone down her aggressive manner, but I could see she was holding herself in check. From what? From reproaching me? From taking her revenge? From dancing on my corpse? My failure is her triumph, but she resents my escaping her wrath. The result is, she hardly speaks to me any more. The atmosphere at our Sunday lunches has become rather strained of late.

Especially as Anna goes on working. She was wise enough to take a civil service job, which pays a modest but regular salary. She runs an office in the Department of Education. The staff are 95 per cent male, and she rules them with a rod of iron – the only thing to do in such a situation. At home she can become a woman again. That's yet another reason for not wanting to change my role.

De Wavre's woman psychologist made no attempt to delve into

my family circumstances. I didn't understand this at first. The strength of the family in France is such that all the predators of the business world claim to be acting solely with their children's best interests in mind. They aren't entirely wrong, either. A father will do anything to retain his daughter's affection, and if that entails buying a stud farm because she's fond of ponies, he'll fight to the death to acquire one. Nothing is more humiliating than having to refuse a child a treat not because you've decided against it for educational reasons, but simply because you can't afford it.

But De Wavre knew all that, just as they knew they had no means of verifying anything I might tell them. When your best friend ruthlessly divorces his wife on the grounds that she has made his life a hell for years, you're utterly taken aback, never having noticed a thing. How could one record that in the boxes of a questionnaire? Anyway, they couldn't care less what sort of life I led. All that interested them was whether it would affect my efficiency and in what way. In my estimation, they had no need to study the character of the members of my family, only mine.

Besides, the life I led was quite innocuous: a troublefree couple, two reasonably well-balanced children (one a little less so than the other), no drugs, no prison record, no shady associates, no disabilities, a household budget prudently administered. No chink or flaw in my armour despite the psychologist's misgivings. I was clean and I wanted to stay that way, because it undoubtedly brought me a sort of happiness, or at least the absence of unhappiness the Stoics aspired to.

One of the great drawbacks of unemployment is the time for reflection it gives you. You review, scrutinize, and dissect your past. This is a mistake. You come to the conclusion that you're responsible for the predicament you're in and must have made a blunder somewhere. I hadn't made any blunder – or rather, only one: I'd underestimated my last employer's stupidity. Nothing to be done. Apart, of course, from starting again from scratch, working harder at school, choosing a better college, studying for the École Nationale d'Administration and becoming a tax inspector, a job in which no one ever pays for a mistake, however outrageous. But, even if I'd had to start again from scratch, I'd still have done all the same things: I would still have married Anna, taken the same jobs (except the last one), and bought the same apartment. I might possibly have tried to give my younger daughter more of the "space" she craves, but that's all. In short, I was on pretty good terms with myself.

Hence my reply to Anna: "All right, I guess."

I felt confident.

Like a lot of seminars, this one started on a Sunday. Executives often go away at weekends, bound for improbable training courses. I used to assume they spent them snuggled up in some hotel with a pretty secretary, and I pitied their wives for swallowing such a crude ploy. But no, the organizers of such get-togethers begrudged the time consumed by travel, reception, checking in, showering on arrival, and all the other formalities that occupied the whole of Monday morning and lost them at least half a day. That's why they now make a start after dinner on Sunday night. I suspect that in 20 years' time they'll begin by welcoming the participants between four and six on Saturday morning, just before sunrise. Later still in the 21st century they'll find some way of abolishing sleep, the most disastrous time-waster of all.

We had arranged to meet just after lunch at the Gare de Lyon. There we were handed our TGV tickets by a young West Indian woman in a blue two-piece – not exactly a flight attendant's uniform, but something similar. There were about 15 of us, but we exchanged no more than a few words in the train: we had yet to bond.

At Grenoble we boarded a bus and set off along the Autoroute des Alpes. Not far from Grenoble we turned off on to a minor road that led through the forest. The further we went, the wilder the scenery. Peaceful pastureland gave way to menacing precipices, dark trees blotted out the sun, waterfalls and scree-covered slopes flanked our route. The air became perceptibly colder as we threaded our way between snow-capped mountains of increasing size.

All at once, on emerging from the forest, we came to the shores of a lake. It was absolutely still, a sheet of zinc more white than blue in colour. The bus pulled up and we were told to get out. The woman beside me was shivering. Opening a large suitcase, she took out a green waistcoat and put it on, then had to run after the driver, who was already loading our bags on to a trolley.

A rickety wooden landing stage reposed on four piles protruding from the water. Moored to one of these was a small motorboat. A very swarthy man had just got out of it. He leapt nimbly on to the landing stage and came towards us with a rolling, nautical gait. Not far from me was a lanky young man.

"Train, bus, boat," he said in a low voice. "What comes next, huskies and a sledge? A microlight?"

The boatman was accosted by another, more rotund member of the party. "You mean there's no road?" he asked plaintively. "Do we have to cross the lake?"

"*Non capisco*," the boatman replied.

The fat man turned to us. "Anyone here speak Italian? I think that was Italian. Are we in Italy? Have we crossed the border?"

A woman detached herself from the bemused flock of sheep we temporarily resembled. There were only four women in the party. She was the prettiest, I noticed fleetingly.

"I speak Italian."

She proceeded to jabber away at the boatman, then came back to us.

"All right, it's like this: we're going to an island in the middle of the lake. That's where the hotel is. The boat can't hold us all, so it'll make two trips. We'll have to split up into two groups. Who wants to go first?"

The boldest among us stepped forward. I did so for interest's sake: it couldn't be a test, not at this early stage.

The crossing was as smooth as a trip on the Grand Canal. There weren't enough seats, so most of us stood holding on to the gunwale and savouring the breeze, which was laden with the tangy scent of pine resin. Without letting go of the tiller, the boatman levelled his finger at a clump of greenery sprouting from the lake.

"*E li che andiamo.*"

The tubby man turned to the pretty woman. "But where are we, in Italy? Ask him," he insisted.

"No, no, he's Italian, but we're still in France."

As we drew nearer we made out a tiled roof, then the walls of a building buried among the trees. The island boasted a landing stage as crude and rickety as the one we'd embarked from.

The boatman deftly wound the painter round one of the piles and leapt ashore.

"*Siam' arrivati. Tutti giù!*" he cried briskly, without turning off the engine.

He helped the pretty woman to straddle the gunwale, almost carrying her in the process, and stood ready to help any other female whose skirt was too tight.

As soon as he saw we were all safe ashore he proceeded to unload our bags, tossing them on to the landing stage with the practised ease of an airport baggage handler. Then he jumped back into the boat and revved the engine.

"Hey," called the fat man, "my suitcase isn't here! What have you done with my suitcase?"

The lanky young man guffawed. "It's like the airlines: lunch in

Paris, dinner in New York, baggage in Hong Kong."

"Very funny," said the fat man.

"Our things are also coming in two batches," said the pretty woman. "They haven't been sorted out yet. Another ten minutes, and you'll get your suitcase back."

"Have you been here before?" asked the younger man.

"No. I've been watching, that's all."

I'd been watching too. They had told me at De Wavre that two-thirds of us would fail to make the grade. The fat man would certainly be one of them, but the woman was proving a danger from the outset. Thanks to her smattering of Italian, she had already staked a claim to leadership. Very soon, if she wasn't stopped, she'd be ordering us around. I didn't have my suitcase either, but I didn't for an instant forget why I was there.

Before heading back, the boatman pointed to a track that led uphill towards the hotel.

"*Su, dai, andate . . .*"

Maybe the first test was an Italian oral, I thought.

"We have to take that track," said the woman.

But I was ahead of her and leading the way before she'd even opened her mouth. The fat man propped his back against one of the piles, determined to wait for his suitcase rather than follow us.

At the top of the track four steps gave access to the hotel itself, which was built into the hillside. Waiting for us on the terrace was a reception committee of one: a jeans-clad female counterpart of the young man who fulfilled the same function at head office. She had the kind of open, smiling, animated face that automatically endears its owner. This was reassuring. If De Wavre always contrived to recruit receptionists capable of disarming the most surly visitor, they should be capable of detecting those whose qualifications would be useful at any level. It can sometimes be harder to find a good flight attendant than a good financial analyst.

The girl disclosed that her name was Natalie. She seemed genuinely delighted to see us and greeted us as if every member of the party were there at her personal invitation. She apologized for the discomforts of the trip and the rather overcast skies. Then, armed with a clipboard, she assigned us our rooms. She repeated each name several times, locking eyes with the person in question – an old mnemonic technique. As every sales rep and politician knows, forgetting a name is the one unpardonable sin. It negates your interlocutors' existence, renders them indistinguishable from the herd, destroys their individuality, humiliates their ego. Most people can't endure such treatment. Natalie had been well trained: after five minutes she knew every last one of us by name and by sight.

"Your baggage will be stacked in the lobby as it arrives," she told us. "There's a problem, though. The porter went sick this morning, so you'll have to retrieve it yourselves."

An executive type in a dark suit and gold-rimmed spectacles raised his eyebrows.

"I see. Tell me, are there any other problems?"

Natalie treated him to a radiant smile.

"Of course. The central heating's on the blink, the cook has just given birth, they haven't delivered any food, and all we've got on TV is a tape of *Fort Boyard*. No, I'm joking, everything else is fine."

After that put-down, the man had no choice but to smile along with her.

"Your rooms are upstairs," Natalie went on. "If your room number begins with one, it's on the first floor, if it begins with two, it's on the second. They're nothing special. No lift and no air-conditioning, but there's always the lake. If you've got a harpoon and manage to break the ice, you could catch a seal – but count me out, if you don't mind. Still, we're lucky it hasn't snowed yet."

"Does the lake freeze over in winter?" inquired the dark-suited executive.

"No. Too big, too deep, not cold enough. You'll have to go skating somewhere else."

"Oh, so they're ice skates. I wondered why your bag was so heavy," a stocky little man remarked to the pretty woman who spoke Italian.

"No, it's my 15-volume encyclopedia," she retorted swiftly, "to help me revise before the tests."

Natalie had succeeded in putting us at our ease with a few samples of that flippant, insufferable badinage which forms a preamble to social intercourse in circles like ours. She gracefully pirouetted on the spot.

"You can now go to your rooms and take a shower if you wish. It's not compulsory, of course. If you prefer to have a drink, the bar is open. Ah, here's the rest of the squad . . ."

Our companions in misfortune invaded the lobby in their turn, puffing and panting. The slope was a steep one, and they'd climbed it too quickly in their eagerness to catch us up. Natalie picked up her clipboard again.

I had inherited Room 211, the last but one from the end of the corridor. It was furnished in the style of a country hotel as opposed to that of the Hiltons and other international caravanserais. A big wooden bedstead, a thick duvet, a rustic bedside table with an ill-fitting drawer, two small red curtains concealing a narrow window, and, in lieu of built-in cupboards, an enormous wardrobe that took up half the available space and encroached on the bathroom doorway. I tested the mattress by bouncing on it a couple of times (hard, but not uncomfortable), then tried the black telephone beside the bed, my room's sole concession to modernity. I let it ring a dozen times. Nobody answered. Perhaps Natalie was alone at the reception desk and too busy dispatching the troops to their billets. Either that, or De Wavre wanted to insulate us from the civilized world.

Obedient to Natalie's suggestion, I took a shower in the tiny cubicle behind the wardrobe and got changed. What sort of look should I aim at? I had long ago learned that dress is the primary medium of communication, the one that registers before all else – in other words, that clothes make the man. My customary uniform, a grey suit and a sober tie, was precluded by the setting. I opted for a beige jacket and blue slacks, a casual but smart and acceptable halfway house between a city suit and rural combat dress. A hint of aftershave, and I was ready to go downstairs.

Now that she had finished allotting us our quarters, young Natalie was officiating behind the bar. My companions and competitors,

40

who turned up one by one, lingered in the doorway for a moment before taking the plunge and joining the fray. The lounge bar was quite sizeable, but they soon filled it. Clearly ill at ease, they milled around beneath the exposed beams, feigning a protracted interest in the scenery outside the big picture window or devoting undue attention to the small coloured prints of mountainscapes that adorned the walls. I felt as if I were attending a private view at which no one knew anyone else and there weren't even any canvases to pretend to admire. The others had reached the same stage, it seemed. They all requested glasses of mineral water, then looked for some quiet little corner from which to watch the throng without compromising themselves.

The rather oppressive atmosphere was dispelled by the live wire that any party of tourists inevitably includes, an extrovert Marseillais who loudly commented on everything that met his eye. He informed us that his name was Morin, that he found the weather really nippy, and that he was in packaging. With the vulgarity of a vaudeville comic, he paid Natalie a series of suggestive compliments to which her only response was a wordless smile. Four or five of the party clustered round him, eager to engage in a battle of wisecracks. The pretty woman who spoke Italian turned to me.

"Incredible," she murmured. "He must be paid by the local tourist board, don't you think?"

I couldn't think of a witty enough reply. Behind me, two older executive types were inspecting the portrait of some animal perched on a crag. One opined that it was a chamois, the other an izard, but their zoological knowledge was too meagre to enable them to settle the controversy. The tubby little man had taken possession of one of the three armchairs and was sullenly leafing through a tourist magazine.

Before long Natalie clapped her hands to attract our attention.

"Dinner is served, ladies and gentlemen. Afterwards, at eight-thirty, you're to assemble for a briefing in the workroom. That's on the first floor, immediately on the right at the head of the stairs. Enjoy your meal."

Standing next to me was a tall, thin man with a preternaturally prominent Adam's apple. "I bet it'll be fondue," he sighed. "They always kick off with fondue in the Alps, to get people to mingle."

He bet wrong. It was raclette.

The dining-room was decorated in the same style as elsewhere: panelled walls, massive beams supporting the ceiling, a big inglenook fireplace – empty at present – flanked by archaic agricultural implements of a mysterious nature. There were four large round tables covered with heavy red cloths. Six settings per table, the fourth one being bare. We seated ourselves more or less at random, Morin the Marseillais in the midst of the little clique that had surrounded him in the bar.

I found myself next to the man with the outsize Adam's apple, for the simple reason that we had entered the room at the same time. No sooner had he sat down than he held out his hand and introduced himself.

"Hirsch. William Hirsch. I'm in information technology."

He had a very deep, very resonant voice. I don't know much about anatomy, but I suspected that it couldn't be related to the dimensions of his Adam's apple. I returned the compliment.

"Jérôme Carceville. Management consultancy."

"Then you're going to need me," said Hirsch.

The thin, very austerely dressed man sitting across the table from us, one of the few to have retained a dark tie and suit, smiled behind his rimless glasses.

"Yes," he said, "generally speaking, the first thing one has to do is rectify computer errors."

Hirsch gave a start, stung by this onslaught.

"There aren't any computer errors. On the contrary, data-processing is entirely logical. Human beings aren't, or not always. *They're* the source of the errors."

"Oh, sure," scoffed the man in the dark suit, "that's what they all say. There are never any bugs, are there? Windows is a stable, rational system. When it crashes, like ten times a day, it's the user's fault."

Thrown by this, Hirsch flushed faintly. The dark suit turned to his neighbour, a big, strapping fellow with a ruddy complexion.

"I didn't mean to embarrass our friend. The thing is, computer experts and computers are rather like men and their wives: they sling mud at them, but they won't tolerate anyone else doing so. Aren't I right?"

The other man nodded vaguely. Hirsch relaxed.

"It's true a few problems do crop up from time to time," he conceded. "Not even we understand them all, but most people fail to locate them in the correct place. They don't complain about something that doesn't work, they complain about something that does work but they can't operate properly. Nine times out of ten they've simply botched the correct procedure."

The dark suit signed a truce.

"Quite right. But don't tell me there's never a problem with hard disks."

"Hard disks present no problems in themselves," said Hirsch. "If a motherboard is defective you replace it, that's all. The only real problem with hard disks is the absence of a standard, so materials aren't always compatible and conflicts arise. But just the same thing happens if you try to install a Peugeot component in a Renault. No, the real trouble is the software. That's where bugs can lurk."

"You're the expert," said the fifth of my table companions, a little man with shifty eyes. "Where do they come from?"

43

Hirsch, flattered by this acknowledgement of his expertise, launched into a long lecture on the undue number of lines in most programmes. Meantime, a silent waiter dressed in blue had deposited an assortment of dishes on the sideboard: slices of cheese and ham, pancetta, pickled gherkins, small onions. There was a roar of laughter at the next table: the Marseillais had heaped his plate with food and inserted it under the portable grill.

"He thinks it's a barbecue," said someone.

The laughter persisted. Morin was now trying to extricate the mass of food, which had got stuck and was starting to smoke. I caught the eye of the man in the dark suit. We were clearly thinking the same thing: Morin had passed the preliminary tests, so he couldn't be as much of a fool as he tried to make out and was cunningly hiding his light under a bushel of banter. On the other hand, perhaps there were two categories present: those who genuinely wanted to win and realized that battle had commenced, and those who, having made it here at the second attempt, were out to have a good time before being rejected as a matter of course. Speaking for myself, I was constantly, keenly aware of the reason for my presence: two-thirds of us would not last the week, and I absolutely had to survive.

I surreptitiously studied the others while chewing my slices of cheese. The dark suit was dangerous, and so was the woman who spoke Italian. Hirsch was no threat to me. He was the best in his field, perhaps, but not in mine, so our interests did not conflict. The little fatty was temperamentally vulnerable and the big, red-faced man too taciturn – he should be easy to intimidate. Morin's companions didn't frighten me. Their penchant for laughter and having fun suggested that they wouldn't be sufficiently focused when the chips were down. As for Morin himself, he would have to be assessed in practice. Three good, seven poor, one doubtful. The five remaining candidates comprised the shifty little man, who was probably incapable of asserting himself but more than capable of making trouble for us, and the four individuals marooned at the third table: the woman in the waistcoat, another rather self-effacing woman, and two men who were eating in silence, one bearded and the other bald. Theirs was the losers' table. Only one of them would make it at most.

I turned to the man in the dark suit, who was also studying me surreptitiously. Our eyes met once more. His were quite expressionless: the blank but watchful eyes of a killer.

"And what's your line?" I asked him.

He hesitated for a moment.

"I trained as a lawyer," he replied.

Yes, I thought, I also started life as a baby and went to school later on. It wasn't the reply I'd been expecting. I opened my mouth to pursue the subject, but Hirsch got in first.

"A lawyer, eh? I can understand why you find computer experts so annoying. You don't have a clue how to handle us."

Instead of contesting this, the dark suit said nothing. Hirsch tried to follow up his putative advantage.

"That's because your laws take no account of what we're doing. We're going much too fast for you. Take the Internet, for example. It defies legal regulation – it's a global network and there aren't any global laws. If you've got two judgements delivered, one in Ohio and another in New Hampshire, how do you propose to apply them in Karachi?"

The dark suit smiled – or rather, slightly retracted his thin lips.

"You're right. One minor point, though: I don't make the laws. On the contrary, my job consists in getting round them. From that point of view, information technology is opening up some fascinating prospects. There are no rules – it's an absolute legal vacuum. Nature abhors a vacuum, so it's said, but we lawyers adore them. Vacuums, I mean. They're the environment in which we thrive and make money."

"You ought to write a book," I put in. "*In Praise of the Void*, by . . . What was your name again?"

He took his dish from the hotplate, carefully grated the cheese, and bisected a small onion with surgical precision. Then he looked up.

"Charriac. Emmanuel Charriac. *In Praise of the Void* . . . Interesting. But if a book is as empty as that, who would read it?"

"So what?" said the shifty little man. "Most books contain a single idea and spin it out ad nauseam. Read the synopsis and you've read the book. The other 200 pages are there to prove the idea – to demonstrate the theorem. You never use the demonstration, you only use the theorem itself."

Charriac eyed him like a frog lying in wait for a mosquito.

"If you'd graduated from a Grande École Mathématique the theory would interest you more than its applications; for another thing, you wouldn't be here."

As I discovered later, this was typical of Charriac's mode of argument. He was always two moves ahead of everyone else. Instead of answering your question, he countered your inevitable objection to his answer. He visualized the implications of every remark and jumped to its conclusion, leap-frogging the intermediate dialogue. Only two members of our party were like that: Charriac and the bald man at the table for four. To hear them arguing was an exhausting experience.

"But I did go to a Grande École," the shifty man protested. "Not the Polytechnique or the Centrale, admittedly, but a reputable one."

"Ah," said Charriac, "I'm fond of the provinces myself."

A normal exchange would have gone as follows:

"A Grande École in Paris?"

"No, in the provinces."

"Of course. The Grandes Écoles proper are in Paris and the merely reputable ones in the provinces. You like the provinces?"

"Certainly I do."

"Ah, I'm fond of the provinces myself."

Charriac had skipped four remarks out of five. Two days later, to neutralize any misgivings aroused by his speed of thought, he claimed to have a horror of wasting time and breath on futile and predictable remarks.

For dessert we were offered slices of Black Forest gâteau. Morin triggered another explosion of laughter by loudly deploring the absence of a cheese platter. Everyone at his table was having fun except the woman who spoke Italian, and the third bottle of white wine had just been broached.

Finally, coffee was served and Natalie reappeared. She hadn't eaten with us, not that anyone found this surprising. She was a member of the staff, after all, and we were at a hotel, not a holiday camp. On the other hand, none of De Wavre's course organizers had shown his face either.

"It's eight twenty-five," she announced. "The briefing is at eight-thirty."

"Synchronize your watches," Morin chimed in.

I experienced that slight twinge of apprehension in the pit of the stomach which precedes a crucial event.

The workroom was divided in half by a sliding partition, which was slightly open. On one side were some 20 chairs, each equipped with a writing surface like the seats in a college lecture hall, and facing them two spartan, ergonomically designed armchairs of the kind you can't sit in unless you're of absolutely average build. In one corner stood a flip-chart easel and a small table bearing a jar of felt-tipped pens. The general impression was low-budget, not to say shabby. It might have been the venue for a training session for the socially disadvantaged.

But the other half of the room, which could be glimpsed through the gap in the partition, looked much more like what we were expecting: rows of computers separated by working surfaces and pot plants, a large video screen on the far wall, and two video cameras on a table – all the toys a modern telecommunicator needs. These were obviously intended for later on.

Two strangers were already in occupation when we entered. One was on the tall side and almost entirely bald, but endowed with a beard so bushy it looked as if the hair of his head had slithered down and lodged on his chin. It was the other man who caught the eye. Around 50, to judge by the wrinkles etched into his tanned, craggy features, he might have been a pirate of old. His cinematic appearance was completed by two green eyes and a set of overly white teeth. Well-muscled, with powerful shoulders and a flat stomach, he was the kind of man whose mere presence transforms the atmosphere in a room. Natalie, who was sitting in a corner, looked almost insipid by comparison.

He welcomed us, then introduced himself as Joseph Del Rieco, De Wavre's course supervisor.

"My job," he announced in a court-room baritone, "is to explore every aspect of your personality. Don't be alarmed, though: everything goes well as a rule. We haven't had an attempted suicide for at least six months."

His opening pleasantry evoked nothing but faint, stiff smiles.

"We shall devote tomorrow morning to some tests," he went on. "After that, we enter the simulation phases. It's rather the same with airline pilots. Before letting them loose on the controls of a jumbo jet costing half a billion francs and carrying hundreds of innocent passengers, you test their response to critical situations in a simulator on the ground. Then you grade them in order of competence: transatlantic airliner, jet fighter, or microlight. That's exactly what we're going to do here: place you in critical situations and see how you react. Afterwards we tell you whether you're fit to run Microsoft or drive a pizza delivery van at most. It's as big a responsibility in business as it is in aeronautics. Put someone who can't cope in charge of a big corporation, and he may also do billions of dollars' worth of damage, quite apart from destroying the lives of thousands of employees and shareholders. We shall also assess your management style and see how you behave as part of a team. When the Japanese engage an executive they send him off into the mountains for a week to teach him that a roped party is only as good as its weakest link, that if someone falls into a ravine they all fall with him, and that a team can't go faster than its slowest member. That's the programme. I can't tell you any more, it would spoil the element of surprise. Questions, anyone?"

Having delivered his little speech, he surveyed us briefly one by one. Not like those lecturers who have learnt to look at each member of an audience in turn, so as not to exclude anyone, but as if he were already trying to lay bare our souls. His expression, a strange blend of cordiality, determination and belligerence, conveyed that he could be merciless.

"It will all seem like a game," he continued in a slightly milder tone, "but it's more than that, you know. There are some extremely serious games, and this is one of them. You all know how much we can do for you if you win. But don't worry, nothing bad will happen to you if you lose. You'll have spent a week in delightful surroundings with some very congenial people, that's all."

He gave a sardonic smile as he uttered the last words, then casually indicated the bearded man behind him, who looked half asleep.

"Jean-Claude, my assistant. He knows how to make everything work – everything I'm incapable of fixing myself: the computers, the video equipment, the microphones – all the gadgets that are forever going wrong. When something doesn't work, it's his fault by definition. That's a very practical arrangement, because it means I never have to blame myself for anything. No, seriously, Jean-Claude is very efficient. If you have a technical problem, consult him. But only on technical problems – he knows nothing about the rest. Natalie you've already met. Don't try weeping on her shoulder – we didn't employ her as an agony aunt, so there's no point in telling her your life story, it wouldn't interest her. We start work at nine each morning and knock off . . . well, when we knock off. If you have any personal requirements – medication, say, or a change of socks – give us 24 hours' notice and we'll obtain them for you. At your expense. Any more questions?"

Natalie cleared her throat before taking the floor. Her voice sounded thin after Del Rieco's baritone.

"Breakfast in the dining room between seven and eight-thirty. We don't serve it in your rooms. Lunch from twelve-thirty to one o'clock, dinner from seven-thirty to eight. There may be times when you prefer to skip a meal. In that case, ask me for some sandwiches an hour in advance. Always go through me, the rest of the staff aren't authorized to deal with your requests. There's a small gym in the basement and a television set in the lounge. I don't think you'll have time for a swim, but if you do, take care, the lake is very cold. Only Monsieur Del Rieco has ever brought himself to dive in."

Del Rieco displayed his flawless teeth.

"Yes," he said lightly, "the time I caught pneumonia."

The woman in the waistcoat raised a timid finger.

"What happens if one of us is ill?"

Del Rieco resumed his serious expression.

"It shouldn't happen in the normal course of events, since you've all undergone the requisite medical examinations. If it's a cold or a sprained ankle, we have whatever is necessary on the premises. Natalie is a trained nurse. A heart attack would be much more of a nuisance – the emergency service would take about two hours to send a helicopter. If the persons in question were in too much pain, we'd consider putting them out of their misery. But we've never had that problem. On the other hand, people sometimes lose their nerve or simply throw in the towel. We evacuate them without more ado, and they're back in their own homes the same night. That seldom happens, though. It simply indicates that there's a defect to be remedied in the tests we carry out at head office."

The man with the outsize Adam's apple put his hand up.

"Do you have any statistics? I mean, on the results here? Just to give us a rough idea . . ."

Del Rieco's eyes narrowed. Without turning round, he gestured to his assistant.

"Jean-Claude, the figures. But there's not much point, you know. Every intake is different. Sometimes we accept hardly anyone, sometimes nearly everyone. The ratio of passes to failures isn't mandatory. To the best of my knowledge, we place approximately one third of applicants after each seminar. Another third remains on our files in case the economy needs everyone it can get, and the rest are eliminated. That's more or less how it goes, year on year, but every seminar has its own relatively tough dynamics."

"That's right," said Jean-Claude, consulting some printed sheets.

"Very well," said Del Rieco, "to end with, we'll conform to custom and I'll ask you to introduce yourselves. Of course, we all know it's impossible to remember 15 names. It's a pointless formality, but there are two or three that will stick in your heads for future reference. Don't worry, this isn't a test."

The tubby little man produced a personal organizer from his pocket. Del Rieco frowned.

"No, no, don't take notes. This isn't a test, I said."

The other man stood his ground.

"If it isn't a test, there aren't any rules and we can please ourselves. You're simply making the job a bit harder. Okay, I'll memorize the names and key them in afterwards."

Del Rieco's face hardened. We all realized that the little man had provoked him deliberately. Even before he'd started to test us, the rebel had decided to test *him*. That's what usually happens the first day in school, and we were curious to see how Del Rieco extricated himself.

"Very well," he said. "I'm supposed to analyse everything that happens, so I'll analyse it. I give an order, and this gentleman proposes to disobey it. Why? Because he wants to see if I'll give way and who is the boss. All right. You can do as you please, but within parameters defined by me. If you don't like the parameters, you can take the boat back. I don't have to justify myself or explain why I do this rather than that. This isn't an elective democracy. It wasn't a test, I said, but you insisted on having a power struggle. Well, now you've got one. Put that thing away. If you want to listen to what is said and write it down afterwards, that's your business, but when I say no notes, I mean no notes. Is that plain enough for you?"

The little man shot him a look of pure hatred and pocketed his organizer. Instead of scoring a point he had lost one. Not very smart of him. To make matters worse, he blurted out an apology.

"I'm sorry, I didn't mean to make trouble. It seemed more practical, that's all."

Del Rieco digested this climb-down and regained his serenity.

"You're right, it *is* more practical. But that's not my idea. You're all on equal terms for the moment. Nobody jumps the gun – the starter hasn't even raised it yet. All right, forget it. Off you go."

As Del Rieco had predicted, I failed to memorize even half the names of those present. I systematically tried to associate each surname with some physical characteristic: Hirsch with his Adam's apple, Morin with his Marseillais accent, Charriac with his rimless glasses. The shifty man introduced himself as Pinetti, the pretty woman who spoke Italian as Laurence Carré. Like Charriac, the red-faced hulk had a name beginning with "Cha" – Chamont, Chavet, Cha-Something – and the bearded man's name sounded Arab. The little fatso who had picked a fight was called Aimé Leroy, and the woman in a waistcoat spoke so softly that no one could hear what she said.

Everyone had a speciality. Hirsch repeated that he was an IT expert, Charriac owned to being a lawyer, Morin was a sales manager, Pinetti a financial adviser, and Laurence Carré had been, in turn, a director of human resorces and a director of communications. As for Aimé Leroy, still seething after his spat with Del Rieco, he described himself simply as a business executive. Also present were a managing director's PA, an engineer (unspecified), a director in charge of staff training, and various other denizens of the human zoo. There were no two persons in the same type of job, that much was obvious, and a wide range of functions was represented. De Wavre must have planned this so as to avoid any direct competition.

Only two of us omitted to volunteer their age – the two oldest, of course. They must have been pushing 50 or just over, which they knew to be a handicap in the present economic climate. (Except in the case of big bosses. They could be 80 without detriment to themselves, even if their subordinates were less than half that age and their secretaries barely a quarter of it.)

One or two people mentioned their place of residence (Paris, for the most part). The rest took care not to. Mobility was essential at this level, and an allusion to your local roots could preclude you from involvement in the globalization process. Morin got round this with a little speech that sounded well-rehearsed:

"I live in Marseille. If I'd said Rennes or Strasbourg, no one would have believed me. I may not have a TV accent, but I speak the same language as you do, or almost, and I aim to show you I'm just as good."

Five or six stated that they were married and had children, a point employers are supposed to find reassuring. The others, even those that wore wedding rings, made no mention of their marital status. One tall, lean, very tanned young man proudly announced that he had once been an Olympic athlete. Nobody inquired what his discipline was.

Our round tour left me in a thoughtful frame of mind. In this type of exercise, what usually happens is that the first one to speak establishes a pattern. The others confine themselves to the same items supplemented by the odd personal detail. Here, everyone was watching everyone else. Far from wanting to shine, we tried to say the bare minimum. No one asked any questions and Del Rieco never intervened at any stage. True, he must have had all our files, so he knew more about each of us than we could possibly imagine. He volunteered no more information about himself and brought the meeting to a close without further comment.

It wasn't ten o'clock yet, and no one felt like sleeping. Morin made up a four at cards, Hirsch leant on the bar and discussed information technology with the man with the Arab name, Pinetti turned on the TV. I strolled down to the lake for a breath of air.

Laurence Carré, seated on a big rock, was smoking a cigarette and looking out over the water, whose surface was shrouded in Gothic wisps of mist. I went up to her.

"You look like Lamartine composing *Le Lac*."

"It wasn't this lake," she replied without turning round. "And Lamartine, in spite of his name, was a man."

I sat down on the ground beside her.

"La Martine. I'd never thought of that. You think he was gay?"

Instead of pursuing my rather inane remark she transferred her gaze to the sky, which was lit by a firework display of stars.

"It's because of the pollution," I said.

She looked at me at last. All I could see in the dusk was a smooth cheek and the curve of her shoulder.

"What do you mean, the pollution?"

Her tone was as cool as the air around us. I was clearly interrupting her train of thought.

"The stars. There's no pollution here, so you can see many more of them."

Slowly, wearily, she turned to face me.

"No, you're wrong. It's because of the darkness. There's too much light in Paris and other big cities. A comet passed near the Earth a few years ago. You couldn't see it in town. You had to go out into the country, where it's really dark. Turn on a light, and it disappeared."

Mechanically, I picked up a pebble. Rising to my feet, I went down to the water's edge and shied it at the lake. To judge by the sound, it ricocheted once before sinking. Then I rejoined her.

"That's more or less what we're going to do, isn't it? Light each other up until some of us disappear."

She didn't reply, so I made my way back to the hotel. Perhaps she'd thought I was trying to chat her up. In fact, I hadn't meant to do any such thing.

I went up to my room and read a few pages of a whodunnit before turning out the light. It was warm beneath the duvet. I stretched luxuriously, feeling sleepy but gripped by that mixture of apprehension and excitement known as stage fright. The stage fright won, and it took me quite a while to drop off.

Although I came downstairs before eight o'clock the next morning, I was one of the last to appear. The dining-room resembled a hair-dressing salon: everyone's hair was still damp from the shower. The men were freshly shaved and overly redolent of deodorant and after-shave. Mingled with the aroma of coffee and hot croissants, these varied scents formed a strange synthesis: the customary fragrance of matutinal dynamism, hygiene, health and vigour. Laurence Carré had donned her war paint again, lips a trifle too red, lashes a trifle too black.

We seated ourselves haphazardly, wherever a chair was vacant when we came in. I found myself between two men whose names I couldn't recall. They were convinced that they had met before. Having worked for the same oil company, but in different divisions, they were trying to pinpoint the period at which their paths might have crossed. They seemed amazed and delighted by this coinci-dence, though it wasn't particularly surprising: every social sector is so small that, if 16 people are gathered together at random, at least two of them will be connected in some way. In the end, by comparing dates, they concluded that they had shared the same employer for only six months.

There was a brief intermission after breakfast. It wasn't nine o'clock yet. The smokers went out on the terrace to pander to their addiction, the rest competed for a look at the local paper or a chance to phone their families. Charriac had opened a laptop and was checking his e-mail.

"I doubt if that's permitted," I said lightly.

He barely raised his head.

"Everything not prohibited by law is permitted. It's in the Constitution."

I wasn't going to let him have the last word.

"Except that this isn't a democracy, they made that clear last night."

"In that case," he said stubbornly, "count me among the rebels."

I gave up.

A diligent morning ensued. Tests and more tests, masses of forms to complete, each of us working individually on our hard classroom chairs. The questions were very diverse. I occasionally recognized traps I had learnt to avoid. For the most part, however, we were presented with imaginary scenarios. What to do in such and such an eventuality? Should an efficient but dishonest bookkeeper be fired or simply hauled over the coals? (Fired; if he went unpunished he would get up to his old tricks again.) Should you blow the whistle on a dishonest colleague, even at the risk of damaging the company's image? (Yes. It would come out sooner or later, and you would be blamed for your inertia.) How to resolve the implacable hostility prevailing between a racist head of department and an African subordinate? (Fire them both. In the event of a dispute, never pronounce in favour of either party; you're running a company, not presiding over a tribunal.) After completing three sheets I'd already fired a dozen people. Irony or sadism? They were asking us, of all people, if our last employers had been right to dispense with our services. But we had already crossed the divide, and a change of location entailed a different point of view.

The other dilemmas they subjected us to were of the same order. Some touched on the private sphere and ethics in general, but most concerned problems of the kind firms encountered in practice. We could answer yes or no and justify our option. None of the questions was too hard. You simply had to look a little further than the end of your nose and assess the long-term consequences instead of solving the immediate problem on impulse. They had been shrewd enough not to include any item pertaining to trade unions or political parties, for fear of incurring the wrath of the freedom of information authority or seeing some malcontent leak their questionnaire to the press. On the other hand, some seemingly innocuous questions did relate to national economic policy. For example: strong currency or weak? (Weak. Only the banks were interested in having a strong currency, and I had no wish to work in the banking sector.) The 35-hour week? (You had to be against it unless you were looking for a permanent post in a trade union or a government ministry. In any case, it was irrelevant to executives of our type.)

My competitors weren't having too tough a time. None of them was gazing fixedly out of the window in the usual examinee's fashion. They were trying to give the impression that it was all too easy, and that they were answering the questions quickly. It wasn't a timed performance, however, and even Del Rieco had disappeared at the outset, leaving us under the inoffensive supervision of his assistant. Nobody was interested in cribbing from his or her neighbour.

We were submitted to a colour test whose purpose escaped me. In conclusion, a blank sheet invited us write a free appreciation of the test. I said it was tricky to give general replies when each case was specific, and that, although it was good to have principles, particular circumstances could provide a pretext for departing from them.

Jean-Claude collected our papers at midday. In the bar, nobody drank anything alcoholic. Morin launched into a long argument with plump little Aimé Leroy on the subject of racism. In his firm, he said, 80 per cent of the labour force were North Africans. If a head of department gave evidence of racism, he had to be fired for fear of provoking a general strike. Leroy carped at this. One Frenchman in three described himself as a racist, according to him, and it was smarter to use persuasion than a big stick. Morin retorted that converting a racist was as impossible as rendering an imbecile intelligent. No one was unwise enough to join in this debate.

Like students emerging from their finals, everyone wanted to know what the others thought of the test. The red-faced hulk (his name, it transpired, was Chalamont) sententiously declared that there were some very bad answers but no really good ones because the situations were such that you always intervened too late.

"The question about divorce was rather personal, I thought," said the woman in the waistcoat.

From which we inferred that she herself was a divorcee.

"Like the colour question," said Hirsch. "Did they want to know if we were colour-blind, or what?"

"No, no," said Pinetti, "it's the latest thing. There are even people who treat illnesses with colours. If you've got tonsillitis, they make you see blue and it cures you."

"You mean it works?" asked Hirsch.

Pinetti burst out laughing.

"No, of course not."

"Unless you believe in it," the bearded man put in. "Given that at least a third of all ailments are psychosomatic, it doesn't matter what cures you as long as you believe in it. Herbal tea, Lourdes – why not colours?"

"Maybe," Hirsch said angrily, "but they're charlatan's tricks."

"What about astrology?" Pinetti demanded. "A few years ago they put you through all kinds of hoops: graphology, the transit of the moon in the Fourth House – the lot. You turned up with a master's from MIT, and they told you your Jupiter was in the wrong place."

Hirsch turned to Laurence Carré.

"Is that true? I can't believe it! Did you use that stuff when you were in human resources?"

"No," she said curtly, without even looking at him. Natalie put an end to the discussion by announcing that lunch was served.

The afternoon turned out to be a lot more interesting. This time Del Rieco officiated in person.

"We're going to play some little games," he announced, "just to relax you. Here's the first. You're the spokesman for a construction company, and you've just heard that there's been an accident on site: a floor has collapsed. There are casualties – you don't know how many. You have ten minutes to draft a press release, which you'll then read aloud to us. Since you could obviously be influenced by what was said by those who preceded you, you'll all hand in your drafts together, and you're not allowed to depart from your original text. Ten minutes. That, be it noted, is roughly the interval that has elapsed between the first reports of the accident and the first journalist's phone call. Naturally, I'll be representing the press as a whole. I can ask questions; you can't. Okay?"

Aimé Leroy raised his hand.

"I wouldn't know how to start, it's not my bag. The ones with experience of such things will have an unfair advantage. If I were the MD I'd have a press officer to handle hot potatoes like this."

"Yes," said Del Rieco, "but the guy you pay to handle them happens to be on vacation and the building didn't warn him of its impending collapse. You're all on your own. Meantime, the journalists are burning up the wires. You have the right to tell them that no one is authorized to issue any information – that's one option. It's up to you. Don't worry, other games will be more up your street. It'll all even out."

Leroy mumbled something inaudible and subsided with a scowl.

"Ten minutes precisely," called Del Rieco.

When the time was up, he put our sheaf of press releases on his desk and invited the woman in the waistcoat to come and read hers aloud. She was hopeless, and most of the others fared little better. Aimé Leroy, still nursing his resentment, curtly announced that he would have to await the investigators' report and could say nothing more for the present. Hirsch spluttered, interspersing his perfor-mance with would-be reassuring smiles that made him look imbecilic. Morin contrived to sound sincere, but gilded the lily by departing from his prepared text, which earned him an icy rebuke from Del Rièco.

Laurence Carré proved convincing, though it's true that she came just after Pinetti, who never looked anyone in the eye. His sly manner ended by persuading us that there were hundreds of fatalities, and that his firm had a lot of guilty secrets. She, on the other hand, outlined the situation in crisp tones and confined herself to the indisputable facts. Del Rieco intervened for the first time. Perhaps because he had left the others to dig their own graves, he decided to needle her.

"Exactly how many casualties are there?"

"We don't know yet," she replied.

"You don't know or you won't say?"

She turned to him, playing the game.

"Look, you're a journalist – a professional like me. You know what happens when disasters like this occur. Days can go by before a final figure emerges. I'm giving you all the information I have; I can't give you what I don't have myself."

"But how many are we talking about," Del Rieco insisted, "two or twenty?"

"Two or twenty, either would be too many. Allow me to spare a thought for the men who are still under the debris – the ones we're trying to extricate. Right now, they're my first priority. I hope we'll get most of them out alive."

"Hey," protested Aimé Leroy, "that's not fair! That wasn't in her draft."

Del Rieco looked tickled. Smiling, he gestured to Laurence Carré to rejoin the others.

She was followed by Charriac, who was equally self-assured and struck the right note from the start. He read his piece with suppressed emotion.

"As for who, if anyone, was responsible," he wound up, "that, of course, will be established by the inquiry. If our company is implicated in some way, if we have made some mistake or other, we shall not evade our obligations but meet them in full. Up to now, nothing has been established and all we have are conflicting theories. But this I *promise* you: you will know everything in due course. We owe it not only to the press but, above all, to the victims' families. This tragedy has shattered us all. We're as anxious to get at the truth as anyone. We want to be able to sleep easy in our beds again."

"Unlike your victims," Del Rieco cut in. "Their sleep will be eternal."

Charriac eyed him with a kind of contempt.

"I envy your ability to make jokes on such an occasion. Personally, I'm devastated. My sense of humour has deserted me completely. It'll be a long time before I regain it."

Dead silence reigned as he resumed his seat. He had been so convincing, we all felt that the disaster was real – that some unfortunate workmen had really been crushed by slabs of concrete.

I came last. Charriac hadn't made my task any easier. Del Rieco handed me my draft, but I suddenly made up my mind to join the revolt and totally disregard it.

The others had already pulled out all the stops and said all there was to be said. I wouldn't fare any better if I followed the same line.

"At 3.23 this afternoon," I extemporized, "an accident occurred on one of my firm's construction sites. The emergency services, who were notified at once, initiated rescue procedures. At 3.44 head office received a phone call from the foreman, whose name and particulars will be made available to you in due course. He informed us that a floor had collapsed, and that casualties had resulted. He was very distressed, and said nothing about the cause of the accident. To date, this is the only direct contact we have had. According to our records, 16 workmen were assigned to this site. They weren't all working on the same floor, but we think that several of them may be among the casualties. The site was closed to the public, so there is no reason to believe that any persons outside the firm may be involved. That is the full extent of our present information. The emergency services are already hard at work, and I shall be joining them at once. The local authority will be opening a press room. I propose to meet you there at about five o'clock, in time for your evening editions. I should then be able to give you firmer and more detailed information. Thank you."

I broke off and returned to my place without looking at Del Rieco. Hirsch, who was sitting beside me, pulled an approving face.

"Very professional," he murmured.

Del Rieco gave me a long, impassive look. He must have been furious, but he didn't want to create another incident.

Having completed his notes, he rose and clasped his hands together like a lecturer, swaying a little on the balls of his feet.

"If this were a training session I should have a number of

comments to make. But we aren't here to improve your technique, even if some of you could do with it. At this stage, it's too late for that. With one exception, you all obeyed the rules, and – "

"Who was the exception?" Aimé Leroy blurted out. "Me?"

"No, not you. Kindly stop interrupting and allow me to run this seminar my way. We're now going to move on to something different. This time it's job interviews – "

"Those we know about," Hirsch whispered. "We're experts."

" – with each of you playing the part of the DHR in turn. Your task will be to – "

Inevitably, Leroy had a bone to pick:

"Listen, there's someone here who's been a director of communi-cations *and* a director of human resources as well. All your sketches are tailored to her qualifications. Why not simply count her out and do something that interests the rest of us?"

"Are you talking about me?" Laurence Carré demanded.

I had never seen her smile, except when talking to the Italian boatman, and her voice would have frozen an Inuit. Leroy stood firm.

"Yes, of course I am. Are there any more like you?"

"What are you implying? That I'm this gentleman's cousin? That I'm his girlfriend? That he's engineered the whole thing for my benefit? I'd be very flattered if that were the case, but – "

Del Rieco thumped his desk.

"That's enough! Monsieur Leroy, do me a favour and wait till the end of the seminar. If you're dissatisfied you can always write to De Wavre International and tell them I was outrageously prejudiced. There are all kinds here, as you've noticed. It's pure chance if someone presents characteristics that give them an advantage on the first day – in theory, at least. But it's like the Tour de France: there are flat racers and hill climbers. The flat racers excel on level ground.

We'll see what you can do in the mountains – if you're capable of getting there."

Leroy scowled and said no more. Laurence Carré tilted her chin disdainfully.

The job interviews varied in amusement value. Del Rieco handed each candidate an imaginary CV and watched to see if the person acting the DHR detected its inherent flaws. Although some of us played the game, others devised insoluble problems for their opposite numbers: chequered careers, irremediable defects to which only fleeting reference was made. Morin evoked roars of laughter with his impersonation of a stuttering Marseillais who happened to be a world expert on rare metals. At the end of each interview the director of human resources had to draft a brief memo stating whether or not the applicant had been accepted. My first pairing was with the man whose name sounded Arab – El Fatawi or something similar. I decided to recruit him as head of security provided he could produce a clean police record. That, as I'd quickly deduced, was the fly in his particular ointment. Next, I faced Chalamont and applied for a job in charge of staff training. He asked the wrong questions, poor man, and never found out that I had been dismissed from a private teaching post for sexual harassment: he hired me.

Towards evening we had to defend divergent points of view in the course of three round-table discussions: one on the taking of performance-enhancing drugs by athletes, one on the liberalization of cannabis, and the last on what to do with juvenile delinquents. This exercise resembled the École Nationale d'Administration orals in which candidates have to spend ten minutes discoursing on an unfamiliar subject without betraying their total ignorance of it. I had attended enough boardroom meetings for this not to present me with any problem. I noticed yet again that I had not been pitted against Charriac or Laurence Carré. The organizers had clearly worked out a pecking order, and the best of us were being shielded from direct confrontation. That, at least, was my immodest inference after the first day's proceedings.

At dinner we sat down in almost the same places as we'd occupied the previous night. It has always fascinated me to see how swiftly habits become crystallized. Each of us now laid claim to a chair; soon this would extend to napkin rings. There were only two or three changes: Laurence Carré, doubtless weary of Morin's one-man show, joined our table, and Chalamont took her place in the party of four. Affinities were beginning to take shape: Morin and his complaisant audience, the only full table; the five rejects; and our own circle, which comprised Carré, Charriac, Hirsch, Pinetti, and me. Morin and his coterie were less noisy than they had been the night before, probably because the day had sapped their energy. At the other end of the dining-room, Chalamont and the woman in the waistcoat were eating in silence, flanked by El Fatawi and the bald man.

"Well," said Pinetti as he sat down, "I'm flattered to be privileged to sit with the leaders in the overall placings."

"We don't know anything about that," Laurence Carré replied.

Pinetti waved his fork.

"Come, come, everyone could tell. It's true one occasionally wonders what they're getting at, but most of the time it's clear enough."

Laurence Carré pulled another sceptical face. A faint smile was hovering on Charriac's thin lips.

"Madame is wary of jumping to conclusions," he said. "To be honest, so am I. They're watching us on several levels. It's as if we're Russian dolls: there's one inside the first, a third inside the second, and so on."

"And what's inside the last one?" asked Hirsch.

Charriac cast his eyes up at the ceiling.

"Who knows? Maybe a diamond, maybe nothing at all."

"I think that depends on the individual," said Hirsch. "They've made no secret of it: they're plucking us like artichokes, leaf by leaf, to see when we crack."

"Artichokes don't crack," Laurence Carré pointed out.

"Okay, so artichokes don't," said Hirsch, "but we may."

Silence fell. The waiter brought us a bowl of green salad sprinkled with morsels of Gruyère.

Pinetti sighed. "I long for a meal that doesn't include any cheese – not a crumb of the stuff. We'll all be as fat as pigs before we're through."

"It's because of the cows," said Hirsch. "Cheese is the only local product, so they've got to get rid of it. Say, talking of cows, did you know their farts are responsible for destroying the ozone layer? Their stomachs generate vast quantities of methane."

Laurence Carré clicked her tongue with a pained expression.

"Do you mind! We're at table. If all you can talk about is ruminants' gastric troubles, I'll go back to Morin, He's coarse, but at least he isn't scatological."

Hirsch flushed at this rebuke. He tried to think of a cutting response, failed, and bent over his plate. Charriac gave him a look of undisguised amusement, transferred it to Laurence Carré, and sat back in his chair.

"Ah, I enjoy a good fight. And with madame here, I don't think we'll be disappointed."

Laurence Carré eyed him askance.

"I'm not particularly interested in the effects of bovine digestion on the environment. Still, if you're all determined to explore the subject, I won't oppose the consensus."

Charriac scratched an eyebrow with the tip of his little finger. Then, planting his elbows on the table, he propped his chin on his folded hands and stared at her appraisingly.

"You're a marvel. When you talk, you sound as if you're reading from a prepared script."

He turned, soliciting our agreement.

"I'm right, aren't I? It's quite extraordinary – almost unique, in my experience. You'd think she writes her replies in her head and then reads them out." He turned back to Laurence Carré. "How do you manage it?"

She bent her head and forked up a lettuce leaf, but he wouldn't let her off the hook.

"Don't be offended, I mean it as a compliment. You've a way of expressing yourself which is completely ..." He thought for a moment. "Literary, that's the word. Listening to you, one would think you were reading a book aloud. Don't you ever relax?"

She slowly raised her eyes to his.

"Not in your company, anyway."

Charriac spread his hands appeasingly.

"Oh, I never hoped you would. Like you, I'm constantly aware that we're, well, competitors, in a sense. It really wasn't a proposal of marriage."

Pinetti broke in.

"They're going to make us fight among ourselves," he said darkly, "you mark my words. It's already started, and it'll end the same way."

Charriac briefly shifted his aim.

"But of course. Why do you think they've put us in a group? If they'd wanted to examine us individually, they could have continued the tests in Paris. They want to see what happens when we're all together – see who survives the frightening jungle of human relations in a climate of competition."

"And I'm the one who talks like a book," sighed Laurence Carré.

With a nonchalant gesture, Charriac returned the ball from the back of the court.

"I read books myself, contrary to appearances, and I also know how to watch every word I say. But it doesn't cost me as much of an effort – I don't have to go as stiff as a poker. Nobody here means you any harm, dear lady. I'll kill you if you get in my way, but I'll send you some flowers beforehand."

There was no doubt about it: Charriac had effortlessly gained the upper hand over all present. All except me. I said nothing, merely watched him. He was drumming on his chest like a gorilla, asserting his apelike superiority over all who might later prove a threat to him. I could see through his game. By bullying each of them in turn he was trying to frighten them, weaken them, with a view to reaping the benefits of this policy in due course. He had already managed to unsettle them to a greater or lesser extent, but he didn't impress me.

He must have sensed this, because he turned to me.

"Our friend here is being very silent . . ."

I was moulding some bread into a pellet. I flicked it into my plate with my thumb and waited a good three seconds.

"You don't tell someone your life story before you shoot him."

Charriac mimed applause with his fingertips.

"Bravo. Sergio Leone, right? The cowboy's in the bath, and he produces a gun from under the bubbles while the other man is explaining how he's going to kill him. A great sequence. I love Westerns, don't you?"

"Yes, as long as I'm on the right side of the gun."

He knit his brow.

"Now what film did that come from? It rings a bell . . ."

The salad was followed by steak and chips. Pinetti pretended to refuse.

"Oh, no, not more cow . . . I really couldn't . . ."

Laurence Carré, annoyed at having been likened to a poker, decided to show she could be flippant.

"I'm curious to know how they're going to make cow sorbet for pudding," she said in a milder tone.

"But didn't you know?" Pinetti retorted. "There's cow fat in everything, even ice cream. When mad cow disease came along, it turned out that they even put it in beauty products!"

Charriac feigned consternation.

"There he goes again! Monsieur Pianetti has decided to spoil our appetite for good! How could you, after what madame – "

"Pinetti," Pinetti cut in. "Not Pianetti: Pinetti."

"Oh, so sorry. For my sins, you may call me Chirac instead of Charriac – but only once."

"I've heard more amusing word games," said Laurence Carré, icy once more.

Hirsch wagged his head.

"You're exhausting, the lot of you."

He wasn't wrong, but he wasn't very sophisticated either. All fashionable dinner parties teem with verbal duels designed to single out the strongest, the smartest, or the most rhetorically gifted – the one who will dominate the rest. Except in those rare instances where the diners are genuine friends with no disputes outstanding between them, food is merely a pretext for the establishment of a hierarchy, a subtle, disguised game whose moves are eagerly discussed when the match is over. In this, the aristocrats of our democratic society are merely aping the habits of the nobility of the Ancien Régime, when counts and barons, no longer able to cross blades, employed ridicule to kill, ignominy to wound, and tongues instead of rapiers.

A basket of fruit replaced the dreaded cow-fat sorbet. By selecting a peach and peeling it perfectly, Laurence Carré gave us a renewed demonstration of her excellent upbringing. Charriac delicately peeled a banana, Pinetti sank his teeth in an apple, I took nothing.

After coffee I went for a stroll beside the lake. I, too, was beginning to develop routines of my own. The moon had risen. Seen by its wan, subdued light, the sombre mass of fir trees looked like a repository of dark secrets. I walked down to the shore and dipped my hand in the icy water. Not a breath of wind; the chill was in the air itself.

I didn't hear Laurence Carré coming. Just as she had the previous night, she sat down on a rock and arranged the folds of her red skirt around her. She looked splendidly at one with the scenery as she gazed into the distance with her profile sharply outlined against the surface of the lake.

I said hello and was about to go back to the hotel when she spoke.

"That man Charriac ... What do you make of him? I don't like him."

"Hardly surprising, after the way he went for you."

She pulled a face.

"Yes, but it isn't that. That's no big deal – I'm used to it. Women often have a tough time in this sort of environment. It was when he said he'd kill me – he really wanted to do it. You didn't get that impression? It was so ... so out of the blue ..."

She spoke with her eyes fixed on the far shore of the lake, as if thinking aloud. I had to draw nearer to avoid missing anything.

"It was just a metaphor," I said.

She shrugged.

"Oh, sure, the eternal power struggle. They talk of screwing their competitors, of shoving it up them, that sort of thing. They employ a very sexual vocabulary when they think you aren't listening. It's an odd kind of sex, though. To them, making love entails humiliating the other party, getting them at your mercy. That's their idea of a loving relationship, hadn't it ever struck you?"

"Yes."

I was rather surprised by the crudity of her own vocabulary. Still, she was only quoting expressions I'd heard my male colleagues use innumerable times. And so, no doubt, had she, even if they made some effort to curb their tongues when ladies were present.

"And then," she went on, "on another level it's violence: kill, beat to a pulp, trample underfoot . . . All right, that's the game, the way of the world. They're just words, but with Charriac it's different. Why did he say he wanted to kill me? Because he's incapable of doing anything else to me?"

She turned and looked at me for a moment as she uttered the last words, then smoothed her skirt down. My surprise gave way to amazement. I'd been utterly unprepared for such straight talking. On the other hand, I told myself, she hadn't got there entirely by chance. Her high horse act was well worth a place in Morin's Marseillais circus. I scratched my chin.

"He didn't say he *wanted* to kill you, he said he'd kill you if you got in his way."

She sighed and gave her skirt another pat.

"It amounts to the same thing. I *will* get in his way, and so will you. We all know there are only a few vacancies, maybe only one or two, and we all want them. If not, we wouldn't have come this far. Why did he say it?"

"To frighten you."

She slowly rose, went down to the water's edge, and stood motionless with her back turned and her arms folded.

"Perhaps. Or to make sure I understood the rules."

She gave a momentary shiver and took a few steps along the shore. I followed her, keeping my distance. She walked with her head down, eyes on the pebbles at her feet.

"Charriac isn't star quality, not really," I said, trying to reassure her. "He wouldn't be here if he was. He may be the best of the reserves, but he's on the bench, not on the pitch. That's why he's angry. You're dangerous because you caught Del Rieco's eye today, so he's trying to eliminate you."

She paused, reducing the distance between us.

"You think he's going to kill me?"

"Are you scared?" I asked.

She smiled for the first time, and her teeth glinted in the moonlight.

"No. If I were scared I'd be a checkout assistant in a supermarket, or running an arts and crafts shop subsidized by a wealthy husband. No, it's simply that I can sense violence in the man. Not just rivalry: hatred."

"I haven't felt it," I said soothingly.

"That's because you aren't a woman," she murmured.

Did she really feel scared – scared to the point of wanting to share her fear? Was she seeking an ally? She didn't know me, knew nothing about me. I might be quite as much of a threat to her as Charriac. Was she trying to get round me so as not to have to fight a war on two fronts?

"I'm in the race too, you know," I said softly.

She kept her eyes lowered.

"Yes," she replied, "I know. Every word can be a weapon, every spark of humanity a weakness, every confidence a betrayal. The others are different. Take Morin and his merry men. They think this is a school exam or a kind of sales convention. You wait: another couple of days and they'll be asking if there's a nightclub around here. They sent off 100 applications at random and replied to 50 small ads. To them, this is just a job interview like any other. Or a game of roulette. They've stuck a 100 francs on number 18, and they're waiting to see if it comes up. Not me, though. Not Charriac. Not you. Maybe not Pinetti or El Fatawi. We're the finalists,

Monsieur Carceville. We're going to tear each other to pieces."

She sighed again, chafing her arms to warm them.

"It's a bore," she went on. "In other circumstances we might have hit it off together. But they wanted it this way. They want to find out if we're capable of being ruthless. I can't allow myself to flunk De Wavre. Anything but that."

This was an interesting piece of information. Casually, I prompted her to go on.

"They're as important to you as all that?"

"De Wavre? They're a must. All the major companies have been using them for the past year or two. If they recommend you, you're made; if they reject you, you're done for. University degrees are fine when you're starting out in business, but later on there's only De Wavre, the ultimate executive search machine. Fail that, and the best you can hope for is a floorwalker's job in a department store. Didn't you know?"

"I've always worked for smallish firms. Their methods of recruitment are different."

"Yes, it's all right when they're small, but I've been in personnel selection, as you know, and I've seen the way big firms work. *Zut*, I shouldn't have told you that, it'll motivate you."

Laurence Carré must have been the last Frenchwoman to say "*zut*" instead of "*merde*".

"Why did they, er . . . ?"

She hesitated for a moment.

"Fire me? Ah, that's my secret. How about you?"

She wasn't expecting a reply – she didn't get one in any case – and walked on. We had strayed some distance from the hotel, of which all that could now be seen was a faint glow above the trees. All at once a rocky spur loomed up ahead of us. The path left the lakeshore and plunged into the woods.

"We'd better come back in daylight sometime, don't you think?"

Laurence retraced her steps and I followed her. At one point she tripped over a stone. She caught hold of my arm for an instant and promptly apologized.

When we reached the foot of the track beside the landing stage, I tried to sound her out a little more.

"What about Del Rieco? Did you know him before?"

She hesitated again.

"No, not exactly. There are one or two gurus at De Wavre. I used to know someone who was recruited after passing through their hands. He called them the 'brain surgeons'. Del Rieco must be one of them."

"You notice they never eat with us?"

"Of course not. When you share a meal with someone it creates a bond. We'd have tried to pump them – to ingratiate ourselves."

"To seduce them, you mean."

She rounded on me.

"You're all the same! Sex! You think that's the only weapon in a woman's armoury. You see it in everything!"

"No," I said haltingly, "I was using 'seduce' in the general sense . . ."

She took no notice. Her look of anger was unmistakable, even in the moonlight.

"You don't seduce one of De Wavre's brain surgeons. It's not even worth trying."

I spread my arms, pleading innocence.

"It never crossed my mind, I promise you. The last thing I wanted to do was . . . I mean, seduction isn't a uniquely feminine activity. There are plenty of other kinds."

She treated me to a sardonic smile.

"Touché! Now and then, when I've had it up to here, I succumb to a brief attack of feminism. Women have a tough time, that's all. Don't hold it against me."

We returned to the hotel without exchanging another word. I went up to my room and re-immersed myself in my thriller.

On Tuesday morning the proceedings began in earnest. Having assembled us in the workroom as usual, Del Rieco announced that we were entering a simulation phase scheduled to last three days. We were to be divided into three teams, each of which constituted the management of a firm. Occupying the same commercial niche and endowed with assets in equal measure, the three firms would fight for the lion's share of the market. Win or lose, it was up to us. There were no rules other than this: Del Rieco was the referee, and he alone would tell us if our initiatives were succeeding or failing. We could organize ourselves and act as we pleased; our ingenuity was subject to no constraints. He would furnish us with the requisite documents: balance sheet, profit and loss account, personnel list, state of the market – all that a managing director keeps in the drawers of his desk. If we needed anything else, Del Rieco would supply it on request.

This, he told us, was a method based on role-play games such as Dungeons and Dragons. There was a small element of chance, but no more so than in real life. We would simply suffer the consequences of any decisions we took. We could go without sleep for all three nights, if we wished, but Del Rieco himself would be unavailable between midnight and six in the morning.

Needless to say, Aimé Leroy was quick to erect a barricade of objections. What form would the scoring take? No scoring, Del Rieco replied. He would simply observe the sequence of events. When would someone have won? It wasn't a question of winning; the teams would end by producing financial statements of a more or less favourable nature. How had the teams been picked? That was Del Rieco's responsibility. Could their composition be changed? No. But if a team was unbalanced, wouldn't that be a disadvantage? You couldn't choose your colleagues when a firm recruited you, Del Rieco said testily – not to begin with, at any rate. What equipment would we have? Computers, paper, and pens. Finally, what product were we supposed to be manufacturing? It didn't matter – anything we liked. Fish-hooks, Pinetti suggested jocularly. Okay, said Del Rieco, fish-hooks it is.

He then read out the teams. Charriac found himself with Pinetti, Morin, and two of Morin's clique. They were Team A. Team B consisted of Laurence Carré, El Fatawi, Chalamont, Aimé Leroy, and another two of Morin's boys. In Team C I inherited Hirsch; the woman in the waistcoat, who confided that her name was Marilyn (but not Monroe, she added swiftly, to banish the extreme improbability that someone might have thought so); the lean, tanned ex-Olympic athlete, whose name turned out to be Mastroni; and the remaining woman, a faded redhead with tired eyes, who introduced herself as Brigitte Aubert. I mentally doffed my hat to Del Rieco: each team included one good one, one or two reasonable ones, and a brace of zeros.

We each had a floor and a room to ourselves. Charriac was on the second floor, Laurence Carré on the first. Our premises – a small room, most of which was taken up by a large table – were downstairs beside the kitchen.

"At least we won't go short of food," Hirsch said consolingly.

While we were settling in, Natalie appeared with a stack of documents. Our little room smelt of fresh paint. There was a computer in one corner of the table, a flip-chart easel facing it, and, as Del Rieco had promised, plenty of paper and ballpoint pens.

I waited until all my colleagues were seated before taking charge of operations without more ado.

"Right, now listen. I'm a management consultant. We'll waste less time if you let me organize things. If I screw up, tell me right away and we'll have a reshuffle. We must act as a team: whether we sink or swim, we'll do it together. We won't have time for arguments, so there won't be any. There mustn't be any secrets between us, either, but not a word to anyone outside this room. From now on it's war: your only friends are in here; everyone outside wants to do us down. I've got to know two or three of the people we're up against, and they're pros. You want De Wavre's seal of approval? Okay, let's flog our guts out and we'll get it."

My warlike tirade had clearly appealed to the two women. Hirsch, who was sitting beside me, also nodded vigorously. Mastroni was slightly less enthusiastic, I sensed, so I addressed him direct.

"Okay, what's your speciality?"

"I'm a marketing man."

"Good. I'm appointing you our sales director. Look through that stack of papers and tell us all you can about the state of the market and the strategy you recommend. You, Hirsch, take a look at the computer and find out what it can do. They must have installed some software – see what you make of it. If you can't, no one can. Marilyn, we need someone to make careful notes of everything – every last detail: the team's memory, a job of vital importance. You're the managing director's PA. Any boss would be half as effective without one, as you know."

She blushed at the compliment. I had motivated each of them

sufficiently for them to get down to work right away. Hirsch, his eyes shining, switched on the computer and started pecking away at the keyboard, Mastroni leafed through the printouts Natalie had brought us. I turned to the redhead.

"And you, what can you do, apart from look decorative?"

She smiled faintly, half flattered, half contemptuous.

"I'm in advertising."

"You'll be much in demand when we relaunch our business after doing the necessary housework. For the moment – "

"I know," she cut in. "It's the first budget to be cut when things are going badly. In the meantime I could nose around a bit – see if I can pick up any information."

"Good idea."

She rose with a mischievous air. At best, she would be able to brief us on the atmosphere prevailing in the other teams. At worst, she would go off for a siesta and get out from under our feet.

Hirsch called to me over his shoulder.

"Word, Excel, spreadsheets, the traditional package. No Internet, but we're linked to some kind of network, that's what worries me. Wait, I'm going to try something. Give me a moment."

A conscientious type, Hirsch. I sensed I would be able to rely on him implicitly. Mastroni extracted some sheets from the stack of documents and pushed the rest across the table.

"I'll take a look at these. The others don't mean much to me, I'm afraid. I've never been able to read a balance sheet."

I waved this aside.

"No problem, I'll get stuck into them."

"Anyone like some coffee?" Marilyn suggested.

Mastroni looked up.

"Bring us a bucket," he said. "And five straws."

I pulled the folders towards me, happy to have cleared the first hurdle without mishap. They were all quite nice, and no one was disputing my leadership for the moment. I hoped Charriac and Laurence Carré were having greater difficulty and wasting valuable time. Generally speaking, an MD spends half his days resolving staff problems. I felt I ought to thank Del Rieco for giving me a team made to measure.

I immersed myself in the firm's accounts. As quickly as possible, I tried to assess the can of worms I'd been handed. The authorized share capital struck me as a trifle meagre in relation to turnover, but this wasn't a serious drawback as long as we didn't have to seek any loans. Our cash flow situation looked healthy, our burden of debt about right. Sales had registered a slight but perceptible decline in the past three months.

I raised this point with Mastroni.

"I noticed," he replied.

"What's been happening, in your opinion?"

His lean face lit up. He was in his element.

"Well, any market gets oversold sooner or later, you know. In the final analysis, all sales graph curves are S-shaped: they end by flattening out, simply because the market's saturated. That's when you have to find a new market, export your products, interest a new range of consumers, or effect a technological breakthrough that renders the stuff outmoded and makes the punters want something else. What's more . . . You want to know what I really think?"

"Of course."

"There are too many of us. There's not enough room in this sector for three firms. Two, perhaps, but not three."

"How about one?" I smirked.

"Ah," he said with a smile, "one would be even better."

I nodded. It was always the same. All they really dreamed of, the smooth talkers who extolled the virtues of competition, was a monopoly. You had only to see what they did once they left the television studio.

So at least one of the three teams had to disappear. De Wavre wanted to know how we went about achieving this and who would be the first to go under. Marilyn came teetering in with a pot of coffee and five cups on a tray.

"Had it struck you?" she asked gaily. "My name's Marilyn and Monsieur Mastroni's is almost Mastroianni. They could have made a lovely film together, couldn't they, Marilyn Monroe and Marcello Mastroianni? Why ever didn't they think of it?"

Her question went unanswered. Hirsch swung round to face us in his chair.

"What shall I say to them?"

"Huh?"

"We're hooked up to a kind of Intranet – we can communicate with everyone in the game: the referee, Team A, Team B – everyone. We can exchange e-mails. They set up the system so we could only get in touch with Del Rieco, but I've tinkered with it a bit. I can access anyone I want."

I bent over, unable to suppress a satisfied grin, and gave him a congratulatory pat on the shoulder.

"Shall I tell them 'Peekaboo!'?" he suggested.

"No, don't," I said quickly. "Better not give the game away at this stage. Can you really get into their computers?"

"Only their e-mails. That was mandatory. When you set up a network, there has to be some means of getting back into it. The only way to evade an intruder is to disconnect. If Del Rieco plans to communicate with us and with each of the other two, there's bound to be a node somewhere."

This certainly opened up new prospects.

"Can you find out what e-mails they've received?"

84

Hirsch thought for a moment.

"No, but it's not out of the question. I'll have to lay an egg in their nest, then I'll be able to go and look at anything I want. But it means getting in touch with them at least once. Do that, and it sticks like a burr. They'll be suckered, and I can get into their knickers any time I want. That's Microsoft and Pentium III for you."

"And you can do that?"

"Maybe. I'll have to see, but it'll take me all day."

"Carry on, we don't need you or the machine at present. But tell me, can you do the same with Del Rieco's computer?"

He massaged his Adam's apple, looking dubious.

"I doubt it. There has to be a password. It's not beyond the bounds of possibility that I could crack it, but it might take me the whole week unless I got lucky. In the old days people used to put the names of their children; now they use unrelated letters. There are seven of them, though, so they have to write them down somewhere or they forget them. Find me Del Rieco's password and I'll tell you what he's got up his sleeve."

"Brilliant. Marilyn, try to find ... what was her name again, the woman with the red hair?"

"Brigitte."

"That's it. Tell her I'd like to see her right away. You'll find her with her ear glued to a keyhole, but we may have a far better method."

Marilyn obediently got up, gave us a friendly smile, and left the room. I turned my attention to Mastroni. He had the wary look of an honest citizen who sees a minor offence being committed and wonders if he ought to intervene.

"You think it's allowed?" he asked. "I mean, won't we all get the chop?"

"Who's to know? Look what happens on the stock exchange: anything goes as long as you don't get caught."

After all, we hadn't done anything illicit so far. Del Rieco had provided us with a computer, but he hadn't imposed a ban on using it. Besides, it rather appealed to me, the thought of taking him down a peg by dismantling his crude system, even at the price of a reprimand. Hirsch set to work again.

"All right, Mastroni," I said. "Give me a rundown on our distributors. We're really fortunate to have someone with your experience in this field."

After devoting so much attention to Hirsch and his computer, I didn't want Mastroni feeling left out. I saw his pupils dilate slightly. In a seduction scene this denotes sexual arousal. Observe the dimensions of the other person's pupils and you know exactly where you stand. There was no question of this in Mastroni's case, but I'd definitely given him a boost. He bent over his papers.

"We have a number of small distributors – retailers of field sports equipment, I guess. More importantly, we have two really major customers: a supermarket chain, which takes a third of our output, and a central purchasing agency, which takes nearly a quarter of it. That's where we're going to clash with the others, I suspect. If we lose one of the two, or simply if one of them reduces its orders, we're a dead duck."

This seemed logical. Manufacturing is only a branch of sales nowadays, and the big boys have the producers by the throat in every sector.

"Are they bigger than us?" I asked.

"Yes, a lot bigger, and they don't just deal in fish-hooks."

So we couldn't buy them out and become our own retailers.

"And are we cheaper or more expensive than the other two?"

Mastroni made a noncommittal gesture.

"Team A is more expensive, Team B less so. I get the impression that Team A's products are more sophisticated, so they're not as dependent on the major buyers. Team B makes bottom of the range stuff."

"You think we could risk a price war?"

He hesitated. Mastroni was one of those people who never feel sure of what they're proposing. You have to chivvy them into overcoming their caution and extract the facts with forceps.

"Perhaps. It's hard to say. Only you can decide if it's worth the risk."

I suddenly felt a lot less grateful to Del Rieco. Middling positions are the worst of all. It's easy to sell dirt-cheap junk or high-priced products of advanced technology. The risks and disadvantages arise when you're midway between them.

Just then, Marilyn reappeared, pushing a gum-chewing Brigitte Aubert ahead of her.

"No luck," Brigitte said with a kind of perverse satisfaction. "They've all barricaded themselves in. I did a bit of nosing around, though, and I know where Monsieur Del Rieco hangs out. There's a kind of chalet hidden among the trees behind the hotel. That's where he is. The waiter was bringing him some paper – I tailed him there."

So Del Rieco had a secret lair in which to hatch his sinister plans. I gripped Brigitte's arm tightly.

"Okay, listen. He'll have hidden a password somewhere – a series of seven letters on a slip of paper. It's probably kept beside a computer. Find it and I'll double your salary."

She burst out laughing. Then, almost imperceptibly, she responded to the pressure of my hand by throwing out her meagre bosom.

"Twice nothing doesn't amount to much, but thanks anyway. Is it important?"

"Very important. Get it for us and we're bound to win. We'll know all the parameters, that's why. Only you can do it."

She narrowed her eyes and struck a pose.

"You don't say! Okay, I'll be back."

Mastroni waited until she had left the room.

"You're the boss, but isn't this a bit risky? We've only just begun and already we're trying to cheat."

"We aren't cheating. De Wavre are the cheats – they have been from the start. They don't tell us even half of what they've got in mind. Afterwards they'll say, 'You, you're a wash-out,' and 'You, you're good,' and we'll never know why. Ask yourself this: have they ever told you the reasons for everything you've undergone to date? Well, have they?"

"No," he conceded grudgingly.

"You see? They want this charade to resemble real life? All right, we'll make sure it does. No holds barred, business is war. They're our enemies, Mastroni – our enemies. You're out of a job, aren't you?"

He shuffled around on his chair in embarrassment.

"Well, yes."

"Do you know why? Is it because you're a wash-out? Is that what they told you to your face? You aren't a wash-out and you know it, but there's a war on. They send for you and say, 'Look, we're really sorry, but the US pension fund managers are demanding a 15 per cent return on their capital and we can't manage it. It's hard luck on you, we know, but we'll have to let you go.' That's what they told you, isn't it? Am I right?"

"Not 15 per cent," he amended with dignity.

"No, they didn't give you a figure, but I'm telling you: it's 15. They line their pockets while you're wondering where your next meal is coming from. You haven't been to a Grande École, you don't have a six-digit income, you don't know how you're going to pay your household bills – and they tell you, 'Don't worry, if the worst comes to the worst there's still the government retraining scheme'. I know those retraining executives, don't you?"

"Yes," he admitted.

My little speech was taking effect. He was starting to revive, but I kept up the pressure.

"Are they worse than the rest? No, it's just that they've got another 50 irons in the fire. How old are you, Mastroni?"

"Forty-six."

"Hm, not long to go. They squeeze you like a lemon for 20 years and then they toss you out like so much garbage. And you still respect them? You want to play the game? Face facts: you played it and you lost. Except that it isn't a game, Mastroni, it's a jungle. If you don't have sharper teeth than theirs, they'll eat you. They're bigger, stronger, nastier. They were born in the right place, and they despise you. Did you know they despise you? They do, all of them. If you're walking down the street and you're stopped by some hulking brute who plans to mug you, there's only one answer: kick him in the balls. That's what we're going to do to them. You think Del Rieco's on *your* side? No one's on your side, Mastroni. Your wife, maybe, but that's all, and even that isn't certain. Del Rieco is on *their* side. He works for them, not you. Has he ever shared a meal with us? Has he ever said a kind word to you, even once? Never. He's paid to find out which of us is the smartest. Well, we'll show him. We'll show him we're even smarter than he is. We'll pull a fast one on him. He wants us to slaughter each other? Okay, we will, but we'll slaughter him too. This is a trap, can't you see? It's one huge, gigantic trap. You really want to be taken for a ride like a 20-franc whore?"

"Speak for yourself," said Marilyn, who was staring out of the window.

"Sorry, I got carried away. I've had it up to here, that's why, but so have you, I guess. What's the point of these stupid games? Should we show them we're good, obedient, well-disciplined soldiers? Not on your life. We'll be vicious – as vicious as they are. We won't play by their rules because they don't play by them either. Box like a gentleman and you'll get kicked in the crotch. This isn't a boxing match, it's all-in wrestling. We're up to our necks in shit. When they come to finish us off we'll bite them in the leg. I'll take full responsibility, Mastroni. If you're asked you can say it was an order. What can we lose, after all? If we play the way they've planned, we'll blow it. I ask you, look at this shitty fish-hook firm with its total dependence on a couple of customers. Tomorrow morning, when you've bust a gut, you'll get an e-mail saying, 'Sorry, cut your prices by 20 per cent or we'll go elsewhere.' Then all that remains is to put a bullet in your head. Is that the kind of game you want to play? Get slapped around the chops and thank them for it? It's a con, don't you see? Well, we're going to con them back. De Wavre can stuff their tests and their international reputation!"

"Well said," commented Hirsch without turning round.

Marilyn looked abstracted and said nothing, but she hadn't missed a word of my harangue. She also seemed favourably impressed. I rose to deliver my final peroration.

"It's no holds barred, Mastroni. There comes a time when even the chickens gang up on the fox. So Del Rieco won't tell us anything? Fine, we won't tell him anything either – no, but we'll *know* everything. I'm sick of being manipulated. Whatever happens, I'm going to leave here with my head held high. Either that, or feet first. This is your last chance, you say? Make the most of it, Mastroni. You've nothing to lose. They think you're already dead. Their selections are cut and dried, or hadn't you grasped that yet? I'll tell you who they are: Charriac and Laurence Carré. The rest of us they'll write to. Except that it needn't be like that. It all depends on you, Mastroni – on you and what you've got in your underpants."

Mastroni had been listening with his head bowed. He looked up and blinked a couple of times. I felt as if I were commanding a platoon in a Vietnamese paddy field. I didn't know where I'd got it from, that two-bit, macho pep talk. It was quite unlike me. Perhaps it had been simmering away inside me ever since I was fired, waiting for an opportunity to boil over. Perhaps Laurence Carré had been right to say that nothing much had changed since the Cro-Magnon era – that excess pressure unleashes atavistic instincts buried beneath the primitive cortex, entombed beneath a mass of ingrained thought processes, beneath a soft, comfortable, post-industrial eiderdown designed to stifle anger and hatred. In the last analysis, perhaps I'd been addressing myself rather than Mastroni.

I gave them all a broad smile.

"Okay, let's cool it. We'll run this firm by the book, but I want you all to know I'll stop at nothing if I have to. Del Rieco wants to see what we're made of, he's said so umpteen times. I'm going to show him, and he'll enjoy the trip. We're all in the same boat. If you think I've gone over the top, if you lose faith in me, you must tell me and someone else can run the show. I won't feel hurt. Is it a deal?"

"It's started," Hirsch said suddenly. "We've got an e-mail."

I chuckled. "The supermarkets? Asking for a 20 per cent reduction?"

"No, they simply say they want to renegotiate our prices."

I spread my arms.

"What did I tell you? Good for us, we foresaw what they were going to do. Tell them to come up with some proposals."

Hirsch pushed his chair back and rose.

"I'm no good at writing letters, it's not my thing . . ."

Marilyn left her place beside the window.

"I can't do much, but letters I can write. May I have a go? I'll draft it on paper to start with. That way, if you want any changes made . . ."

I gave her the thumbs up.

"It sticks out a mile," I told them. "Naïve, almost. They want to know we're capable of making economies and tightening up the management – if we can still get by with lower prices. And how do we do that?"

"Staff cuts!" chorused Hirsch and Marilyn. I joined in their laughter and Mastroni deigned to crack a smile.

"Right first time," I said. "Downsizing. They want us to show we can be ruthless, so we'll fire a few people to please them. Personally, though, I'm going to look for some real economies. Hirsch, now is the time to get in touch with the others and lay those eggs of yours. I think they'll have received the same e-mail, but I'd like to check."

Mastroni came round the table and leant over my shoulder.

"Mind if I watch? Figures have never been my strong point."

I spread the accounts sheets in front of me.

"It's quite simple. You look at the major items of expenditure. You're told they're sacrosanct, so you crack down on postage, phone calls, trifles of that kind. That saves you a couple of francs, and when you've finished fighting with everyone in sight, all you're left with are the staff. The theory is, you can get through the same amount of work with fewer people – you're paying a bunch of idlers and haven't pushed them hard enough. If you don't believe that, you don't listen to them and you go back to the major items. And you realize they're far from sacrosanct."

Hirsch straightened up and made the V sign without taking his eyes from the screen, then converted the gesture into a two-fingered salute.

"Know what I did to them?" he cried. "I signed the name of the supermarket chain and simply added 'Urgent'. They'll think they're being pressured and won't give it another thought. They'll never know I've accessed their systems."

"What if they haven't received the same e-mail from the same sender?" Mastroni objected. "They'll realize there's a problem right away."

Hirsch sat down again.

"Damn, I hadn't thought of that. Between what hours are you permitted to drown yourself in the lake?"

"Don't worry," I told him, "they received it all right – everyone did. It's kick-off time. Things'll start to diverge from now on. By the way, what's Brigitte up to? You don't suppose she's having it off with Del Rieco, do you?"

"She wouldn't be that conscientious," said Marilyn, who seemed unruffled by our barrack-room humour.

"I hope not," I replied, but only for Marilyn's sake. For our sake I rather hoped the contrary. There was a knock at the door and Natalie came in, looking brisk and cheerful. Hirsch glued himself to his screen like a guilty schoolboy and Mastroni bent over his papers.

"A message for you," she said brightly.

She handed me a fax. It was a copy of the e-mail we had received.

"We already got that by Intranet."

She raised her eyebrows.

"Oh, so you've discovered the Intranet? That's good. I'll tell Monsieur Del Rieco, it'll save me a journey. In future, everything he sends you will come by that route."

I looked dismayed.

"You mean you won't come to see us any more? Me and my big mouth! If only I'd known . . . Never mind, drop in for coffee now and then, we'd like that."

"I promise," she said, turning on her heel.

Hirsch clicked his tongue reproachfully when she had gone.

"You're crazy, we'll have to keep hiding everything."

"Don't you believe it, she won't come. I only said that because it's always good to cultivate junior members of the staff. They exist too, you know, and they like to be noticed. They can let things slip . . ."

Marilyn handed me the letter she had just drafted.

"See if that suits you. I'll go and smoke a cigarette outside, if you don't mind." She turned as she opened the door and looked me in the eye. "I'm glad I'm in your lot – we may stand an outside chance. You're a real bastard . . ."

She closed the door on this unexpected announcement. Mastroni nudged me gently.

"Don't be miffed, I think it was compliment."

Hirsch stared at the door, looking dumbfounded.

"Well, I'm damned, Mother Marilyn's got spirit. You could knock me down with a feather."

"Yes," I said thoughtfully, "there are unsuspected depths beneath that prim exterior."

"She's put in a lot of flying time, too," said Hirsch.

"That's just it," I said. "When I was young I wanted to play tennis. I bought a fantastic racket, some brand new tennis togs, took lessons and everything. One day I came home and told my father, 'I've just been thrashed by a guy with holes in his shoes and a battered old racket.' All he said was, 'You see, my boy? If he's in that state, he must have played a lot. You should have been wary of him.' That lesson stuck. I've never forgotten it."

I ran my eye over Marilyn's draft.

"This is perfectly worded – really first-class. A trifle surprised, a trifle hurt, a trifle chilly, but cordial for all that. Her late employers had a pearl on the premises, and they never noticed."

"Like the husband who comes home to his wife after a dirty weekend," said Hirsch. "Give it here and I'll send it."

I went and opened the window while he was tapping away. We must all have been sweating without realizing it, and the little room was starting to smell like a stable. Marilyn had obviously noticed this sooner than us, hence her escape.

I drew in a big breath of forest air. Rather humid and resinous, it smelt fresh and soothing like shower gel. The sky was overcast. From where I stood, all I could see were trees and the glint of water. No sign of any human presence.

Mastroni was examining the staff list when I sat down again. The man was an inveterate slogger. He traced some lines with his finger.

"You're wrong, you know. We *could* make some economies. Look, four people in reception – four! And two chauffeurs. What about those guys? Do we need them?"

"They're your chauffeur and mine. Surely you're not going to deprive me of a chauffeur?"

"What about me?" Hirsch complained.

"You can take the subway. All geniuses are poor."

Ignoring his jocular protests, I tapped Mastroni on the shoulder.

"Of course," I told him. "Fire the chauffeurs and two of the receptionists. Tell me, do we also manufacture fishing rods, or only hooks?"

Mastroni burst out laughing.

"But we don't even manufacture those. I don't know what we *do* manufacture. We sell a product, that's all – it could be anything. It was that idiot Pinetti who came up with the idea of fish-hooks and everyone leapt at it. I ask you, fish-hooks! They'll end by getting them stuck in their pants."

"We'll have to diversify. The best product in the world won't keep you in business for three years, not if it's the only one you've got. We'll have to invent something. Do we have an R&D department?"

"A what?"

"Research and development. A laboratory staffed by guys who invent things."

"No. At least, I don't think so."

"What the hell is this lousy outfit they've landed us with? We can't expand, we can't innovate, we can't swallow our competitors. What *can* we do, apart from firing receptionists and chauffeurs? How about selling the whole caboodle and converting ourselves into a property company? What do you reckon?"

"That could be one option," said Hirsch. "Maybe it's the conclusion they want us to come to."

I took the remark seriously. What did they expect of us? That had been the whole question from the outset. This wasn't a simulation or a war game; it was still, and would continue to be, a test – an experiment carried out on us, De Wavre's Pavlovian dogs. Perhaps they didn't give a damn whether or not we improved our financial status – perhaps they simply wanted to test our nerve. All at once an idea pierced the fog enshrouding my brain. I clicked my fingers.

"Hey, do you think they're keeping tabs on us? CCTV? Microphones? I wouldn't put it past them."

Hirsch paled a little. He rapped the wall with his knuckles.

"At least there's no two-way mirror. I can't see any cameras, either. They couldn't miniaturize them sufficiently."

He drew back and eyed his screen suspiciously.

"If they're watching us, it's with that."

Mastroni, infected with the prevailing paranoia, ran his hand over the underside of the table and up-ended the chairs. He was still bending down when we heard what sounded like a child's musical box playing the first few notes of "Dixie". It couldn't be a mobile phone: they'd warned us that there was no reception in this remote area, with its lack of relay stations. For all that, what Mastroni produced from his pocket looked very much like one.

"I didn't think it would work here," he said apologetically, before putting it to his ear.

"If it's your wife," quipped Hirsch, "tell her you'll be late for dinner."

"No, it isn't her, it's . . . Someone said 'Urgent' and hung up."

Removing the phone from his ear, he stared at it with a mixture of surprise and suspicion, as if it were smeared with some evil-smelling substance.

"But I didn't think there were any relay stations around here," he insisted.

"That's no problem," I said. "Some of them go via satellite – for explorers and so on. They don't need any relay stations."

"But it costs a bomb. Sixty francs a minute!"

"So? You think they'd quibble about 60 francs? Hey, Hirsch, isn't that what you sent to the others: 'Urgent'?"

Hirsch nodded.

"In that case, someone must have spotted we've tampered with the network."

"Del Rieco!" Hirsch blurted out. "We're cooked!"

That was one hypothesis: Del Rieco was letting us know that he'd spotted us and wanted us to stop. But there was another possibility. Charriac had made no secret of his laptop, and heaven alone knew what it harboured in the way of software. He was quite capable of having a satellite phone as well.

It had been great fun, scaring ourselves, but now we had to get down to business in earnest. We delved into the files again, working fast but meticulously. Mastroni, who really did know the ropes when it came to sales, sent messages to our most important customers via the referee, aka Del Rieco. In other areas, however, he was no help to me. Hirsch recalculated all the items in the balance sheet and detected a minor error in our unemployment insurance contributions. He then showed Marilyn, who had reappeared after her nicotine fix, how to enter what he wanted on a spreadsheet. Brigitte Aubert returned from her mission empty-handed. Del Rieco had closeted himself in his chalet, and there was no way of getting near him. She loafed around for a bit, then helped Mastroni to plan an advertising campaign.

Late that morning we received another e-mail, this time from the central purchasing agency. They were complaining of irregular deliveries. Mastroni got out the hauliers' file. He sent off a fax laying the blame on our main carrier and asked Del Rieco if he could bring the forces of competition into play. He received a list of four haulage firms by return and promptly asked them to state their terms.

"Shall I invite them to tender?"

"No, too many rules. We aren't going to amuse ourselves by steaming open envelopes and resealing them immediately in the usual way. Just sound them out. It won't cost money or commit us to anything."

Five minutes later the supermarket chain contacted us in its turn. All things considered, they requested a 2.5 per cent discount, claiming that one of our competitors had offered them 3 per cent.

"They could be bluffing," Hirsch suggested. "Like me to access the other firms' systems and see what concessions they've really made?"

"No. True or false, it makes no difference. They're asking 2.5, and the reason they give you for courtesy's sake doesn't matter. Offer them 1.5 and see how they react. At worst, we'll have gained a little time."

Brigitte Aubert raised her eyebrows and smiled incredulously.

"You sound like a couple of carpet sellers in a souk. How about a nice cup of mint tea?"

"Basically," I said, "that's the way it always has been. It's just that we wear Oxfords these days instead of Turkish slippers. The technique is a tad more sophisticated too, but the principle hasn't changed. A and B both want a bigger share of the cake, so they have to compromise. A quotes twelve, B counters with three, and they eventually agree on seven, which is what they knew they'd settle for in the first place. Another six months, and they start all over again."

Just before twelve-thirty Natalie came to tell us that lunch was served. Hirsch caught her by the arm.

"Tell me something, sweetheart. Could we have a phone?"

"What for?"

"Well, to phone people. The other teams, for instance."

She shrugged.

"I'll have to ask Monsieur Del Rieco, but I don't see why not. Except that I'm not sure there's a socket in this room. If you only want to speak to the others, you could always climb the stairs."

We had such a strong sense of being imprisoned in a kind of submarine that this hadn't occurred to us.

"A simple but brilliant solution," Mastroni said in a neutral voice.

I got to my feet.

"The rest of you can do as you like. Personally, I'm going to have some lunch. There's nothing worse than hypoglycaemia. It's beginning to play havoc with us already."

Lunch was a strange affair. Everyone realized that we were now in direct competition. At the same time, we tried to maintain at least a modicum of our former conviviality. We were like examination candidates seated in the same dining hall: united by our common status as victims of De Wavre International's machinations but opponents notwithstanding, alert to anything the others might let slip and on guard against divulging anything ourselves. This lent our conversation a peculiar flavour compounded of vague hints and oblique references, veiled allusions and suppressed sarcasm. I had never heard so many lies told, even at a press conference.

Charriac's team entered the dining-room in a body and took exclusive possession of one table. Now and then they uttered a loud remark intended for our ears, but most of the time they whispered together. Morin had not only forsworn his clumsy jokes; he even seemed to have forgotten his Marseille accent. Charriac was clearly the boss. The others hung on his words and looked at him before venturing to speak. He resembled the central figure in a painting of the Last Supper, stiff and erect, with his apostles gathered round him. All he lacked was a halo – and, perhaps, a Judas.

One of the remaining tables was deserted, the other occupied only by Aimé Leroy and El Fatawi, both of whom belonged to

Laurence Carré's team. I sauntered over and joined them.

"How's it going?" I asked.

"It's a grind," replied El Fatawi, who looked worn out. "If this was a handicap we'd have to be the best, considering the extra weight they're making us carry. We're having organizational problems, too. You're a management consultant. Care to advise us?"

I spooned a little mound of grated carrot on to the side of my plate and added two slices of ham.

"I'm expensive, you know . . ."

He gave a world-weary shrug.

"Your fee doesn't matter – we couldn't pay you anyway. We can't pay our taxes, we can't pay our suppliers . . . If you're interested in promises, on the other hand, we've got plenty of those."

"Is it that bad?"

"No, far worse. Pass me the bottle, Leroy, I'm going to drown my sorrows in drink."

"Muslims don't drink," Aimé Leroy pointed out.

"No, like Catholics don't lie, don't kill, and don't cheat on their wives or try to get rich at others' expense. Pass me that bottle."

Hirsch walked into the dining-room and sat down beside me. For some obscure reason, he stocked up with five or six slices of bread and propped them against his glass. Perhaps he was afraid of rationing.

"What's new?" he asked.

"Nothing much. They've just been telling me what fun they're having."

Chalamont completed our table. He was unfolding his napkin when El Fatawi inquired after Laurence Carré. Chalamont replied that she was still hard at it.

The last two members of the Carré team came in just as we were attacking our spaghetti Bolognese, followed almost immediately by

Mastroni and Brigitte Aubert. Sitting down at the table for four, they proceeded to discuss the unpredictable mountain weather and the likelihood of rain. We were casting around for an equally uncompromising topic when El Fatawi heaved a sigh.

"Fish-hooks, I ask you! Anything else would have done. Who was the schmuck who thought of fish-hooks?"

"The schmuck was me," Pinetti called from the next table.

Which proved he wasn't missing a word that passed between us.

"Sorry," El Fatawi mumbled half-heartedly.

"I tried to think of a product whose technology would be accessible to us all," Pinetti said triumphantly. "So as not to put you at a disadvantage. You ought to thank me."

El Fatawi had no wish to argue. He raised a limp hand.

"Okay, consider yourself thanked."

But Pinetti, having sunk his fangs in El Fatawi's calf, refused to let go.

"You're in a bad way, from what I hear. You spend an hour-and-a-half debating who's to run your firm, and even then you can't agree."

I was still wondering how he knew this when Laurence Carré appeared, the last of us to do so. She looked paler than yesterday, and her lips were ever so slightly pursed. The remaining vacant place happened to be immediately across the table from Charriac. She hesitated for a moment, staring at it with a gloomy expression, then sat down. Charriac leant forward solicitously.

"You're looking tired, my dear. Come, relax. A little wine?"

She shook her head.

"Just imagine," Charriac went on, "my worthy associate Monsieur Pinetti has been teasing your people. He's discovered, I don't know how, that you've been having some minor structural problems –"

"In the paper," Morin cut in. "He read it in the paper."

"– and the foolish fellow thought it might impair your efficiency. That's absurd, of course. Back-stabbing is the main occupation in all large concerns, but they continue to function perfectly well."

"Mind your own business, Charriac," she retorted.

Listening to her voice, I sensed the weariness she felt and the effort she was making to overcome it. She wasn't the kind of woman to give up easily.

Charriac slapped his thigh.

"Mind your own business ... What an original riposte – I must remember that one." He smiled. "Never mind, I think my plans are going to suit you."

Laurence turned her head and caught my eye. Although it wasn't a plea for help, I felt sorry for her. Was she losing the game already, or had she simply been drained of energy by a bad night's sleep?

Hirsch indicated Charriac with an almost imperceptible jerk of the chin. "There's something about that man I don't like," he whispered, almost exactly echoing Laurence's words of the previous evening. I inferred from El Fatawi's spuriously absent expression that he had heard the remark and endorsed it. The waiter asked if he could clear the table and earned a curt rebuke from Charriac.

"No, no, Madame Carré hasn't finished yet. We'll wait for her."

Silence fell. Marilyn, trying desperately to keep the conversational ball rolling, said, "Know what I like least about being in the mountains? Thunderstorms."

"I think there's one brewing, too," said Charriac. "Personally, I adore thunderstorms. You can never be sure where the lightning's going to strike, that's the amusing part."

"As long as one isn't the target oneself," said Hirsch.

"I always take care not to stand beneath a tree," Charriac replied.

"Sure," I said pointedly, "but if someone else did, I bet you wouldn't warn him not to."

Charriac's grey eyes met mine, magnified by his rimless glasses. His expression hardened. "I'm not my brother's keeper," he said. He held my gaze for a moment, then looked down at the tablecloth and started toying idly with his fork.

"On the other hand," he went on, "I'm not averse to passing on a friendly word of advice. Take our present situation. What if one of us were to cheat – what if, just for the sake of argument, he tried to access the other teams' computers? Well, there are no judges here, no police or industrial courts, but it would be an extremely reprehensible thing to do. Naïve, what's more. Why? Because my team, for example, includes our friend Delval here, the world's foremost computer expert."

He jerked his thumb at one of Morin's coterie, a man so self-effacing that I'd never noticed him before.

"He'd be quite capable of retaliating by infecting the intruder with some frightful virus," Charriac went on, "and the result would be total chaos." He gave a thin-lipped smile. "But this isn't a war. We share the same interests, after all. The estimable Monsieur Del Rieco – our lord and master for this week, at least – was absolutely clear on that point: De Wavre will accept all the good candidates. Well, we're all good, so we ought to be mutually supportive instead of stirring up trouble for each other."

I was about to reply when Laurence Carré got there first.

"Said the big bad wolf as he blew the little pigs' house down."

This remark evoked an avid smile from Charriac. He eyed her like a cat contemplating a goldfish.

"My dear lady, you've no idea how deeply you distress me. I've always treated you with irreproachable courtesy, yet you don't like me. No, no, I can tell: you don't like me. Why not abandon your irrational prejudices and listen to the voice of reason?"

He leant across the table and took her hand.

"Why, oh why, don't you like me?" he groaned with histrionic fervour.

His team members tittered admiringly. The others, impressed by his performance despite themselves, remained silent. Laurence, possibly reinvigorated by the proteins in her steak, withdrew her hand.

"You want me to tell you? All right, I will. I used to belong to your world, Charriac. The one you come from – the one you still inhabit. I've ridden around in limos and spent weekends at luxurious country hotels, I've drunk vintage champagne in first-class restaurants and attended conventions in Venice. I've had all those things, like you. And then, one day, I was slung out. That was when I first saw your world from the outside. It's a heartless, violent, hypocritical place – a phoney place, and I hate it."

Charriac tried to stem her flow of words.

"Look," he said, "someone gave you a push and you fell off and hurt yourself. It's only natural, but we're going to help you back into the saddle. You'll soon forget your little bruises, believe me."

"But I don't want to forget them!" she exclaimed, thoroughly infuriated. "I've seen it all and done it all, thanks very much. I've lost interest in listening to a boardroomful of suits making financial decisions that put a thousand poor, unsuspecting devils out of a job!"

Charriac spread his arms.

"Oh, my God, a trade unionist!"

"No, no, Charriac, I don't even believe in that, not any more. It's just that – "

"May I ask you a question?" he broke in.

She nodded briskly. Beside me, Hirsch propped his elbows on the table, stroking his lower lip with the tip of his thumb. I, too, was interested to see where all this was leading.

"My question is this," Charriac said deliberately. Then, raising his voice, he almost shouted, "If you really feel that way, what the hell are you doing here?"

"And you, Charriac?" she replied in the same tone. "What about you? Did you get the boot too? No, I don't believe it: you resemble them too much – you're just like them. You're on their side, Charriac, but to what extent?"

He gulped, looking uncharacteristically taken aback.

"Just a minute, I've lost you. What are you accusing me of?"

Laurence stuck to her guns.

"We're all shaking in our shoes and hankering after a job we may or may not get – all of us except two. *They're* relaxed. *They* crack little jokes, *they* needle everyone and know everything. Who am I talking about? Del Rieco and you. I put one and one together and, oddly enough, I get two."

Charriac was looking genuinely disconcerted now.

"Just a minute," he repeated. "You think I'm working for them? You think I'm here to spy on you? An additional test? You're crazy!"

She crouched over the table like a boxer seeking an opening.

"Listen, they know everything – we can't blink an eyelid without them finding out. They don't eat with us, they don't sit in on our deliberations, and there aren't any hidden cameras. So?"

Charriac had recovered his composure. "A traitor?" he said slowly. "Think what you like, I know it isn't me. Mind you, they may have inserted one in every team."

"Stop talking bullshit, Charriac!" snapped Laurence. "It won't wash. What is this, the new game? You want us all to suspect each other? There's only one traitor here, and it's you!"

He stared at her without a trace of his former sarcasm.

"Or you. This could be a double bluff on your part."

To everyone's surprise, Chalamont, the beefy, red-faced man

made a ponderous attempt to quell the argument.

"Look," he burst out, "what are you trying to do, drive us all nuts? Now it's traitors around every corner. What is this, a selection process or the CIA?"

"Madame Carré has advanced a theory," drawled Charriac. "We mustn't turn it into a fixation, but we can't dismiss it out of hand."

He readdressed himself to Laurence.

"Believe what you like," he went on. "I 'got the boot' myself, as you so elegantly phrased it. Circumstances conspired – it happens, even to the best of us – but I'll be back on board the train in no time. If it amuses you to remain on the platform, vegetating, that's your problem. And if there's a traitor in our midst, he can go and tell Del Rieco. It's not a statement of principle."

"And if you have to climb aboard over my dead body, I know you will," Laurence said sullenly.

"Quite so. Because I'm not tired or disillusioned, and I still aspire to those fleshpots you despise – I've developed a taste for them. And if anyone here would sooner live in the sticks and get up at five in the morning to catch a suburban train to work or queue for income support, let him stand up and say so. That way, we'll have found the traitor in double-quick time."

The waiter brought us some *poires Belle Hélène*. Morin, who was back in form, cracked a joke. It was less vulgar than vapid.

"Instructive . . ." Hirsch mumbled through a mouthful of chocolate.

The game began to take on greater intensity during the afternoon. The referee's e-mails, which arrived at ever shorter intervals, introduced a succession of minor incidents such as occur in the everyday running of any business, presenting us with the sort of traditional teasers any management team has to solve. There were no really strategic problems, just a series of tactical setbacks. We had some hitches with various government departments, which made me feel that De Wavre's scheme of things needed updating. Our public services have made a lot of progress in recent years. The youngsters they employ are far more on the ball and their response times far quicker, even though they're still hamstrung by an avalanche of confused and contradictory blanket regulations. We also had some customer relations problems of the usual kind, psychologically speaking. Forgetful, scrupulous, bombastic, diffident, nit-picking, offhand – all these types were represented among our smaller distributors. Some unoriginal spanners were thrown into the works, ranging from mechanical breakdowns to a carrier who failed to deliver an important consignment on time. Finally, there were one or two claims by staff members dissatisfied with their holiday times and pension schemes. Hiccups of this kind tend to throw managements into a tizzy. My own team tackled them calmly and efficiently, without ever losing their sense of humour. We argued briefly once or twice, but all our decisions were unanimous. The wheels were turning smoothly. I felt we had managed to come up with the measured responses Del Rieco required, so I was pretty satisfied with our work.

By evening only two or three files were still open, and the signs were promising. We were awaiting the bank's response to a loan rescheduling plan worked out by Hirsch; Brigitte Aubert had marginalized two vindictive customers by resorting to litigation; Marilyn was drafting some fearsomely ambiguous letters; and Mastroni, who combined marketing and production, was concentrating on technological innovation. We had abandoned piracy, sobered by Charriac's allusions to it. Our lunchtime paranoia had subsided. All they wanted to know, quite clearly, was whether we were capable of surmounting everyday management problems, and I couldn't detect the smallest trap in the exercises they had set us.

Dinner was a more relaxed meal than lunch. We now knew what Del Rieco was getting at and had no further grounds for anxiety. The organizers could easily have defused the explosive atmosphere that had almost become established, simply by being more specific about the object and rules of the game. I would definitely have told them so, had we been subjected to the end-of-day evaluation customary on training courses, but Del Rieco was lying low. We hadn't seen him all day. Natalie and his assistant hadn't shown their faces either – and, apropos his assistant, I wondered what use he was, given that none of us had ever heard him open his mouth.

The teams did not split up at dinner. Each of them monopolized one table. Instead of two tables of six and one of four, there were now one of six and two of five. This was a detail, but the kind of detail I'm always alert to. It's quite spontaneous, my observation of the way people arrange themselves within a given space, the subliminal signs they exchange, and all those little, almost imperceptible trifles that end by building up a general impression. Our senses register these, analysing them without our knowing it, and we finally form a judgement that always – although we're incapable of justifying it – proves correct. I was a little ahead of the others: I could register fleeting expressions or gestures and interpret their meaning; I knew that our bodies constantly betray us, and that one only needs to watch them.

A buzz of conversation is indicative of mood, not of the actual subject under discussion. In our case the music of the voices was slow, gentle, serene, and indicative of relaxation after a tiring day. There was no clash of steel or blare of trumpets as there had been at lunch. Faces, bodies, limbs – all betokened that the warriors were at rest. No one was preparing to mount an attack: the air seemed to purr like an engine ticking over.

After coffee I went outside for my ritual walk beside the lake. The sky was still overcast and the pine needles were stirring in a gentle breeze. Marilyn was smoking a cigarette on the terrace. Hirsch had retired to the bar for a game of chess with Delval, Charriac's computer expert. For all I knew, they might be trying to improve on "Deep Blue", the world champion in their field.

Laurence Carré was already there, seated on her usual rock near the landing stage with her long skirt spread out around her. I leant against one of the piles.

"It's none of my business, I know, but you really are looking tired."

She drew a deep breath.

"I had some news from home before lunch, that's why I was late. Only a minor problem, but not an aid to concentration. I took it out on Charriac. His bad luck."

"I was fortunate not to get in the line of fire."

She smiled. "Yes, but you took care not to."

"He was trying to test you."

"Of course. Del Rieco initiates the process, and now everyone's testing everyone else. Rather exhausting, don't you think? I didn't put a stop to it at once because I'm not a hundred per cent on the ball. It's the stress – one thing on top of another, know what I mean?"

I didn't respond. If she wanted to tell me about her personal problems, she would do so of her own accord. In any case, I wasn't sufficiently interested to press her. I liked the woman – I even rather admired the way she stood up for herself – but I never forgot why we were there. That obsession overrode everything else. She was pretty, I had to admit, and even prettier now that the dusk concealed her pallor, but my hormones remained strangely well-behaved. I had never even looked at her breasts or her hips. If I'd shut my eyes I would have been incapable of describing them.

She glanced at the woods.

"It's really dark tonight. We won't find out what lies at the end of that path, not this time."

"You see? You don't keep your promises."

"I know, that's why I never make any."

I stretched lazily, smothering a yawn.

"I know what's at the end of the path," I said.

"Oh? What?"

"Another path, and beyond it another."

"You mean it never ends?"

"Yes. When you've completed the round trip you end up back where you started."

"So let's stay here," she said. "What's that, a haiku?"

"No, a haiku is supposed to make one think. A sense of futility inhibits thought."

She uttered a little grunt of amusement.

"Don't worry. A little Prozac, and you'll get over the feeling."

Our flagging dialogue was interrupted by Charriac. We hadn't heard him coming. All at once he was there between us. His suit and tie looked out of place in such wild surroundings.

"'Hello, young lovers wherever you are,'" he warbled.

Laurence looked at him with a mixture of surprise and distaste, as if she'd found a slug in her salad. I found her reaction excessive. Why did she hate him so much? Because he had been clumsy enough to attack her while she was trying to come to terms with some personal setback, or was there something else?

He launched into a Fred Astaire dance routine and hummed the opening bars of "Change Partners".

"Push off, Charriac," Laurence said curtly.

Ignoring her injunction, he leant against the pile beside mine and adopted the same pose.

"No, no, I've got things to tell you. I suppose you're aware of the fact that today was just the hors d'oeuvre. What am I saying? Just the drinks and nibbles – a warm-up, nothing more. Now we're convinced that everything's running smoothly, the real problems will crop up."

Laurence emitted a weary sigh.

"You're being a bore," she said. "What are you trying to do, destabilize us? Scare us? I don't get you, Charriac. Is this your Dracula act?"

"It isn't just me you fail to understand," he replied. "You don't understand a thing – it's hopeless. Carceville here, *he* understands." He paused. "All right, I'll spell it out for you. Everything we've done to date could just as well have been done in Paris. They've brought us here because they want to see how we perform in competing teams. That being the case – do you follow me so far? – something is going to happen. Something that will put us at daggers drawn – irrevocably so. Right, Carceville?"

"Possibly."

"Probably – no, certainly. We *haven't* been competing up to now. We've been running our little businesses in peace and quiet. But that's pointless. They want us to slaughter each other, and they'll see to it that we do."

Laurence sighed again.

"Is that all you dream of, Charriac, bloodshed and murder? What were you in private life, a serial killer?"

He took a step towards her, then paused and raised his hands.

"There's a Thai proverb: if someone tells the truth, give him a good horse – he'll need it to escape. Where's *my* horse? Think for a moment: what's their objective? They want to know if we're good soldiers, if we're capable of inspiring a team and persuading it to massacre the competition without a murmur. They've let us form personal ties and get friendly, and now we've got to open fire on our buddies. You're familiar with the world outside, the one we may be reinjected into, you told me so this morning. You said it was harsh and merciless, and it's true. There isn't enough money to go round, and everyone wants more than the rest. It's dog eat dog. If you want to know what you've got, a toy poodle or a Dobermann, what do you do? Leave it all alone in its kennel, or toss a bone into the fray and see what happens?"

Laurence's resistance was crumbling.

"What are you getting at?" she asked in a milder tone.

"Just this. I suppose you've analysed the market. If you haven't, go away and play ping-pong, this isn't the place for you. What conclusion have you come to? In the long term, is there room for three firms?"

"No," I conceded.

He took this as an encouraging sign.

"Exactly. So one of us will have to disappear. By tomorrow night there'll only be two of us left. We'll come down to this landing stage and escort the reject to the boat, our handkerchiefs wet with tears. I don't know how they'll go about it, but it's inevitable. Right, Carceville?"

I nodded, unable to detect any flaw in his reasoning.

He rubbed his hands.

"Good, we're making progress. In political science – yes, I studied that too, of course – there's a theory that has never been disproved. When three parties are involved, two will always join forces against the third. Alliances may change, but the rule stands: three equals two against one. That leaves us with a very interesting clutch of possibilities."

"You're boring me, Charriac," Laurence said half-heartedly.

In fact, she was listening intently. He crouched down and drew a line on the ground with his finger.

"One, Carceville allies himself with me and we eliminate you, then play each other in the final. That's the most logical alternative – the one I'm sure you've been trying to counter by engaging in this improper flirtation."

"You're sick," said Laurence, but he didn't even hear.

"Two, Madame Carré joins forces with me and we eliminate Carceville. That's a possibility worth considering. It isn't really in my interest because I could manage perfectly well on my own. On the other hand, it would preclude the third possibility and make the fighting less of an effort. I can't ignore that advantage, dear lady, and you ought to give it some thought. Three . . ."

"Us versus you," said Laurence.

Charriac looked up and smiled.

"Ah, so I interest you after all . . . Quite so: the two of you against me. That would definitely be the most well-balanced contest. Not because of our individual qualities – those I'd sooner not pronounce on – but with an eye to our balance sheets and respective commercial positions. When you play chess you look at the board, not the opponent who's trying to impress you. The only thing is . . ."

He rose and wiped his finger on his other hand.

"If we do that, it means we go straight into the final. If I detect even a hint that you're ganging up on me, I'll be compelled to bomb you. Be warned, I'll do a NATO on you, and the result will be like Kosovo: a sea of rubble and everyone loses. Smooch beside the lake as much as you like, but don't lay a finger on me. That's my message."

Laurence stared at him blankly.

"You're incredible, Charriac."

He smiled without showing his teeth.

"I still can't fathom why you dislike me. Do I remind you of someone who rubbed you up the wrong way? There's no room here for sentiment, favourable or unfavourable. France is the only country where people use takeover bids to settle their personal disputes. Love, hatred, friendship – the place for those is at home. Here, we're machines. No one will be grateful to you for having a heart. You're paid to have a brain. It's your intelligence they're buying, nothing else. I mean you no harm; I mean you nothing but good. I keep my eyes on the chessboard. I don't even know if there's anyone behind it."

Turning, he prodded me in the chest with his forefinger.

"*You* know what I mean. Explain it to her. Here's a second message for you: if you want to join me, either of you, you'll be welcome. It would be in your interest as well as mine . . ."

He inclined his head in a parody of a bow.

"I trust I haven't spoiled your evening. Enjoy the rest of it."

Then he walked off, whistling. Laurence shut her eyes.

"It's starting again," she said in a low voice, "this atmosphere they create. The kind where everyone suspects everyone else and we're forever wondering what the others have in mind. Do you think they're trying to break our nerve? I can't shake off the idea that Charriac is in cahoots with them. He puts us under pressure at every opportunity. It's true I don't like him. He's . . . well, insidious, slimy. And that air of superiority, that conceit, those lectures of his. I hate that."

"He's intelligent," I said.

"Cunning, you mean."

"No, intelligent. But not intelligent enough. There's a fourth possibility. Strange he didn't mention it."

"What's that?"

"The three of us versus Del Rieco. If we joined forces we might be able to blow his system sky-high. We're the sole manufacturers, there aren't any others. If we all adopted the same position, what could he do?"

She jumped to her feet, abruptly reinvigorated.

"Brilliant! Are you going to suggest it to him?"

"Yes, if you agree."

"Good. If he refuses, it'll be because I'm right and he's in league with Del Rieco. Go and ask him right away, I'll wait for you here."

I advised against it. The breeze had died away, and wisps of cold, damp mist were beginning to rise from the lake. Conditions had changed in a matter of moments, and so did our state of mind. While walking up the track I had to fight off a sense of unease. I half expected to see a witch or a grimacing goblin appear from behind every tree. The mountains around us seemed to loom over the lake, guarding its secrets. The lights of the hotel reassured me for a moment; then I wondered who could have had the idea of building such an establishment on this remote and inaccessible island. There were no signs of any ordinary guests, yet the place was equipped with everything one could wish for. While we were on the subject, I would ask to examine the hotel's books – *if* I could get hold of the manager or someone who resembled one. The only employees we had set eyes on so far were the waiter and the Italian boatman, but there had to be someone in the kitchen, chambermaids, and so forth. Where were they? Why did we never see or hear them?

We were halfway there when it started to rain. Isolated drops at first, fat and heavy as gooseberries, then a crepitating, penetrating downpour. I grabbed Laurence by the elbow and forced her to run the last few yards. Once inside the lobby, I left her wringing out her wet hair with both hands.

My interview with Charriac resembled a scene from a thriller. Like a pair of conspirators, we took refuge in his bedroom on the second floor, he seated on the bed, I on the only chair, while the storm beat down on the roof overhead, punctuating each remark with a roll of drums. He had turned on the bedside light, but it was overwhelmed by the stroboscopic flashes visible through the little window, which lit up our faces and sculpted them into pallid masks. I remain convinced that things would have turned out quite differently in another environment. Closeted in air-conditioned premises with artificial lighting, we have become unused to feeling the effects of the elements. When they do erupt they take possession of ancient circuits in our brain and turn our reactions upside down.

Charriac, who did his best to ignore the pandemonium, gave an imitation of a robot with a mechanical half-smile glued to its lips.

"Your attitude amazes me," he said. "It's irrational. You're annoyed because you're being led by the nose, and you don't like it. But this isn't a match against Del Rieco. It's us against De Wavre, an immensely influential concern. Del Rieco is only a pawn, a mercenary, an executive agent. He does what the programme requires him to do. I completely fail to see how it would benefit us to pick a fight with him. On the other hand, I do see what our chances of winning would be: zero."

"Change places."

"I'm sorry?"

"Change position. You aren't looking at the situation from the right angle. You're a chess player, aren't you?"

He bridled. "Just a humble amateur . . ."

"If you know exactly what your opponent's next move will be, doesn't that give you an advantage?"

"A substantial advantage."

"That's what I'm suggesting. Let's pool our information. If we manage to discover what Del Rieco is cooking up for us, it'll be much easier."

"What guarantee do I have that you won't keep the only important information to yourself? I might give you all I have in return for a few measly crumbs from your plate. How could I check on that?"

"Trust, Charriac. All business relations are based on trust. You're sure your banker isn't going to run off with your money. What guarantees that he won't? The certainty that, if you doubted him for a moment, the whole system would collapse."

He pondered my theory for a moment, staring at the floor.

"That's true on the macroeconomic level, but not on the microeconomic. I trust my bank because it can't survive unless everyone trusts it, and it knows that. If it gives me the slightest reason to mistrust it, it's dead. I'd demand a colossal indemnity – one it couldn't afford. But you, Carceville, if you conned me, what could I do?"

"What could you do in real life?"

"There are laws. Contracts. Penalties."

I shrugged.

"Come on, Charriac, that's a fiction. Laws, contracts, cheques, banknotes? They're only paper – trust committed to paper. No, not even that: figures in binary code keyed into a computer. It's like religion: it works only because people believe in it. Pull the plug and everything goes phut. We could try pulling the plug on Del Rieco."

Charriac got up for a moment, hands in pockets, but bumped into the wardrobe and sat down again.

"No. If someone doesn't play the game he's either a criminal or a madman. Whichever he is, they lock him up. The Inquisition burnt people at the stake. The system doesn't support deviants. Speaking for myself, I'm *in* the system. I'm not going to help to destroy it. Certainly not."

I blew an imaginary fanfare.

"Which brings us back to my original question: to what extent *are* you in the system? To what extent are you collaborating with Del Rieco?"

"Hell's bells!" he exploded. "Do I really look as two-faced as that? This is incredible! I'm beginning to ask myself some questions of my own!"

"You'd do well to."

The storm had released a shutter, which started banging. Charriac got up again and half opened the window. Having secured the shutter he sat down, wiping his glasses on the edge of the blanket.

"Damn this weather! I'm not worried about myself. I know perfectly well where I stand. It's you. You're invited to attend a seminar designed to display your prodigious competence, and you've barely arrived before you wonder how to sabotage it! What are you, a revolutionary? If you don't like the game, stay home and don't play it. I *want* this job, Carceville, and I'm going to do everything they tell me – everything. They want to find out if I'm a good little doggie? Fine, that's me. Chuck me a bone, preferably one with a few scraps of meat attached."

"But the game is rigged. Good God, you're an intelligent man!"

"Of course it's rigged!" he snapped. "All games are rigged. Even my son cheats, and he's only six. You're well off? They give you more money. You're poor? You'll get even less. And they tell you you're all starting on equal terms. Del Rieco cheats, you cheat, I cheat, and the Pope must split his sides laughing every time he says Mass. The only thing is, there's a white line somewhere, and behind it a policeman waiting for you to go that little bit too far. As long as you cheat within certain limits, okay. It's like radar traps. Technically the speed limit is x. As long as you don't exceed x + 10 they leave you alone; take it into your head to drive at x + 50 and you'll have problems, so be sure to keep a gun in your glove compartment. I'll tell you what you are: an extremist. Everyone cheats a bit. You notice that, and it riles you so much you start firing from the hip. That's the sign of an inflexible personality. Judges and terrorists are very much alike, you know, hence their mutual comprehension. *They* believe that certain norms are sacrosanct. Not like us, with one foot on either side of the law. They're both on the same side – they both play the same game."

Charriac was listening to the sound of his own voice, revelling in his own theories. Aware that we were wasting time, I cut him short.

"All right, listen. I made you an offer. Here it is again: (a) we pool any information we may have about Del Rieco's dirty tricks; (b) we confer whenever a problem crops up. It wouldn't commit you to anything. You'd still retain your freedom of action."

"A free trial, you mean?"

"In a manner of speaking. Look, you also got an e-mail from the supermarkets demanding a discount of two-and-a-half per cent, didn't you? Well – "

"Two-and-a-half? The buggers asked me for three!"

"You see? And what did you do? You offered them one."

"One point three."

"Okay, and you'll settle for one-seven. If we'd got together, the three of us, we'd all have said no and that would have been that. They'd have had it. Zero."

He relaxed a little.

"There's something in what you say, certainly in this particular case. But I'm not sure we're entitled to – "

"Of course we aren't. But what do civil engineering companies do when they're invited to tender? They get together: X, Y and Z all quote a rock bottom price. It's strictly against the rules, but if they don't do it they get beaten out by big European conglomerates that slash their prices to eliminate the competition. And the authorities aren't allowed to favour a French firm if it's more expensive than an international monster. The European firm cleans up and your unemployment contributions are increased because of job losses. 'Ah,' they tell you, 'but it's not the same fund.' You think that's acceptable? I tell you, it's the rules that stink."

"You're a revolutionary," Charriac said mockingly.

"No, I'm defending myself. They want my hide, and I'm defending it. Who made the rules? Are they written down somewhere? The hell they are! Del Rieco makes them up as he goes along. So De Wavre want to see what I'm made of? All right, but I want to see what *they're* made of. That's fair enough, isn't it?"

Charriac considered this for a moment.

"Not altogether. They can do something for us, something that means a lot to us, but we can't do anything for them. Our relative positions are unbalanced. We're playing chess. They've got a queen and we haven't."

Then, quite suddenly, he made up his mind.

"All right, I'm happy to accept your proposal. We've nothing to lose. After all, criminal conspiracy is a pretty common strategy. If we're all in it together they can't pick on anyone in particular – unless this room is bugged. Now, to change the subject . . ."

Satisfied with his reply, I felt tempted to relax. I did nothing of the kind. This was the most dangerous moment, the one when, having settled the matter in hand, someone turns in the doorway and hurls a grenade at you. Charriac leant over until our foreheads were nearly touching and I could smell his rather fetid breath.

"Madame Carré . . ." he murmured. "Do you really need her? Are we obliged to include her in our agreement? If you and I got busy on her, she wouldn't last a day."

"What good would it do us to eliminate her?" I asked, forcing myself to sound conciliatory.

He pursed his lips like a mischievous adolescent.

"Well, I don't know. It's the game, isn't it? The idea is to win. What are we after, all of us? A chance to become the richest, most powerful person in the world, no?"

"Why? Will it make us immortal?"

He sat back and assumed his former pose, planted his fists on his thighs.

"I was wrong: you aren't a revolutionary, you're a philosopher. That's far worse. No, we'll all die sometime. The question is, what kind of life will we have first? Pleasant and comfortable, or lousy? Know something, Carceville? I've never looked at a price in a shop and I don't intend to start now. All right, about this lady: what do we do with her?"

I ostentatiously rose and stretched.

"For the moment, nothing. We'll see."

"Ah . . ." He bowed his head, looking disappointed. "Are you planning to form an alliance with her? You think she'll be easier to screw that way?"

"Stop it, Charriac. I never mix business with pleasure."

That was the kind of language he understood. He nodded approvingly.

"One last piece of advice, my friend: take a good look at the chessboard, and before you do something stupid, work out what you really want."

I gave him a friendly pat on the back.

"Thanks. I'd like to do you a favour in return – a token of my goodwill, so to speak. Del Rieco hangs out in a cottage behind the kitchens."

Charriac's eyes lit up. "So that's where he goes to ground – I was wondering . . . Shall we meet again tomorrow morning?"

"Yes, preferably outside. Down by the lake at ten, say?"

"I'll be there." He threw up his arms in a dramatic gesture. "What a start to a glorious friendship!"

Laurence was waiting for me in the workroom, where the sliding partition was tightly closed. She had dried her hair and changed into a hip-hugging navy blue two-piece. I told her the result of my interview.

"What was your impression of him?" she asked.

"He's a *millefeuille.* You're never sure what you're dealing with. You think it's icing, but underneath there's cream, and when you start on the cream – surprise, surprise – you find some jam and puff pastry, and after that . . ."

". . . more cream," she broke in, "and then a layer of something really hard, then nothing at all. I know the type – I even married one. We were together nearly ten years. When I told him I was leaving he said, 'I don't understand, I've never refused you anything.' That was when I realized he'd bought me. In his head, he was paying for me. It was just a commercial transaction."

I said nothing. She stared fixedly at one corner of the room for a few moments, then bade me an abrupt goodnight. The storm had abated, but it was still spitting with rain. I waited until the door had closed behind her before inspecting the place she had been looking at. There was nothing to be seen but an almost invisible scratch on the paintwork.

The night was still. Nature was catching its breath, and the air had become fresher. When morning came, the sun peeped out from between two clouds like a pretty neighbour opening her shutters. Then, doubtless unimpressed by what was happening down below, it retired behind a rampart of cumulus.

I was in the shower when someone knocked on my door. I just had time to turn off the tap and grab a towel when Brigitte Aubert invaded the cramped little bathroom.

"All right," she said, with an unabashed glance at my semi-nudity, "get a move on. I'll wait outside."

"Would you be kind enough to pass me a few clothes?"

I heard her open the wardrobe. She threw me a pair of underpants and a shirt.

"Ah, men . . ." she sighed.

Brigitte wasn't unacquainted with the opposite sex, one could tell, so I didn't have to make any allowances for a long lost sense of decorum. I put my head round the door.

"You can talk, I'm listening. Mind if I shave at the same time?"

"No, no, feel free. The thing is, I went for a stroll near Monsieur Del Rieco's chalet when I got up, and guess who I saw going in?"

"No idea. Natalie? Charriac?"

"Neither. Morin – you know, the guy from Marseille."

"Really? What was he doing there?"

"Good question. Afraid I don't know the answer."

This information raised some interesting possibilities. I finished lathering my cheeks.

"Maybe the bar ran out of pastis. Maybe he went to lodge a complaint."

Brigitte lost patience. Framed by the doorway, the reflection of her weary little face appeared in the mirror. "But how did he know where Del Rieco . . ."

"I told Charriac last night."

She looked mortified. "What's the point of me busting a gut if you go and tell them everything?

"Strategic considerations . . . I can explain . . ."

I pondered her revelation while shaving. None of the rest of us had gone to see Del Rieco – we weren't even supposed to know the location of his hideout. If Morin had waltzed in there without being barked at by guard dogs or fired on from watchtowers, it must mean he was on their side. Charriac wasn't the only traitor; his whole team was involved. He must have laughed up his sleeve when I passed on my exclusive information, and this morning he'd sent someone to report our conversation to Del Rieco. We were on opposite sides. My offer of an alliance had been a monumental blunder. De Wavre now knew I wasn't playing their game.

I had gone too far too soon. There was nothing for it but to go and see Del Rieco and try to sort out Charriac's status. And protect myself from the consequences of my faux pas.

"Mastroni wants a word with you," Brigitte went on. "Some e-mails came in during the night."

I turned on the tap to sluice my razor and dabbed my chin with a towel.

"Really? What time did you get up – or haven't you been to bed?"

"Six o'clock. We've been on the job since seven."

"Fine. Carry on, I'll join you later."

She clenched her fists impatiently.

"But you're needed right away. There are decisions to be taken."

From that point of view the simulation was a success. The third day had hardly begun and I was overbooked already. I went out into the bedroom. Brigitte stood aside to let me pass. I liked what I saw in her eyes: expectancy, hope, the imploring gaze of a dog on the look-out for a bone. That's what makes power worthwhile: you suddenly become important to a host of people and feel twice as alive as usual.

"May I?" she asked.

She deftly straightened my tie. I had decided to wear one today: the holidays were over. Then she inspected me from head to foot, flicked an imaginary speck of dust off my sleeve, and gave a satisfied nod. I let her have her way. Like wives, secretaries, mothers and advisers, personal assistants are rather like a champion's trainers. They want their boss to shine, to be handsome and brilliant, and they feel responsible for his shortcomings.

"I'll be with you."

"When?" she entreated.

"As soon as I can. It's a tough business. Any amphetamines on sale here?"

She went out, dragging her feet.

Once outside I found it rather hard to get my bearings. The kitchen had to be situated behind the dining-room and built into the slope. Our third day here, and I still hadn't taken the trouble to carry out a full reconnaissance. Seen from the front, the hotel appeared to have only one entrance, but it was skirted on the left by a narrow path that had so far escaped my notice. I set off, bending low to avoid the branches of a tree that brushed the wall.

The path led to a small, unpaved yard containing a rubbish bin. It was bounded on two sides by windowless walls and on the third by a barn. The fourth side was open to the woods. Just beyond the yard and slightly higher up the slope stood a sort of timber-framed chalet. Without pausing for thought, I climbed the two worn planks that served as steps and knocked on the door.

Del Rieco opened it at once, wearing a red sweater that set off his tan. He looked at me without a trace of surprise.

"Monsieur Carceville," he said slowly. "I was expecting you. A little sooner, to be honest. Come in."

I found myself in a small, low-ceilinged room cluttered with computers and television screens. An untidy tangle of electric cables snaked across the worn carpet that covered the floor. Jean-Claude, Del Rieco's assistant, was sitting at the back of the room. He flipped some switches and the screens went dark. A bare bulb was suspended from a beam.

"We're a bit short of space here," Del Rieco said apologetically. "I've been requesting bigger premises for years, but you know how it is. A cup of coffee?"

I shook my head. Del Rieco leant back against the bare wooden wall.

"So what can I do for you?"

"Monsieur Del Rieco," I began.

"Joseph, please," he cut in. "And may I call you Jérôme?"

"Of course. Well, er, Joseph, I've a couple of things to tell you, and I also need some information."

"It's not really allowed, you know," he said, looking faintly aggrieved. "We're not supposed to have any contact with each other before Friday, technically speaking, but this seminar is taking a strange turn. I should perhaps have been more explicit, but your files didn't prompt one to foresee that eventuality. Never mind, it's instructive. It's people like you that help us to refine our methods. You're furthering the cause of science, my dear Jérôme."

He was putting me down. We were arm-wrestling again. I wouldn't come out on top, but I could at least attempt some damage limitation. He hadn't invited me to sit down, which was a good thing. Being an inch or two shorter, he couldn't dominate me physically.

"I'm going to put my cards on the table, Monsieur Del Rieco – Joseph, I mean."

"Not before time," he said sarcastically.

"You've placed us in a competitive situation. Very well. A quick analysis of our respective positions leads me to conclude that there isn't room for three firms in the relevant sector. I'm sure you'll stop me if I'm wrong."

"Don't count on it," he said, rather more curtly.

I continued to look him in the eye.

"Consequently," I went on, "one of us will have to go. But Monsieur Charriac won't have failed to inform you of what he has learnt in the course of his studies, and what he was kind enough to remind us of: that a triangular situation inevitably breeds alliances."

I paused for a moment, but he said nothing.

"As he informed us on your behalf, just in case we hadn't worked it out for ourselves, there are three potential permutations: Charriac and Carré versus Carceville, Charriac and Carceville versus Carré, and Carré and Carceville versus Charriac. Am I right?"

"It's one theory," he conceded grudgingly.

"But there's a fourth possibility: the three of us against you. Because this isn't a game for three, it's a game for four. That's where the trickery comes in. Except that I may be wrong and it's a game for three after all: Carré, Carceville, and Charriac-Del Rieco combined."

He wagged his head dubiously, as if making an effort to follow me.

"Are you interested in football?" he asked out of the blue.

"Who isn't?"

"There are twenty-two players on the pitch – supposedly. No, twenty-three – or rather, twenty-five, counting the referee and linesmen. I, my dear Jérôme, am the referee, and our friends Jean-Claude and Natalie keep watch on the touchline. Some teams, Italy for example, make a systematic attempt to get the referee on their side – to exert pressure on him. For his protection the authorities invented a new offence: the simulated dive in the penalty area. That earns the offender a yellow card, and that's precisely what you deserve for coming here. I ought to get out my card."

His voice had hardened still more. I responded by trying to look still more unruffled.

"No, Joseph," I told him. "That would be true if it was a fair fight, but it isn't. You've introduced a team of your own, which means we have to compete against it and you both. This morning, one of its members came to see you and receive instructions. We aren't on equal terms."

"No one ever said you would be. When you take an examination the examiner knows the answers better than you do. You're taking an examination here, Jérôme."

I almost lost my temper.

"But it's a charade! A third of the intake consists of stooges belonging to you! Is that what we were supposed to find out? Okay, we've found it out. Do we stop now?"

His infuriating smile returned.

"I see, so you spied on our friend Morin, who did indeed come to see me just now. Not exactly the kind of attitude our organization favours, but still. In case you hadn't noticed, I should tell you that Monsieur Pinetti is currently lurking behind the tree facing my door. As soon as you leave here he'll scuttle back to Charriac and inform him that you're an actor in my pay. We're headed for a pretty complicated situation, don't you think? Actors spying on actors – a fascinating game of mirrors ... But hadn't it occurred to you that Morin may have come to tell me the same thing as you? You think the opposite and so does Pinetti, but for your own reasons. A friendly word of warning: you're well on the way to destroying your chances – all of them. You're an intelligent man, there's no denying it, so you'll come to the same conclusion as me: spend two days looking for spies instead of working, and you'll fail on both counts. If you become paranoid enough to infect the whole intake with your psychosis and sabotage my scenario completely, it won't do you any good. Nor me, I grant you. But all I'll have to do is revise my methods, whereas you'll go home and draw your unemployment benefit. Is that really what you want?"

Still holding his gaze, I detected a hint of weariness in his eyes.

"I'll put my cards on the table too," he went on. "We keep you under constant surveillance. How? That's my business, but nothing you do escapes our notice. Some bosses bug their telephone exchanges and install CCTV in their offices. Well, it's something of that kind. I ask you, would I pay an entire team? In the satellite era? Come on! Here's another piece of advice for you: We aren't interested in your ability to play Sherlock Holmes; there are some excellent detective agencies for that sort of job. All we want to know, quite simply, is whether you succeed in selling ... what was it?"

"Fish-hooks," said Jean-Claude, who had been following our conversation without appearing to do so.

"Quite so, fish-hooks. Strange idea, that. Your immediate predecessors settled on the wholesale meat trade. An unfortunate choice: they had problems with mad cow disease, but it was interesting. Listen to me, Jérôme: run your firm, team up with anyone you like – both of your competitors, for all I care – and forget this espionage business. Nobody wants to employ James Bond, so be a good boy and stop telling horror stories. In other words, Jérôme, cool it."

He underlined the last injunction by prodding me in the chest with his forefinger, then opened the door.

"Oh yes, one more thing, just so you didn't come here for nothing: Charriac isn't working for me. Whether or not you can trust him is another matter, but I give you my word he isn't in my pay. Back to work now, and don't let me see you here again."

There are 17 physical clues to duplicity. If someone displays nine of them, he's probably lying; 13, and you can stake your life on it. Del Rieco displayed none, and his line of argument had shaken me.

I left the chalet and made for Pinetti's hiding-place behind a large fir tree.

"Come on, Pinetti, we'll go and see Charriac together. And the next time you hide behind a dark-green tree, don't wear a white shirt."

It wasn't very fair of me. I mightn't have spotted him if Del Rieco hadn't told me, but I had to win a set against someone.

When I entered Charriac's office on the second floor, Delval, the computer expert, hugged his screen to conceal it from me and Morin hastily slid a blotter over the papers spread out in front of him. Mutual trust reigned supreme. I pushed Pinetti ahead of me.

"Here's your spy," I said. "He's not very good at it. I told you I'd be clean, Charriac, and I am. I've just been to see Del Rieco, and I'll tell you everything he said. It wasn't worth sending your bloodhound after me. If we compare my info with what Morin was told, maybe the picture will become a bit clearer."

In fact, the ensuing discussion did little to clear the air. Charriac reproached me for having gone to see Del Rieco without letting him know in advance; I reproached him for having done the same by sending Morin. Morin, with every outward sign of innocence, repeated what I had just said, almost word for word. Del Rieco had delivered exactly the same speech, and Morin's motivation had been the same as my own. Charriac sprang to his defence, claiming that Brigitte Aubert had made an identical approach last night, and that I had concealed this from him. If there was a traitor in our midst, said Charriac, it could only be me. All Del Rieco's reasonable, straightforward arguments collapsed, plunging us once more into a shadow theatre where no one knew who was who, where every curtain concealed an assassin and the only light in the gloom was the glint of his dagger. In the end I lost patience.

"Charriac," I said, I'm revoking all our agreements!"

He stared at me.

"What agreements? You haven't kept to a single one – you've taken me for a ride from the start. You're the biggest phoney I've ever met. I'm amazed you're in business. With your talents you should have been in politics!"

Like all businessmen, Charriac cherished a profound contempt for politicians. This was the ultimate insult, coming from him, and I took it as such. I shrugged and went downstairs.

My little team was hard at work. Hirsch had just printed out a bunch of e-mails. He handed them to me.

"Hang on," I said, "first I'd better put you in the picture."

I told them what had happened, withholding nothing. Brigitte Aubert flushed when I mentioned that Charriac had accused her of treachery.

"I swear to you, by all that's holy . . ."

I brushed this aside.

"We believe you, Brigitte."

When I'd finished my briefing, Mastroni summarized the situation.

"I see," he said. "In short, we've made no progress."

"Too true, but we're going to act as if we have. Del Rieco has a point: it makes no difference whether or not there are spies among us. The only thing is, we can't rely on joining forces if we need to. A pity, the three of us could really have put the screws on them. How's business?"

"Sales are going down," said Mastroni. "The fishing season is almost over. One day equals three months in this game. What are we going to do during the close season?"

"We've got some cash reserves, haven't we? We'll diversify. What can we go into that's open all year round?"

"Brothels," suggested Hirsch.

"I've had an idea," said Mastroni. "Fishing freaks think of nothing but fishing. When they can't fish they get bored. Well, we could bring out a video game – you know, a CD-ROM like the ones for golf or football. The number one seller in the States is a video game based on hunting. The guys zap deer on their computers. Virtual reality. These days, it's a bigger money-spinner than reality itself."

Hirsch rocked around on his chair.

"It's a question of one particular niche in the market. You can't try your hand at everything and anything. If we're into fishing, just sports fishing, we can make the CD, but we could also make lines and reels and rods and waders and God knows what else. I'm no angler."

"Sure," said Mastroni, "but rods and waders pose the same problem: they don't sell out of season. Except to poachers, and there aren't enough of them."

"I'm for it," I cut in. "We'll make the CD. There's only one little snag: we don't have the technical expertise. How long would it take?"

"To develop a video game? A month for a crappy one, anything up to four years for a class act."

"That's too long. Isn't there someone who's already produced an angler's video game – one we could import under our own label?"

Hirsch swung his chair round to face the computer.

"I'll check."

"You see? It takes a firm six months to change direction and a government department 15 years. We've done it in three minutes flat. Any coffee going? Thanks to Del Rieco and his bullshit I missed breakfast this morning."

Marilyn smiled and got up. Everything seemed to be going well – very well. Charriac had been wrong to nudge me in the direction of politics; that was where I felt at home. My team was running smoothly. I trusted them. All the subtle cruelties of the outside world were effaced by the simple, soothing realization that I was surrounded by decent folk. Perhaps I had been wrong to want to swim in the shark aquarium with the Charriacs of this world. Perhaps this industrialized, globalized planet still had room for a few quiet little concerns with limited ambitions, firms whose employees merely tried to do their job without sinking their teeth into the opposition. I briefly daydreamed along these lines, then came down to earth with a bump: those weren't the kind of people De Wavre International was looking for.

Brigitte Aubert touched my arm with the tip of a lacquered fingernail.

"You're looking stressed out. You should try to relax."

"Really? How do you relax in the middle of a wolf pack?"

"Oh, there are plenty of techniques. Meditation, relaxation therapy . . . Lots of people use them, you know, even yuppies. It's essential, otherwise you crack."

Mastroni looked up.

"I knew a guy who used to shoot himself full of vitamin C. To give himself a lift, I mean. He carted a whole pharmacy around with him."

"And to think they give athletes the chop for smoking cannabis. Not to mention these boardroom drug tests . . ."

I made do with the coffee Marilyn brought me.

Here, as in an old folks' home, meals represented the focus of communal activity. People turned up for lunch at irregular intervals, so the teams were prevented from reconstituting themselves. This time I found myself seated next to Morin, who launched into a long lament about the reputation of his part of France. According to him, northerners had always despised southerners in every country on earth.

"Marseille is France's second city," he said. "Try uttering the name in Paris: people shrug their shoulders and laugh as if we're all comedians down south. They go there for their holidays, so they think we're permanently on holiday ourselves. They don't take us seriously. Suppose you go to the best brain surgeon in France. If he tells you he's going to trepan you in an accent like mine, you'll run a mile. If he says exactly the same thing in a northern accent, you'll trust him. I ask you, is that fair? It's the same in business. Say I offer you a deal: if I talk like a TV announcer, okay, it's a deal; if I talk the way I do, you think I'm going to con you and call the police. You think we spend our days swilling pastis and figuring how to fleece tourists. I open my mouth and everyone sniggers. You think I enjoy that?"

The whole table burst out laughing at Morin's indignant tirade. He pretended to lose his temper.

"What choice do I have? If people take me for a buffoon, even when I've just lost my entire family in a plane crash, okay, I play the buffoon. That way they don't distrust me – that way I can get by. Alternatively, I have to write to them. You can't hear someone's accent when he writes to you."

The man had a point. His comic turn was a covert way of warning us not to judge by appearances.

"I exaggerate my accent," he went on. "If people don't like it I lay it on twice as thick. They talk about France, France . . . It doesn't exist, I tell you! In Paris one time, I went to a newspaper office to hand in a press release, and a journalist told me, 'This piece of yours is too complicated. Some of our readers live in the sticks, remember.' In other words, Paris is for intelligent folk; in the provinces they're all country bumpkins. Even guys from my part of the world drop their accent when they come to Paris. They change their shirts and their accents on the plane. Why? Because if they don't, and even if they explain the quantum theory to you, you'll think they're village idiots and won't believe a word they say. Talk about the French Revolution! It hasn't happened yet, believe you me!"

"All the same," said Chalamont, "some of our big industrialists are southerners."

"Yes: Ricard! See what I mean? Quote me another – name me a government minister who doesn't have a Parisian accent."

"But they're all elected by provincial constituencies," Delval objected. "Or nearly all."

"Oh yes, they're elected there, I don't deny," Morin retorted scathingly. "They don't turn up their noses at our votes, but that's as far as it goes."

Chalamont stiffened. "You aren't going to talk politics, I trust?"

The dessert arrived and we changed the subject. I studied Morin out of the corner of my eye. He radiated a violence, rancour and frustration I'd never detected before. Beneath his extrovert exterior lurked an embittered man. Charriac's team was decidedly dangerous: Pinetti, the personification of duplicity and ruthless ambition; Morin, the nurser of grievances; and Charriac himself, intoxicated with an intelligence that strayed into abstract parameters, who regarded humanity as a colony of woodlice fit only to be crushed underfoot. Delval apart, they were a bunch of psychopaths.

After coffee I joined Laurence Carré, who was strolling beside the lake. She showed no surprise when I turned up – she must have been expecting me – and treated me to a bright smile.

"Shall we see where the path leads to, now it's daylight? If we don't do it now, we never will."

"Sure. Let's go."

We set off through the trees, whose branches afforded sporadic glimpses of the overcast sky. The weather was still unsettled.

"Let's hope it doesn't rain. I haven't got a mac with me."

"Don't worry," I told her, "we won't be going far. Anyway, it's a small island – there's no danger of getting lost. We can always turn back if the worst comes to the worst."

The path zigzagged up the hillside, skirting any trees that encroached on it. We were steadily climbing. Laurence walked with a springy, almost balletic step – not, perhaps, the most effective mode of progression for a walk in the country, but undeniably easy on the eye.

At the top we came out into an open field. The whole of the lake was visible from there. Looking down, we could make out the roof of the hotel and even Del Rieco's chalet. Behind us, all that separated the island from the shore was a narrow strip of water. Laurence frowned.

"Why didn't they make everything face the other way? On this side they could almost have built a bridge instead of compelling the hotel guests to cross the lake at its widest point."

"Yes, but this side faces north. Hotels face south, otherwise they don't get the sun."

"We never see the sun in any case."

I bent down and examined the grass. There were bare patches where it had been torn out in tufts.

"They must graze goats here. Or a cow. Look, it's all been eaten..."

"Oh," she said mockingly, "so you majored in agronomy as well."

She knelt down beside me, near enough for me to smell her slightly spicy perfume. It wasn't a covert invitation, though, and I continued to avoid touching her. She swivelled on the spot and sat down. I followed suit, hugging my knees.

"I had a talk with Charriac at lunch," she said. "The man's completely insane. He came out with the most incredible theory about women."

"I had the pleasure of Morin's company. He was bad enough."

"At least he's funny. Charriac is sick. It was deliberate provocation, of course, I realize that. He tried to make me lose my temper, but don't ask me to repeat what he said. That brand of utter contempt ... He exudes it from every pore. It wasn't just the ingrained conservatism of someone who can't get used to seeing women emerge from their traditional role – there are plenty of men like that. No, it was ... I almost threw my glass in his face."

"I think he feels the same way about men as well, you know. He despises the whole human race."

She plucked a blade of grass and put it to her lips, then opened her fingers and let it blow away.

"No, it was more specific than that. A hatred of women. I don't know what they've done to him, but he deserved it."

"He's married. At least, he's got a young son."

"I didn't know that. I'm amazed. Maybe he had a messy divorce."

"Is there any other kind?"

She gave a little hiccup of amusement.

"Not that I'm aware of. In the end, though, it was almost fascinating. First there's himself, Charriac, and a few other masters of the universe whom he respects because they're powerful. Then there's a bunch of slaves who sometimes have their uses. Finally, right at the bottom of the heap, come women, who are ruled by their hormones, good for nothing but reproduction, and solely interested in finding a male well-heeled enough to secure their children's future. It's rather as if . . ."

She hesitated for a moment.

" . . . as if he's a superior being – one who has succeeded in flushing out all the mediocre lies told in the name of love, affection, compassion. To him they're contemptible emotions that inhibit pure thought. You know what? I think he's a kind of Nazi. He'd be quite capable of torching Oradour-sur-Glane or opening a branch at Auschwitz, yawning behind his hand. The Nazis must have been just like that. They haven't suddenly vanished, have they? Their attitude of mind, I mean . . . It's simply that they're senior civil servants or captains of industry, and these days they're liberals. But they continue to regard the rest of humanity as insects."

She lost her balance, steadied herself by resting her hand on mine, and swiftly removed it.

"Excuse me . . ."

"Do you hate him?"

"I can't even bring myself to do that. I feel sorry for the man. He must have been very unhappy. It must be frightening, the dam he's built to hold everything back, not to mention what's festering behind it. No, what alarms me is his utter lack of restraint. He's so sure of himself. Other people don't exist; they're merely reflections of his ego."

I glanced at her. She was looking genuinely upset.

"Let's not spend the whole day talking about Charriac. Tell me about yourself."

"Not here, later. In Paris, if you like. There's something about this place that . . ."

Laurence didn't complete the sentence. She rose abruptly.

"Shall we? I must go and face my team. Some team! I've seldom come across such a collection of broken reeds." She ticked them off on her fingers. "Leroy: nothing's ever right for him – he moans the whole time. El Fatawi looks shy, but he's the same – constantly dissatisfied. Utterly defeatist, too, and stubborn as a mule. I'd need a pitchfork to budge the pair of them. As for Chalamont, he's as thick as two short planks. His one asset is, he knows it so he keeps his trap shut. That's invaluable: most knuckleheads think they're smart. The less said about the other two the better. I don't think they've ever opened their mouths, but at least they don't bug me. If that's De Wavre International's idea of selection, I don't think much of it."

We made our way back down the path, walking gingerly because the carpet of pine needles made the surface slippery. Laurence clung sometimes to my arm, sometimes to the nearest tree trunk. Her remarks had given me food for thought. It was true that, discounting four or five of our competitors, most were not of the calibre one would have expected.

"There could be another possibility," I said. "I mean, in view of the fees they charge, De Wavre may only want to test a couple of applicants – well, three or four, let's say. The rest may be here simply to complete the simulation and confront us with the sort of problems you meet in a real firm. You know, the fanatical surfer who doesn't give a damn, the complacent idiot who's proud of all the boobs he makes, the ageing executive who's within a year of retirement and spends his time playing golf, and the boss's nephew, who's clearly out of his depth. We don't have any of those, but still, they've found us a pretty representative sample."

She paused for a moment and started to laugh.

"You may be right. It would be very flattering for us. *If* I'm included in the elite, I mean."

"Of course you are, otherwise Charriac would leave you in peace. He simply wants to see if you're going to raise the usual feminist objections: women are given a hard time, there aren't enough of them, nobody ever listens to them – all that stuff."

She wagged a forefinger at me.

"Ah, if you're going to start that too . . ."

"No, it's true, employers are men like any others. They hate that kind of talk. It makes them feel guilty."

"Sure, it rubs their nose in their own mess. It's a fact, though, isn't it? That women are under-represented, I mean. Is it unfair to demand greater representation?"

"Of course not," I said, "but when you're unemployed it poses a threat. There aren't enough jobs to go round, and we're told to make room for you."

"If you won't make room, you'll have to be pushed!"

She thrust out her chin, torn between amusement and anger. Without thinking, I took her by the shoulders.

"Laurence, I'm afraid our interests don't coincide . . ."

She didn't shy away, but I detected the challenge in her eyes and released her. She attracted me, that was undeniable now, but I had no wish to start an affair. I love my wife, and besides, I had too much on my plate already.

We walked the rest of the way in a rather awkward silence, separated by the sort of wary void that opens up between two people when something that might have happened hasn't.

Hirsch was eagerly awaiting me on the steps of the hotel. He cast an inquisitive glance at Laurence, then grabbed me by the elbow and whispered, "I got a reply – it looks quite promising. Please come."

He showed me the e-mail he'd just printed out. Del Rieco had condescended to inform us that, yes, an angler's video game did exist, and yes, the American designer was interested in exporting it to Europe. Mastroni was already drawing up a contract.

"What do we do," he asked me, "open a new branch?"

We debated this for a while. There were advantages and disadvantages, not least the time factor.

The question had still to be settled when Laurence suddenly burst in on us. Her cheeks were flushed and her eyes filled with tears. She gave Hirsch a nervous smile, then turned to me. She was looking alarmed.

"Jérôme, may I have a word?"

It was less than half an hour since we'd parted.

"What is it, Laurence?"

She shook her head. "In private, if you don't mind . . ."

I'd seen similar symptoms only once before, and that was when a secretary of mine had just heard that her son had been knocked down by a truck. Something serious must have happened. I gave Hirsch an apologetic tap on the arm and followed her outside. She walked a few yards down the track, then swung round to face me.

"Charriac is raiding my share capital!"

"How do you mean?" I said, puzzled.

She wrung her hands. She was trying to put a good face on things, but the effort was too much for her. Her eyes bored into mine.

"Do you know the composition of your share capital?"

Mentally, I gave myself a resounding slap in the face. I'd thought of everything but that. Having proceeded on the implicit assumption that I was the majority shareholder, I hadn't bothered to check that fundamental point.

"Er, no . . ."

"Well, take a close look at it. That's what I've just done."

"Are you quoted on the Bourse? Has he launched a takeover bid?"

"Not even. It's a lot simpler than that. I hold a third of the shares, and so do two other people. Charriac has just bought out one of my fellow shareholders and is flirting with the other.'

"Where's the money coming from?"

"How should I know?" she snarled like an angry cat. "Maybe he's got cash reserves – maybe he did a deal with a bank. Tell me the truth, Jérôme, I beg you: it wasn't you, was it?"

"No." I smiled broadly. "Cross my heart."

Her look of relief was quickly replaced by a worried frown.

"You've got to help me, Jérôme! If he collars the remaining third I'll be a minority shareholder in my own company, and I may as well pack my bags. It's out of the question, Jérôme! I've simply *got* to be selected, I'll explain why."

It was pointless. We all had our own reasons, and they were tragically similar.

"What do the unions say?" I asked. "They don't like mergers. Mergers spell redundancies."

"The unions don't give a damn!" she hissed. "There's too much money on the table."

"How much?"

She named a figure. It was about as much as we had decided to invest in importing the video game. She gripped my wrist.

"Listen, Jérôme, I've no alternative: you must buy the third block of shares. Then we'll be on level terms: a third apiece to him, you, and me. If we join forces we can fight him off. All he'll have is a blocking minority – in fact he's got that already."

"What if you increase your capital? He won't be able to – "

"Too late. I should have done that before, but I was too gullible. I'm in your hands, Jérôme. Everything depends on you."

"I'm not a lone operator, Laurence. I've got a team to think of."

She saw what was plain to see: a definite reluctance on my part. Her eyes filled with tears. With a final look at me she turned away, hugging her shoulders as if she were cold.

"If you desert me too," she said in an oddly expressionless voice, "I'm done for."

"It's only a game, Laurence . . ."

"No, it isn't. If it is, then life is a game."

Feeling ashamed, I cravenly tried to hedge.

"Listen, I didn't say no, I said I'd have to discuss it with my team. I have to think of them too. I'm not ruling it out, but you've got to understand my position."

She looked at me wearily.

"Oh, I understand it all right. It's everyone for himself."

"But it's been that way from the start, Laurence. Don't panic, here's what we'll do: I'll tell my people what's happened. We may have to protect ourselves first. We've just changed gear, so we'll need time to get our bearings. After that, if there's any chance of our risking the operation, you must come and explain to us why it's in our interest. Give me all you've got, your financial statements, your share of the market, et cetera. We'll have to study all those things."

She shivered.

"In other words, I sell myself to Charriac, but first I give myself to you. May I ask you a question?"

"Go ahead."

"Would it have changed anything if I'd gone to bed with you?"

"No," I said promptly.

"Thanks. I needed to know that."

I took her by the shoulder and shook her.

"Snap out of it, Laurence, the game's not over yet. Don't act the little girl who's broken her doll – not you, not that! Know what?

You're looking beaten already. Go and take a shower, get changed, pull yourself together and take up the cudgels again. Jesus Christ, haven't you got any guts?"

She gave me a wan smile and walked off. I returned to my lair – slowly, because I needed to review the situation on every intersecting level. Charriac's offensive was certainly designed to eliminate Laurence. That had been his original plan, and he'd never disguised the fact. But it might also be designed to test me. Torn between the interests of my firm and my well-known liking for Laurence, which way would I jump? Del Rieco was clearly expecting me to join in the hunt without hesitation, or even to dispatch the quarry myself. Perhaps he hadn't been evaluating two or three candidates from the outset, only one: me. Were De Wavre looking for a killer? All right, I would give them one.

I rejoined my associates and gave them a brief account of the latest developments. Mastroni was the first to react.

"I'm not surprised. It had to end like this."

"One firm too many in the trade?"

"No, no. Financial coups. You don't make money by manufacturing something or satisfying the consumer, not these days. You make it on the stock exchange. That's where the grass is greener. What they call sacred competition consists in buying out rival firms and closing them down. What does our capital structure look like?"

Hirsch was already punishing his keyboard.

"I took a good look at our cash flow, but I didn't pay any attention to our working capital. I knew we weren't quoted on the Bourse, so I thought we were safe." Hirsch paused. "Well, what do you know! There's no majority shareholder – the biggest has only 11 per cent. There are three banks, though. Their combined holdings would amount to 27 per cent."

"Too little."

"Yes. As long as no one verges on 33 and a third . . ."

"We don't have enough cash to buy Laurence's third, I suppose?"

"No way."

"Then she's had it," said Mastroni.

"Serves her right," said Brigitte Aubert. "She's always got up my nose, her and her airs and graces . . ."

"Maybe," I cut in, "but Charriac's getting a bit too big for his boots. That's not good. If he marginalizes us he'll be able to corner the market. Laurence's demise could be the start of our own. I don't think there's anything to be gained by it, do you?"

"Still," said Mastroni, "the playing field wasn't really level. Madame Carré has three shareholders, we've got umpteen. What about Charriac? Can we access his capital structure?"

"I'll see," said Hirsch, continuing to fill his screen with figures.

Mastroni scratched the nape of his neck.

"A financial scrap . . . I don't like that – for that you need pros. We were stupid, we should have suspected it. Who cares about manufacturing fish-hooks? It's all about money. We've been playing rummy, they've been playing poker."

I looked at them all in turn.

"By 'we' I assume you mean me. Mastroni's right, I haven't been playing the right game. Old-fashioned capitalism. I'm surprised I didn't invest all our liquid reserves in Russian imperial bonds. You're absolutely right, you don't make money by manufacturing things, you make it by pinching it from other people, so that's what we're going to do."

Still with his back to us, Hirsch said, "Charriac's capital is on a par with ours. The biggest shareholding is 17 per cent, all the rest are eight or less. He's laughing like us."

"In other words," said Marilyn, "only poor Laurence was for the high jump."

"She should have played it safe," Brigitte Aubert decreed. "It's easier to control three people than 50, surely?"

"Wrong," Mastroni retorted. "It's a lot harder."

At that moment El Fatawi came in. He deposited a sheaf of papers on the table.

"I was told to bring you these. Hey, guys, any chance of our teaming up?"

"There's a major objection, of course," Mastroni told him without a smile.

El Fatawi stared at him uncomprehendingly. Then he ventured a cordial grin and left the room. Mastroni sat back in his chair.

"I agree with Jérôme, more or less," he said. "It won't do us any good if Charriac swallows Team B. Not unless he exhausts himself financially in the process."

The more I listened to Mastroni the better I liked him. He was calm, intelligent, competent. I knew I could depend on him far more than I had done hitherto. He had a gruff manner and lacked charisma, but for my purposes that presented no problem.

Hirsch straightened up with a jerk.

"Got it!" he cried triumphantly. "I've got the answer. The American, the video game guy, he's going to bring some cash with him. He's prepared to take a 15 per cent stake in our business. If we've got some ready cash we won't need to invest – we can fall back on the financial market."

I whistled. "And you dreamed that up all by yourself?"

"Sure. There are workers and wankers, it's the way of the world. Now let's take a peek at Team B's finances and see if we can't snap up a lousy firm that's heading for the rocks."

I'd been so busy defusing the charges laid by Del Rieco, Charriac and co., I'd failed to keep a sufficient grip on my team. Hirsch and Mastroni were putting on speed and starting to grow wings. If

I wasn't careful, the real threat would come from inside.

We made an offer slightly in excess of Charriac's. It wasn't difficult: believing himself to be the only bidder, he had offered the bare minimum. By four that afternoon we were co-owners of Team B.

It was a pretty good deal. Laurence and her people hadn't run the firm very efficiently, but they did possess certain assets. By sacrificing one or two poor product lines we might be able to break even this year and start making a profit in less than three. A score of redundancies, no more. Taking early retirements into account, we would probably get by. The business was fundamentally sound.

Ten minutes later Charriac sent us an e-mail. He was convening a Firm B board meeting at six o'clock. Each director could bring an assistant.

"What right has he?" Mastroni protested. "Madame Carré's still the chairman and managing director, isn't she? If the board meeting isn't convened in due form, we can request the commercial court to annul it."

"Yes," I said, "but let's keep that up our sleeve in case things go sour. I'd like to hear what he's got to say. I also want to see the look on his face."

I couldn't wait to savour Charriac's come-uppance, but I was disappointed. He was more triumphant than ever. We met in the workroom, which Laurence had occupied until then. I was accompanied by Mastroni, Charriac had brought Pinetti, and Laurence had installed an anonymous member of her team in a corner, his sole function being to take notes of all that was said. Charriac, impeccably dressed as ever in a dark blue suit, opened the session.

"Well, there have been a few minor upheavals . . . Madame Carré must inform us of her intentions. As I see it, she has only two remaining options: either she takes the boat back tomorrow morning or she remains in business, but under our control. I won't keep you in suspense: it's all the same to me. Just as long as she consents to do as we dictate. If she decides on the second alternative, I'm sure we shall be able to count on her loyalty."

"Just a minute," Mastroni broke in before I could stop him. "She's still chairman."

"Oh, no!" Charriac laughed derisively. "She'll be whatever we decide. We could obviously waste a few minutes arguing about conventions, but it wouldn't affect the final outcome."

Laurence was looking straight ahead, seemingly unconscious of the torture to which Charriac was subjecting her.

"I think conventions matter," Mastroni said angrily. "In the normal course of events, she's the one who presides, who calls on people to speak and decides the agenda. Where is it, by the way, the agenda?"

Charriac adopted a patient, schoolmasterly tone.

"Monsieur Mastroni, in a real-life situation we could afford to flounder around for a while – it might even be amusing. But this isn't a real-life situation. One day counts as three months, so one hour counts as roughly four days. If we agree that these legal quibbles normally take three hours, real time, we ought to devote – let's see . . . about two minutes to them. We've already done that."

Laurence interrupted the proceedings. She addressed us in profile, so we couldn't see her eyes, as she did all too often.

"Monsieur Mastroni is right, it's my job to open this meeting. I'm dazzled by Monsieur Charriac's capacity for mental arithmetic, but I feel, as he does, that we're wasting time. I suppose the first item on the agenda you ask for is the election of the chairman of the board. I suggest we proceed to it right away."

"Now you're talking," Charriac said approvingly. "Let's get on. I propose Monsieur Pinetti here."

I couldn't help smiling.

"You can't be serious. There's no reason for you to take over."

"I'm not taking over. Think for a moment. It can't be me, nor can it be you, Carceville. Nor can it be Madame Carré, who has brought this firm to its present pass. So it must be a fourth party – a kind of Gulbenkian. You know who Gulbenkian was?"

"I'm sure you're going to tell us," Mastroni said resignedly.

"Indeed I am. Two oil companies were contesting the mineral rights of some country or other – Iran or Iraq, perhaps. Neither of them could muster a majority shareholding; more importantly, neither of them wanted the other to have it. So they each took 49.5 per cent, went down into the street, accosted the first tramp they met, and presented him with one per cent of the shares free of charge, on the strict understanding that he didn't interfere with anything. A sort of UN peacekeeper. That one per cent made him fabulously wealthy. He led a life of luxury, opened famous museums all over the world, set up an artistic foundation, and always kept his promise to do absolutely nothing except prevent the formation of a majority. My idea of heaven! Unfortunately, such a combination of circumstances arises only once a century."

"Nice of you to compare Pinetti to a tramp," said Mastroni.

Charriac was unruffled. "Oh, Gulbenkian wasn't really a tramp, he was a carpet dealer or a shopkeeper, I don't recall exactly. Of course, if Monsieur Pinetti agreed to take on the responsibility, he would resign from my team at once."

"I don't have one per cent," Laurence put in coldly, "I've got 33 and a third."

I took the floor in my turn. It was time to stop Charriac in his tracks.

"Okay, so Charriac has tried to foist Pinetti on us. Presumably he's gambling on our having lost our wits before coming in here – a thousand-to-one chance. Let's be serious, Charriac: tell us what you've really got in mind."

"But I already told you," he said, looking hurt. "This is incredible: I explain in advance what I think, and no one takes a blind bit of notice. All right, not you, not me, not anyone present. In that case, who? If it can't be anyone from your lot, or mine, or Madame Carré's, who does that leave? What about the deputy director of her team, subject to a supervisory board? Those associates of yours, Madame Carré, what are their names? Whom do you recommend?"

Pinetti pretended to leaf through his papers.

"Let's see . . . She's got Chalamont, El Fatawi, Leroy . . ."

"There we are," said Charriac. "How about Chalamont? Not Leroy, he'd be moaning down the phone all day long."

"You must be joking," I said.

"Look," Charriac said wearily, "in real life we'd import some big name from outside. Here, we're on an island – there isn't anyone else. Either we make do with what we've got, or we give up. I made some genuine suggestions – Pinetti, who would resign from my team; or Chalamont; or even the Arab, if you like – but you reject them all. I don't see what we can do, apart from shut up shop. Well, I'm listening . . ."

So that was what he'd been aiming at all along. He had entangled us in a line of argument whose inevitable outcome was a cessation of activity. I fixed him with a broad smile.

"Charriac, you haven't studied the chessboard closely enough. Your holding amounts to 33 and a third per cent, no more. I propose Madame Carré, and I request her to proceed to a vote."

"This is ridiculous," he said, throwing up his hands. "I see no point in giving her artificial respiration. She's beaten, Carceville. If she had a spark of decency, she'd have resigned and gone off to pack her bags by now. You really want to keep her here in a coma?"

Laurence's cheeks were burning. I sprang to her defence.

"Madame Carré is entitled to play the game to a finish."

"But she's a total write-off," Charriac objected. "She doesn't have a shot left in her locker. Any profits she makes – *if* she's got the gumption to make any – will end up in our balance sheets. More probably, she'll continue to run this firm like a stupid cow, and *we'll* have to absorb her losses. What do *you* do with corpses, Carceville, embalm them? Personally, I incinerate them. It takes up less room."

His brutal remarks were clearly aimed at Laurence. By humiliating her, Charriac was trying to get her to crack. She stood firm, however, and her stony expression conveyed that the argument didn't concern her. Charriac fired a parting shot:

"I propose we put the firm into liquidation."

"Oh, yes," Mastroni burst out, "so you can snap it up for peanuts! There's absolutely no reason. The firm isn't losing money. It hasn't any debts. This is just a change in the capital structure."

"A minor detail!" Charriac retorted. "You haven't understood a thing, Mastroni. Reread the instructions: the object of the game is to make money, no matter how. Madame Carré is a thoroughly delightful, likeable person. In real life I should be very happy to invite her out to dinner, if she granted me that pleasure, and swap the latest gossip with her. Here, I couldn't care less."

Mastroni struggled in vain to keep his temper.

"No matter how?" he exclaimed. "Why not import drugs while you're about it?"

"Who says I'm not doing that already? Another ten years, and they'll be legal in any case. Drugs account for five per cent of the world economy, my dear Monsieur Mastroni – the *world* economy! One can't afford to disregard that five per cent simply because the FBI has decided that alcohol is all right and drugs are not. They'll be permitted if there's a market for them, and there is one. Prohibition lasted less than 20 years. It's just a question of time."

"That's not the point at issue," I broke in. "Your flights of fancy are becoming tedious, Charriac. I propose we take a vote."

"I was answering your sidekick," Charriac protested. "*He* raised the subject. Vote as much as you like, if you still think it's worthwhile. I hold a blocking minority – I can paralyse you, so it won't affect the final outcome. Listen, Carceville, let's not spend the whole night here. Here's my last word: Chalamont chairman, you and I deputy chairmen. That's if you absolutely insist on keeping this firm in existence."

"Let's vote," I said stubbornly.

Charriac rose. "Count me out. What is this, a business or a love affair? I hope you'll invite me to the wedding." He shook his head. "I'm going to make your lives a misery, believe me. You won't be able to sleep at night."

He took three steps and came to a halt in front of Laurence.

"Tell me the truth, Madame Carré: it's my aftershave, isn't it? That's what you've never liked about me – I knew it! I swore I'd change it, and then I forgot."

"No," Laurence said deliberately, "it's your lousy face."

Charriac took this in his stride.

"How I love the cordial boardroom atmosphere!" he exclaimed. "It's so nice to be able to speak one's mind among friends. Naturally, I shall put a dozen spokes in your wheel. When force fails, there's always the law . . ."

On which sardonic note he left the room. His departure was followed by dead silence. We proceeded to gather up our papers, Mastroni with a look of weary resignation.

I remained seated while the others made their exit. Laurence turned in the doorway and raised her eyebrows.

"Aren't you going? What are you waiting for?"

"Well," I said wryly, "a word of thanks, maybe."

She slowly retraced her steps.

"Good God! What for?"

"For having saved your neck, among other things."

She propped one buttock on the table.

"You didn't save me. He's right, I'm finished. I'm only staying on for curiosity's sake, to see how the game turns out."

"I did my best . . ."

She put a hand on my chest as if fending me off.

"Yes, for your own sake. You couldn't accept Pinetti, Chalamont would have been a disaster, and you didn't want me to bow out. Charriac would have had too great an advantage, and you need some time to negotiate with your American."

"You know about him?"

Her eyes narrowed. There was no gentleness in the bitter set of her mouth.

"I know plenty, Jérôme. I've been watching you closely, you and Charriac. He makes a lot of noise, generates a lot of hot air. You economize on saliva, but you're both the same breed. You're built along the same lines and your minds work the same way. You observe certain conventions, that's the only difference. Go on, tell me I'm wrong."

I lowered my gaze. "It's the game that's like that, Laurence. I'd even go so far as to say that life is like that."

"Life!"

I looked up. She seemed on the verge of tears, but she pulled herself together.

"Life! What do you know about life? *C'est la vie*, take the rough with the smooth! That's cheapjack philosophy, Jérôme. It's on a par with the stupid things people say at funerals. For a moment – a moment of weakness or optimism – I thought you were different. It didn't last, though, and my disappointment wasn't too bitter. Even now, I hoped you'd protest, deny it, tell me I'm wrong. I gave you a last chance, but you didn't take it. If only you hadn't spotted it, but you did."

"Grief has unhinged you, Laurence," I said, trying to be jocular. She opened her bag and took out a packet of cigarettes.

"Mind if I smoke?"

"Of course not."

"Would you mind if I died? A little bit, admit it just to please me. Charriac's a sadist. He gets a buzz out of killing; you merely find it distressing. You're genuinely sorry I found myself in the line of fire, but it didn't stop you pulling the trigger."

"That's really unfair of you, Laurence," I protested. "You want the truth? Okay, here it is. You're right, it wasn't in my interest to close your firm down, but the situation is such that it's neutralized in any case. Charriac wanted Chalamont. I could have proposed El Fatawi. He would have played along – or pretended to – just to make peace with me. It was you who told me El Fatawi's a dud, but maybe he isn't as bad as all that. I fought for you. I could have played for time, negotiated a truce. Now I'm at war with Charriac. It's a head-on confrontation."

"In the final," she muttered with an effort.

"Yes, in the final. It's come sooner than I wanted. I did it for your sake, I'm sorry you never noticed. Some nerve, levelling your reproaches at me, when I'm the only one that doesn't deserve them. Blame Charriac, Del Rieco, De Wavre – blame anyone you like, but not me. Alternatively, do as you damn well please!"

This time she buried her face in her hands, her back bowed beneath the nervous strain of the last few days. She emitted a brief sob. I put out a tentative hand and stroked her hair.

"You haven't done all that badly, Laurence. You bear a grudge against the whole world, I know, but things could be worse. Life goes on . . ."

"Stop banging on about life!" she burst out. "It's exasperating –

I've never heard such crap! That's not the point. I wanted to succeed with De Wavre, I really did. I was ready to do anything – anything, you hear?"

Two or three times my office had been invaded by women who'd let their skirts ride up their thighs and said exactly the same thing. It saddened me to see Laurence suddenly resemble them. I removed my hand from her hair.

"I can't give you what you're after, Laurence. Del Rieco's the only one who can. You've nothing to lose. In your place I'd concentrate on him."

She looked up sharply. "What do you suggest I do?" she asked, wiping her eyes.

"Here's the picture as I see it. Charriac is riding high. He's screwed you, and he'll do the same for me if I make the smallest slip. Del Rieco holds the key. If only we could access his programme and doctor the data a little . . . You've retained your status, but it'll be no use to you any more. Your position couldn't be worse if you were selling fish-hooks in the middle of the Sahara. You can't recover lost ground that way. You must try another angle – the only one that counts: Del Rieco. He's the one that holds all the cards. Stock exchange, judiciary, government – he's all of them rolled into one. He dictates who wins or loses. If he'd wanted to save you, all he had to do was say that the other shareholders were too attached to the firm and refused to sell, period, but he didn't. Still, these things happen – it wouldn't have conflicted with his logic. It was Del Rieco who gunned you down. Not me, that's for sure, and not even Charriac. If it's revenge you want, go to the right address."

She looked at me more closely. "And you?" she said. "What would you gain by it?"

I blew out my cheeks. "Possibly nothing at all, apart from the pleasure of having dried your tears. Possibly a great deal, if you share your information with me – if you stop believing that I've got it in for you."

Laurence walked over to the window, rested her fingertips on the sill, and gazed out at the trees. She did the opposite of most people: she never looked at you when she planned to say something important. You sometimes had to strain your ears to hear her.

"I'm looking for the trap," she said in a low voice. "You make a habit of saying A when you're thinking of B and aiming at C."

"Who, me?" I said indignantly.

"Yes, you – all of you. I never imagined it would be so hard."

"Nor did I. Everything's twisted, and it's our job to get used to it. Charriac thinks he's straight, but he's as bent as a corkscrew. The most twisted of the lot is Del Rieco. Think it over on your own, Laurence. I'm not the one who's been laying mines everywhere."

She bowed her head as if she hadn't heard me.

"I can't wait to get out of this place. Just now, when he tore off my clothes and dragged me along by the hair, I nearly snapped and chucked the whole thing. I can't wait to be back among normal people!"

"There aren't any, Laurence," I said gently. "Here we're stripped naked, and we don't have much time, so we see things more clearly. That's the only difference."

She turned, her figure outlined against the dark mass of the trees.

"You know, when I was young I thought you could only truly know a man when you'd made love with him. I thought the skin couldn't lie, but even that isn't true . . ."

"*Mondo cane*," I said lightly.

I didn't know what she intended to do, but I knew what *I* was going to do.

*

Our conversation left me feeling uneasy. I was surprised that Laurence's aggression, which was only natural after what had happened, had been directed primarily at me. Perhaps she expected more of me than I'd imagined. She knew as little about me as I did about her. We had barely touched, or rather, we'd been careful not to. Knowing full well how De Wavre's scenario was likely to turn out, I hadn't wanted to form any personal ties. I had allowed one or two branches to become entwined despite myself, but I decided to ignore the fact. The game, with its many levels of duplicity, was complicated enough without my introducing a tangled skein of emotional relationships and individual psychologies. I had to concentrate on priorities. If there was to be a sole winner it couldn't be Laurence. But it could be me. And then, from the victor's rostrum, I would try to intercede in her favour. She deserved it for her courage and tenacity.

At dinner Pinetti subjected us to a long diatribe against the unions. Although they had so far left us blissfully alone (keeping their powder dry for day three, no doubt), he had targeted them for some unknown reason. He declared that the class struggle was an appallingly anachronistic and outmoded concept in the Internet era, that technological and social upheavals had abolished such obsolete ideas, and that he couldn't understand why they were still cited by otherwise intelligent people who regarded employers as their enemies. According to him, all the associates of a firm had a major common interest in seeing it develop. In a fiercely competitive international context, no one could afford to foster internecine strife or entertain suspicions and claims that were incompatible with common objectives. Brigitte Aubert pointed out that this little speech was just as anachronistic as the attitude it condemned; there had always been rich and poor, and she failed to see how the Internet was changing that. Equality was a dream that must be abandoned, Pinetti retorted. All the systems that laid claim to it had gone bust, whereas those that took account of disparities and exploited them to the best of their ability were demonstrating their effectiveness every day. El Fatawi laid a trap for Pinetti by asking if he thought of society as a human body with limbs adapted to various functions and specialized cells of which each had its proper place.

"Absolutely," said Pinetti.

"Then you're an out-and-out fascist," El Fatawi retorted. "That corporate vision of yours is the very basis of the fascist theory."

"My God, an intellectual!" Pinetti said pityingly.

"That's typically fascist, too," said El Fatawi.

Pinetti lost his temper.

"Okay, professor, where are the guard dogs? Where are the watch-towers? Seen any political prisoners lately? Society has never been freer, I tell you!"

"Yes, because you've succeeded in smashing every collective undertaking. There's nothing left but individual egos – and, right at the top, a few people who decide for everyone in the name of technocratic efficiency. Revolution may be dead, but there are plenty of murders, plenty of nervous breakdowns and suicides. No more political prisoners, it's true, but four times as many prisoners under common law. There have never been so few strikes or so many people behind bars."

"That's because they don't play the game," said Pinetti. "Obey the rules and you won't have any problems. Force has been replaced by law. Isn't that a step forward?"

"Who makes the law?"

"You and me, through the people we elect."

"Bullshit! Two hundred technocrats subject to nobody's control and scared stiff of the reactions of the financial markets. No need to call out the riot police: you simply draft a decree and leave it to the courts. Everything always favours the same interests: those of the multinationals and the United States, which amounts to the same thing. You have to be a schmuck like Milosevic to get yourself bombed to blazes. One fine day, if you're civilized, your currency depreciates by zero point one per cent and you know at once you've made a booboo. So you come to attention and toe the line."

"Sure, because there are rules governing profitability, and they're the same everywhere. They're economic laws as immutable as your need to breathe, eat and pass water, and there's nothing you can do about it. Didn't they teach you that in your faculty? If you break them it's like refusing to breathe: you die."

"Obey them and you die too. But it isn't the same ones who die, that's the whole point."

"Will you be much longer?" Morin complained. "Anyone would think this was a school debating society."

"Well, well," Laurence said innocently, "so Monsieur Morin's school had a debating society. What a surprise. I always thought the Marseillais settled arguments with their fists."

The atmosphere was becoming downright poisonous. All the members of Laurence's team were exuding resentment and taking out their sense of failure on Charriac's minions. I felt convinced that if Pinetti had presented an apologia for Stalin, El Fatawi would have extolled the merits of free enterprise. They were making long, subtle detours in order to convey, without ever uttering it, the simple sentiment: "You're a bastard and I loathe you." That, in most cases, is what underlies any so-called ideological debate; the rest is just a smokescreen.

We were in for a surprise at coffee time: His Excellency Joseph Del Rieco deigned to join us. He was wearing a navy blue blazer and a pair of immaculate white slacks. Jean-Claude and Natalie followed him in, preserving their usual discreet silence. He treated us to one of his broad Hollywood smiles, every tooth bared, green eyes alight with brotherly love.

"I trust I'm not intruding?"

"Not at all, not at all," said Pinetti, pulling up a chair. "We see far too little of you."

"Far be it from me to encroach on your freedom of decision," Del Rieco said apologetically. "We complete this exercise tomorrow evening. On Friday there'll be a little obstacle race, and that's the end of that. On Saturday morning you can forget all about me."

He warmly thanked the waiter, who had just poured him a cup of coffee, radiating exuberant solicitude. One could have mistaken him for an American politico on the campaign trail.

"Well," he asked, stirring his coffee, "how's it going? Not too tough for you?"

Laurence took the plunge.

"Some of your decisions need explaining," she said.

He turned to face her with a radiant smile. For a moment I thought he would kiss her.

"I'm not responsible for many of them, you know. We have a sort of model based on our observations. Whenever you take an initiative we consult a set of pre-existing parameters. The number of things people can reasonably do is far from being infinite. Don't be annoyed if I say this, but your actions are relatively predictable. You know those books in which you yourself are the hero?"

"First you'd better explain to Monsieur Morin what a book is," El Fatawi said scathingly.

"Very funny," Morin retorted with a shrug.

"They're books for children – or adolescents, let's say. Every page presents you with a choice. Choose A, and you go to page 51; choose B, to page 19. Then it starts again. Some choices lead you up blind alleys, others help you to progress. This seminar of ours is somewhat similar, but more complex and realistic. It presents you with scenarios in which you can take any turning you please. If you do this, that happens. That's all there is to it. As I told you at the outset, it's based on the role-play principle. It's a kind of game . . ."

"A very entertaining one, too," Laurence put in.

Del Rieco either ignored or failed to detect the sarcasm in her tone.

"Yes, it can be. A kind of Monopoly. There is an element of luck, but it's very small – just as it is in real life. Your chances of success are greater or smaller according to what you've done to date. The computer continually adjusts the parameters. If you ask for a loan, the bank's reaction will depend on what security you can offer."

Charriac had remained on the fringes but was listening intently.

"In short," he said, "when you're doing well you do better and better; when you're doing badly, worse and worse."

Del Rieco nodded. "Quite so. That's what generally happens, you know. It's the quicksand theory: step on the stuff, and you've had it."

"What if someone breaks the mould?" I asked.

"That very seldom happens," Del Rieco replied. "We have a library. If someone diverges very slightly from the norm, I make a decision based on what seems logical to me – on my experience. If it's a totally unprecedented case, which is very rare indeed, I pick up the phone and consult an expert or two. One crafty individual cited a law I'd never heard of. It was several hours before I realized he'd invented it."

"Did you approve?"

"Yes and no. You can get away with a lie in real life, but people tend to mistrust you somewhat."

"And *did* he get away with it?"

"We added a few words to his assessment. Some employers aren't scared of cheek, others are more cautious."

"Will you be writing an assessment on each of us when this is over?" asked Charriac.

"Naturally. That's the whole point of the exercise."

"Can we see a sample assessment?"

Del Rieco shook his head and laughed. "No, no, they're our property."

"But we're legally entitled to see any file containing information about to us," said El Fatawi.

"Oh, sure. Like a company balance sheet. Any shareholder is entitled to access it. The official balance sheet, that is; the real one remains under wraps. We can show you your file if you like. You'll find it contains your CV and little else."

"You're sailing close to the wind, legally speaking."

"Listen," Del Rieco cut in good-naturedly, "is it legal to employ someone on the strength of his star sign? Yes. You think that's preferable? Personally, I try to gather the most objective information possible. That's what employers want, too. That way, everyone is happy."

"Except the ones you reject," said Laurence.

Del Rieco flapped his hands.

"No, it doesn't work like that. The preliminary selection process took place in Paris. Here we test candidates for what they have to offer in action. How they behave in a group, how they react when they hit a snag – everything their CVs don't tell us, in other words. Then we divide them into batches: the ones we aren't going to recommend; the ones we'll try to place, but in the right niche – somewhere where they'll be able to display their best qualities and minimize their shortcomings; and the ones we're going to recommend unreservedly. If you need a confectioner and you're offered a first-class welder, you aren't interested, and vice versa. The same goes for an organization, a team. There are times when you need a fighter, but if you've already got three they'll tread on each other's toes and start fighting among themselves. There's room for all kinds, you know."

"There are three million people in this country who aren't convinced of that," El Fatawi muttered.

"Because they haven't found the right niche – or because they've got some manufacturing defect. The streets are teeming with second-raters. Good ones are harder to find; very, very good ones are few and far between. At De Wavre we're only after the very, very good ones. That's why there are so many rejects."

"How many of those are there here, in your opinion?" asked Charriac.

"How about you?" Del Rieco shot back at him. "How many would you employ?"

Charriac didn't evade the question. "Pinetti. Delval. Hirsch, maybe. That's the lot."

"Thanks very much," said Morin.

Charriac gave him an odd look. "You've already got a job."

To my surprise, Morin didn't answer.

"This *is* nice," Laurence said drily.

"It's certainly interesting," said Del Rieco.

"You still haven't answered my question," Charriac insisted. His little eyes never left Del Rieco's face.

"I'll answer it," Del Rieco said. "On Friday night I shall see you all in turn and explain the reasons for our decision in each particular case. If you're rejected you will at least have gained that: a complete personal inventory – a check-up."

He slapped his thighs, swallowed the last of his coffee, and rose.

"There, now you know everything. Everyone is in possession of the same information. I wish you all the best of luck."

"If you don't mind," I said, "I've got a question too. Is this unique to our intake, or do you do it every time?"

"Do what?"

"Come and have coffee, all buddy-buddy, and drop a few friendly hints."

"Oh, I see," he said, quite unruffled. He had nerves of steel, that man. "No, sometimes I come at drinks time, sometimes not at all.

I do what you do: adapt to the particular situation."

"So what *do* you think of our intake," asked Brigitte Aubert, "collectively speaking, I mean?"

Del Rieco just smiled at her and made for the door without a word.

Charriac looked at me.

"He came to repair his frontier defences – to see if we're escaping. I think we're getting to him."

The lake lay spread out at my feet. My brain had divided into two. One part kept mulling over what it had registered of Del Rieco's remarks. He must have come for some good reason, not just on a friendly impulse. He'd had something to tell us, and he'd said it. That the simulation would end tomorrow? We'd known that from the start. There had to be something else: a detail, a word. At some point an alarm bell had rung in my head, and I was desperately trying to remember why.

But another convolution, another circuit in my grey cells, tended in a philosophical direction. Why had we begun by taking the track that led down to the lake but hesitated to take the path that led upwards through the woods? Why hadn't we explored the rear of the hotel, the hillside behind it? Was there something fascinating about this motionless expanse of water, some suggestion it would bring forth the truth, yield a revelation? Did our files already contain a note of this tendency to choose the easiest, most reassuring route, the one they had signposted in advance – this reluctance to lose sight of the other shore that linked us to civilization? Or was there an innate disposition in the human being, a magnetic attraction to the primeval waters from which, one day, there emerged the unicellular creatures that had, by a process of natural selection, laboriously mutated into insects, reptiles, and humankind?

None of this was getting me anywhere. Closeted on this island, we were in a cul-de-sac – a crude metaphor for our botched lives. For those who managed to extricate themselves, the seminar might be a springboard; for the rest, the ultimate scrap heap. We had 24 hours in which to eliminate the competition, 24 hours or even less in which to brush aside the opposition, exterminate our adversaries, and show, in a definitive manner, who were the best, the only ones deserving of survival.

Just as I had the first night, I played ducks and drakes and bent down to watch the pebble skim the surface. It ricocheted three times before sinking into the depths. When I straightened up she was beside me, an erect, silent figure.

Not Laurence. Laurence wouldn't come again, not now. It was Brigitte Aubert, engulfed in an enormous sweater that reached to her thighs.

She didn't sit down on the rock or spread out her skirt – how could she, wearing a skirt as short as hers? Her presence made me miss Laurence all the more. Although nothing had happened between us, we had experienced something together – something that had left a lasting residue: the fragile spider's web of what had remained unspoken between us.

"I was sitting beside baldylocks," said Brigitte. "Just now, when our Führer was giving his spiel."

"Baldylocks?" I wasn't really listening.

"The bald guy with the beard. Del Rieco's right-hand man."

"Oh... His name is Jean-Claude, I seem to remember. Jean-Claude what, we were never told. What about him?"

"I looked to see what he was doing. He had a list. He wanted to check we were all there. He was ticking our names."

"So what?" She was boring me.

"And we weren't. All there, I mean."

"Really?"

"You don't understand," she said with an exasperated sigh. "We weren't all on the list. There were three names missing. Are you listening?"

"Sure I'm listening, but I don't know what you're getting at."

She pretended to shake me.

"Hey, Carceville, wake up! Don't you see? The list of people on the seminar – it wasn't complete. There were three missing."

"So?"

She shut her eyes incredulously. "There are times when I wonder just how bright you really are. Like me to draw you a picture?"

Laurence's image faded. I came down to earth.

"You mean three of our number aren't on the course?"

She spread her arms and bowed her head in a mock obeisance.

"Bravo, you got there at last. Shall I explain the implications, or will you work them out by yourself?"

"It means they aren't testing three of us. Three of us are on their side, not ours. Who?"

"You see, you can do it when you want to," she said, still mockingly. "The starter motor sticks a bit. You'd better remember that the next time you're in for a service."

"Three snitches . . ."

"Afraid so." She checked them off on her fingers as if anxious not to leave one out, pausing between each to heighten the suspense. "Aimé Leroy. Morin. And Marilyn."

"One in each team . . ."

"Great, you're putting on speed, we'll be able to take off soon."

I snapped my fingers. "Morin! And Charriac knew it – that's why he told him he didn't need a job, he'd already got one."

"And why Marilyn went out to smoke a cigarette every five minutes.

It wasn't nicotine addition: she went to report on us."

"And why Aimé Leroy kept carping at everything – to convince us that he wasn't in cahoots with the organization . . ."

"Three of the bastards," Brigitte concluded. "What are we going to do?"

Just then I heard footsteps and Laurence emerged from the gloom. She had been running. Her chest was heaving. She drew a couple of deep breaths.

"I've got something to tell you, Jérôme . . ."

She caught sight of Brigitte and stopped short. Brigitte looked her up and down as if wondering what wave could have deposited such a trashy piece of jetsam on the lakeshore. Strangely enough, the sentimental thrill I'd felt when thinking of her had abruptly subsided. We were back in the game again.

"That's to say," she said breathlessly, "it's confidential."

"Carry on, Laurence. There's nothing Brigitte can't hear."

She hesitated before taking plunge.

"I saw the assessment forms. The three of them went off to the kitchen after coffee. I've no idea what they were going to do there . . ."

"The washing up, maybe," Brigitte said sarcastically.

"Anyway, I made a dash for the chalet and managed to get inside. They'd left the forms on the table. They were blank – just our names. And guess what?"

"There were three missing," said Brigitte. "Don't you have a harder question for us?"

Laurence stopped short again, thrown off her stride.

"How did you know?"

"We all have our own methods, my dear," Brigitte said with a mixture of distaste and contempt.

Their mutual animosity was almost palpable. I wondered what

could have set them against each other. They'd barely exchanged a word up to now. If there was such a thing as love at first sight, I supposed there had to be equally instantaneous, inexplicable hatreds that blossomed just as quickly.

"They know everything," said Laurence, ". . . everything. They haven't missed a trick."

Brigitte turned to me. "You're the boss. *If* you've recovered your wits, that is." She paused. "And if you can keep your mind on the job . . ."

Her sarcasm was beginning to annoy me.

"We must interview them," Laurence suggested. "I'll go and see Leroy and have it out with him."

"No," I told her impatiently, "don't do anything without my say-so. It isn't necessarily in our interests to put our cards on the table right away. They don't know they've been rumbled. First let's exploit that advantage."

"That's why he's the boss," Brigitte said to Laurence. "He can see further than the end of his nose."

Laurence stiffened but said nothing.

"Right," I said, thinking aloud, "first I must have a word with Charriac. The little swine has known about this longer than we have, and Morin knows that he knows. The pieces of the puzzle are falling into place. That was the little detail I was trying to remember just now. The only thing is, why have they left Morin with Charriac? Is Charriac blackmailing him? No, that's impossible. Or maybe he's hoping Morin will give himself away . . . I've got to know! I'm going."

Laurence looked smug, like someone who finally sees her case proved.

"Charriac is playing their game. I said so from the start but you wouldn't listen. The final has already taken place, Jérôme: it's

174

you versus me. We may as well spend tomorrow skiing, it'll make no difference."

"What's she talking about?" growled Brigitte.

I shut them up with a gesture. "Don't go away," I said. "I'll have a talk with Charriac and see how things stand."

Brigitte gave a mocking laugh. "Tarzan goes swinging through the trees and hurls himself at the lion! At your service, boss. If you don't mind, though, I'm going in. It's getting a bit chilly out here, and the company could be more desirable . . ."

Laurence deliberately gave me a wink that hovered on the threshold of vulgarity. The two women weren't squabbling over me; despite my excellent opinion of myself, I had no such pretensions. It was just a classic case of rivalry: ill-favoured Brigitte envied Laurence her satin complexion. There was almost nothing to be done about such a state of affairs apart from leaving them to needle each other. I had be careful not to become a bone of contention between them, that was all. For the moment, I had other worries.

I failed to find Charriac either in the bar or in his room. He was working overtime in his team headquarters on the second floor, curtains drawn. He had opened his laptop, plugged in an ultra-flat printer, and was busy consulting some documents. Pinetti was sitting idly in a corner.

Secretive as ever, Charriac swiftly slid the documents under a sheaf of papers. He glanced at me briefly, then gave Pinetti his marching orders.

"Unless I'm much mistaken, Monsieur Carceville wants a word with me in private."

Pinetti made a reluctant exit. I sat down facing Charriac and stretched out my legs. Seen in the light of the bare bulb suspended from the ceiling, the scene resembled a poker game between two crooks. Charriac produced a small cigar and lit it very deliberately. He could have saved himself the trouble: that in itself was a sign of nervousness. After four days, everyone was taking up smoking again.

"Yes?" he said.

"One question: how long have you known that Morin was working for Del Rieco?"

He inclined his head in mock admiration.

"Congratulations, Holmes. To be honest, I suspected it right away.

They obviously knew my every move. They answered my messages quickly. A shade too quickly. Then your friend Madame Carré started to suspect me. She was looking in the wrong place, but she guessed something was up. That started me thinking. After that, well, it was easy. Politicians do it: they give four different versions to four different people and see which one appears in the press. You identify the leak very quickly that way. In my case the leak was Morin."

"What have you done about it?"

"Nothing." He smiled helplessly. "What did you expect me to do? I told him I wanted him to pass things on to Del Rieco. I converted the mole into a double agent. Brainwashing. Then I watched him. I made a note of what caught his attention. You know, like the children's game: you're getting hotter, no, colder. That helped me to get my bearings. What have you done about yours?"

"Marilyn? The same as you."

"Oh, so that's who it is. I wondered. Personally, I'd have put my money on that flat-chested redhead of yours. They needed someone who's not too obtrusive but not too self-effacing either. Someone who's inconspicuous but knows everything. The MD's personal assistant, eh? Perfect – I should have thought of that. What about your girlfriend's stool pigeon? Who was it, Chalamont?"

"Leroy."

He sat back with the tip of his cigar aimed at the ceiling.

"Leroy . . . Not bad. A bit of a caricature, though. Morin with his overdone Marseille act, Leroy and his grouchy manner. Too theatrical. Marilyn wasn't that obvious – she's best of the three. Even I might have missed her . . . So they screwed you, huh?"

I propped my elbows on the table, surreptitiously scanning the papers that littered it. They were extracts from law books, commentaries on judicial rulings.

"You didn't give me a straight answer, Charriac. To repeat: exactly how long have you known?"

"Oh, dear," he said in mock terror, "you aren't going to give me the third degree, are you? I can't tell you exactly when. Like you, I became suspicious. It was a hypothesis, one of several possibilities. I was 60 per cent sure, then 70, then 80. It's like when you're being cuckolded."

"I wouldn't know, I never have been."

"That's what you think. But if you have, I swear I'm innocent. I've never had the pleasure of meeting Madame Carceville."

"When did you tell him you knew?"

"I hesitated. I wanted to let him stew in his own juice, but I couldn't resist the temptation. 'Human, all too human ...' Know who? Nietzsche. We aren't as uncultured as our Arab friend assumes. I've even read Mao Tse-tung, if you want to know. I'm ready for them any time."

The smoke from the vile weed he was sucking made me cough.

"This is like being at the dentist," I said. "Your answers have to be extracted one by one."

"Of course. What are you offering in return?"

"I've given you Marilyn and Leroy."

"True. They're no use to me, but it's a token of goodwill. All right, it may be in both our interests to engage in limited cooperation – I've been trying to convince you of that for ages, God knows ... When did I tell him I knew? This morning. I put the squeeze on him late this morning. Man to man."

"Didn't he try to deny it?"

"Yes, of course. But (he imitated a Hollywood Gestapo officer): 'Ve haff vays of making you talk ...' At first he tried to make me believe he was a psychologist. You know, like the ones they foist on you at weekend seminars for budding executives. A psychologist with a watching brief. In the end he says: your style of leadership is too authoritarian, too permissive, too this, too that. You slip him 10,000 francs and say thank you very much. Morin a psychologist? You could have knocked me down with a feather! My grandmother would have done better."

"One last question, then it'll be over – then we can sew you up again: what did he tell you?"

"Absolutely nothing – yet. He's very worried. If I sell him to Del Rieco, Del Rieco will fire him and he'll be out of a job like us. That would be a laugh, wouldn't it? He hopes I'll keep my mouth shut. He'll have to make it worth my while, of course. I don't want much."

"Our scores, the result of the tests, that sort of thing?"

"Something of that order. A little tinkering with the printouts, for instance. But we'll be on equal terms. You'll do the same with Marilyn, won't you? Even Madame Carré will put Leroy on the spot. It's going to be an absolute scream. A quiz where everyone knows the answers in advance – what do you think of that?"

"I think it'll leak out. They'll simply scrub the whole seminar."

"Don't you believe it. Any idea what Del Rieco charges for this shambles of his – how much he earns for running three seminars a month for years on end? If we screw him up and the story starts circulating in Paris, he's dead. We've got him by the balls, Carceville."

Charriac could have been right. He blissfully savoured another puff of cigar smoke.

"We've got De Wavre taped," he insisted. "I'd sooner have been on my own, of course. A pity we have to share the same bone. Still, you were absolutely right to come and see me. We might have messed things up if we hadn't had a word together. We must cooperate, Carceville. Let's be realistic: does Madame Carré really have to be in on this? Sacrifices are unavoidable – we can't expect Del Rieco to endorse all three of us. Now it's your turn to come clean: Who knows, out of your lot?"

It irked me to come to terms with him, but I didn't have many other options. Charriac might be antipathetic, but Del Rieco was the real target. We listed the initiates: Charriac himself, me, Laurence, Brigitte Aubert, and Pinetti, to whom Charriac had divulged the secret. Five out of 13 (since we'd never been 16). That was the ratio De Wavre was expecting.

"Right," said Charriac. "Let's all get together in, say, ten minutes. That should be time enough to round up the others. And mum's the word – one more person in the know would be one too many."

The five conspirators assembled in Charriac's team headquarters at eleven o'clock that Wednesday night. I had to dig Brigitte Aubert out of bed, whither she had calmly retired unaware of the bomb she had dropped. She looked rather incongruous in her dressing-gown and slippers. Pinetti, although innocent, couldn't manage to divest himself of his stage villain's mask. Laurence was her usual erect, queenly self. She ostentatiously avoided looking at Charriac.

Charriac had cleared the table of his legal files, which were now useless. He opened the meeting by calling on me to speak.

"My friends, the situation has changed considerably. Monsieur Carceville will now summarize the main developments."

I briefly described the new prospects that had opened up, then embarked on an analysis.

"There are – as usual – several possible courses of action. We each manipulate our own spy: that's the first solution, but I'm not too keen on it. Morin appears to be scared of Charriac, but I don't know how Marilyn would react. If one of the three goes and tells Del Rieco we're trying to blackmail him or her, things could turn sour. Del Rieco might put the blame on us and cut his losses. He might simply decide that we're a bunch of incompetents and reject us all. We can't afford to act indiscriminately. The second solution is, we concentrate on one person only: Morin, who seems vulnerable. We forget about Marilyn and Leroy and try to turn Morin. We collectively ask him to work for us."

"I don't get it," Brigitte grumbled. "We ask him what, exactly?"

"For a start," said Charriac, "to lift our files. Then, depending on what we find in them, to doctor them a bit. He feeds a few lines into the computer when nobody's looking and none of us says a word. He keeps his job and we get ours. Nothing very difficult about that."

Brigitte raised her eyebrows. "You mean you're going to cheat?"

"Well, yes. We're going to change the rules a bit. I think that's fair enough. Look where present methods of employment have got us. If you're bound to lose a game under the existing rules, you must change them, that's all."

When Charriac was on form he could have converted the Ayatollah Khomeini to Catholicism and enrolled George W. Bush in the Communist Party of America.

"Hang on, does that mean we give everyone 18 out of 20?"

"Not everyone, just us. It would be too obvious otherwise."

"What about the others?"

"My dear girl," Charriac said patiently, "this is a jungle. Jungles contain lions and antelopes. Which species ends up on top, do you think, and which would you rather belong to?"

"Lions and antelopes don't live in jungles," Laurence muttered contemptuously.

I quelled the looming altercation by tapping the table with my finger.

"We aren't here to discuss geography. Or zoology."

"Just a minute," Brigitte insisted. "What about Mastroni, say, or Hirsch? You mean we make the grade and leave them in the lurch?"

"Some people die and others survive," Charriac retorted. "Some have jobs and others haven't. Life's a lottery. Today, luck happens to be with us – the ones in this room."

I tapped the table again, this time with my knuckles.

"I'm not through yet, if you don't mind. There's a third possibility: we zap the middlemen, go straight to Del Rieco, and put him in the picture. To me, that seems the safest course of action. If things get really nasty – if he digs his heels in – we'll laugh it off, tell him it was just a bit of fun."

"I prefer the second solution," said Charriac. "Morin will do as I say. I control him."

"That's just what doesn't appeal to me," said Laurence.

"Well, I refuse to rat on Mastroni and Hirsch," Brigitte said firmly. "It's not right, teaming up and then going solo. They need a job as badly as we do."

"The matter's still open to discussion," Charriac said in a conciliatory tone. "We haven't decided anything yet. All the same, I don't see how we can sneak everyone through. The principle doesn't worry me – I mean, we're only a dozen out of three million unemployed. A few more wouldn't make any difference, but they'd be noticed. It's like the *Titanic*. There comes a time when you've got to choose who survives and who drowns. Otherwise, everyone goes to the bottom."

"Well, I've chosen," Brigitte said stubbornly. "I don't like cheating, especially when my friends have to pay for it. I think I stand a fair chance anyway."

"That's just where you're wrong," Charriac told her brutally. "Either cooperate with us, or you're as dead as Tutankhamen. I know its a nuisance, but we'll all be done for if we don't pull together. Whatever we decide – and we'll put it to the vote, if you like – the minority will have to give way. We need absolute solidarity."

"That's great, coming from you! No, I'm not playing."

Charriac gave me a strange look, half saddened, half menacing. He was figuring out what would happen next.

"You don't have much choice," he said softly. "Get this straight: we're all in the same boat. If one of us rows in the opposite direction, the boat veers off course. And that we can't allow."

"Really? What would you do to me?"

It was time for me to step in.

"Let's not get worked up about this, it's pointless. Listen, Brigitte: we're in a very tricky, very delicate situation. I've taken careful note of your position. It's perfectly reasonable and it does you credit, I quite appreciate that. You've swayed me, but you aren't alone. There are four other people involved, and it's your turn to bear that in mind. We'll continue this discussion at our leisure. Meantime, I'm asking you as a personal favour not to breathe a word to anyone. I'll do my best, I promise you, but we're too deeply committed simply to bow out and say sorry. That would be even harder. Will you trust me?"

She hesitated. "Yes," she said grudgingly.

"Do I have your word?" I insisted.

"Only until tomorrow. And as long as you don't do anything irrevocable."

"Agreed. What about the rest of you?"

"I'm with Emmanuel," said Pinetti.

It took me a moment to remember that this was Charriac's first name. Laurence was looking tired – not unnaturally, after the day she'd had.

"I don't think we've had enough time to decide on anything," she said in a subdued voice. "This needs more thought. I suggest we meet again tomorrow. We could have a working breakfast here in this room. Let's sleep on it."

Like me, Charriac sensed that the time wasn't ripe. He abandoned the idea of forcing the issue.

"Very well. Shall we meet at, say, seven-thirty?"

The others nodded. I hate discussions over the breakfast table, but there was no alternative. Brigitte gathered the folds of her dressing-gown around the pink nightdress she was wearing, Pinetti slithered out of his chair like a snake, Charriac shuffled his papers together. I remained seated, trying to marshal my thoughts. Laurence tapped me on the shoulder.

"You're going see Del Rieco tomorrow morning, aren't you? Whatever anyone thinks, I mean?"

I didn't deny it. "Perhaps. It's the smart thing to do, no?"

"I want to be there too."

"Out of the question," said Charriac. "Two is a friendly chat, three is a delegation. Don't think I'm being personal, it's a question of psychological effectiveness – one doesn't discuss things the same way in a crowd. You can come, but only if Carceville gives up his place to you."

"You may be right," she conceded. "Perhaps I wouldn't be any good."

"Enlightenment dawns," sneered Charriac. "Better late than never."

She gave him a murderous glare before leaving the room. Charriac removed his glasses and started polishing them. He looked up.

"Shall we meet at seven? Before going see Del Rieco, I mean."

"You've given up the idea of turning Morin?"

"Yes. One has to face facts. I could do it if I were on my own. With those three getting under our feet, all with ideas of their own, it would be too dangerous – quite impracticable. We must act in concert, the two of us. Let's say here at twenty to seven. By the way, what about your pin-up in a dressing gown? Sure you can keep her under control?"

"For a while, yes. After that . . ."

"I'll put Pinetti on to her. He's the SAS type: tell him to kill, and he kills. He doesn't ask questions. If she gets in our hair he'll take her for a boat ride on the lake."

"With her feet in a bucketful of concrete?"

He chuckled. "Not a bad idea – she wouldn't be much of a loss. No, no, just to take her out of circulation. A visit to the zoo while the grown-ups get on with the things that matter. He'll feed her candyfloss and keep her out of our way."

"We'll see. I'm off to bed."

"Twenty to seven, Jérôme. Set your alarm."

"I'll be there, Emmanuel."

We parted like bosom pals. I wasn't feeling particularly proud of myself when I got back to my room, but splashes are unavoidable when you've been unexpectedly dunked in a vat of liquid manure. I really did need a job. I was prepared to do anything rather than have to face my wife's compassion when I got home. That was what I forgave her least: the inexhaustible kindness, the maternal concern for a hurt child, the sympathetic acceptance of my personal setbacks. I would have preferred insults, or the contempt I deserved. I could read my own downfall in her eyes. She had never uttered a word of reproach. Our friends thought her a paragon. She was the heroine and I the villain; she had a steady job and took care of her unfortunate husband without a murmur. No one could have failed to love such a gem of a woman. I was the failure, the plucky but unlucky individual who would do better next time. I hated her for not hating me. I went to sleep thinking of her, dreaming that I had returned home in triumph, and that life would resume its former course.

At some point in the night I was awakened by the sound of someone scratching on my door – Laurence, I guessed. She probably couldn't sleep and wanted to talk things over for the umpteenth time. I stayed put and pretended to be dead to the world.

At a quarter past six my alarm sliced through the middle of a dream. I got shaved and spent a long time under the shower. Like the others, I was showing signs of fatigue: the sensation that I was swathed in cobwebs, that the whole world was out of kilter and slightly unreal.

Then I went off to join my new-found friend Emmanuel Charriac. He was still in the same place, ensconced behind the same sheaves of legal documents and pecking away at the same laptop. If he hadn't just shaved and drenched himself in cologne, I could have believed he'd spent the whole night there. I sat down the way I'd sat the night before, legs spread and hands clasping the nape of my neck in an attitude of total relaxation. Charriac keyed two final instructions into his machine, then lost interest in it and turned to me. He had changed his shirt and tie, but not his suit.

"Well," I said, "what are we going to say to Del Rieco?"

"Pah, we went through all that last night. I was in favour of a frontal attack, then you came along with the Vaseline. Quite predictable, given our different temperaments."

"So what *do* we tell him?"

He donned his spuriously innocent expression.

"The truth, what else? I don't like lying, you always catch your feet in the carpet. We'll tell him he's a bungling idiot, that he foisted three spies on us, that it's out of order and we're going to blow his outfit sky-high."

"Oh, is that all?"

"Yes. We wouldn't be pushing our luck, you see. I put the squeeze on Morin last night, and he cracked. He went to get our assessment forms for me – the real ones. Then I came and tried to tell you, but you were out like a light."

I wasn't too surprised. I might have guessed it if I hadn't been so tired. As it was, I felt a pang of uneasiness. Charriac was better than me – each new development proved it. He was quicker, sharper, more unscrupulous. Smarter, too, beyond a doubt. He had pictured the scene in advance, foreseen Del Rieco's replies, identified the flaw in our case and promptly taken steps to remedy it.

"What did you say to him?"

"To Morin? I threw a scare into him. I threatened him. The vast majority of people are cowards, and he's no exception. No balls."

"But if you show our cards to Del Rieco, he'll fire him"

"Sure, but that's life. I made him no promises. Look, Jérôme, don't be like our redhead. It's him or us. He isn't a Marseillais, by the way. He's from Avignon."

"Okay, let's see those forms."

"Not on your life!" Charriac smiled broadly. "The game isn't over yet, not by a long chalk. I love you dearly, Jérôme, but I have to allow for every contingency. Who knows what the future holds in store for us? I'll show them to you if we KO Del Rieco, I promise. It'll motivate you, you'll see."

"That's not what we agreed."

"If you'd hung around instead of going off to stew in your pit, we could have worked on Morin together. No, I'm joking. I have to make the most of what I've got, that's all." He paused. "Very well, I'll give you a hint – for friendship's sake, let's say. The general picture looks pretty good, but your girlfriend Laurence and her team are all kaput, all for the chop including her. 'Over-emotional.' That really staggered me. She's a marble statue, that woman. She turns up here, strikes a pose and holds it, and they think she's over-emotional! Jesus, what do they want, a lump of wood?"

"What about me?"

"Oh, you . . ." He grinned like a mischievous schoolboy. "That's my little secret. Tell yourself that whatever you think of yourself, they do too. Chew on that. Shall we go?"

We went.

Del Rieco hadn't turned up yet, so we sat down to wait on the steps of the chalet. The sun, still smeared with wisps of cloud, was rising beyond the trees. The lake glittered in its slanting rays. Peace reigned inside the hotel. A morning like any other, so it seemed. We might have expected to hear a rooster crowing, the clatter of cups in a kitchen fragrant with hot coffee, the blithe footsteps of an angler off to do a spot of fishing. We might have, yes, if we hadn't been under such pressure.

At seven twenty-five Del Rieco crossed the courtyard with martial tread, his blazer hooked over one shoulder like an uhlan's cape. He walked past as if he hadn't seen us.

"I'm not at home to visitors, I thought I made that quite clear."

"Yes, but this is different," said Charriac. "You'll be interested in what we have to tell you."

"I strongly doubt it," Del Rieco retorted curtly.

But he didn't slam the door in our faces, so we followed him inside. He went over to the little east-facing window and opened it, then blew a speck of dust off the table.

"Well?"

"You haven't been playing fair with us," I said in a reproachful voice. "You told me there weren't any spies and there are."

"Really?"

"Morin, Leroy, and Marilyn what's-her-name. Just imagine, they tried to pass themselves off as psychologists!"

"Are you accusing me of lying, Jérôme? I wasn't guilty of any inaccuracy. It's all down on tape, you know. I can play it for you if you like. You came to complain that Charriac was working for me – in fact you were positively hipped on the subject. Now you know you were mistaken. I said you were under constant surveillance. What was wrong with that? Nothing I told you was untrue, not a word. They're neither bit-part players nor psychologists, they're . . . observers, let's say. You didn't ask the right questions, that's all."

"Oh, come on, Mons . . . Joseph! That's just a quibble!"

"Now listen, my friend," Del Rieco said sharply. "I run this seminar the way I want. If you don't like it, nobody's keeping you."

Charriac, who should theoretically have been charging him hell for leather, said nothing. Feeling rather uneasy, I tried to stand in for him.

"All the same," I said, "it was out of order. Your people haven't been silent and inert, far from it. An observer normally says absolutely nothing in such cases, but they've never stopped talking, making suggestions, steering us in one direction or another."

"Quite so. They're part of the test. This isn't a sample group for a university experiment in social psychology, it's a seminar with a predetermined purpose. I manipulate the variables whenever I think I can learn something of practical value. I told you: I'm not here to improve your technique or give a diagnosis, I'm here to see how you react whenever I inoculate you with some new bacterium. It's a training exercise with live ammunition. But Emmanuel isn't saying anything . . ."

Charriac was pretending to study the ceiling. At last, very reluctantly, he broke his silence.

"The question is, what happens now? Are you going to call off your stooges or leave them with us?"

"It's as you like," Del Rieco replied, far from disconcerted. "I'm rather inclined to call them off. It'll falsify the situation, but . . ."

"You're the one who falsified it."

"No, I set it up. In my own way."

"If you withdraw them, everyone will know there was a trap."

"A secret is something you hear an hour before everyone else," Del Rieco said sententiously. "I don't see how it can be avoided."

"I needn't tell you what a poisonous atmosphere it'll generate."

"Oh, so you think the present atmosphere's healthy, do you? I've seldom seen such a – how shall I put it? – such an obstreperous group. You spend the whole time trying to sneak round the sides. You regarded me as an enemy right away, Jérôme. You were wrong. I'm here to help you to show what you're made of, but your immediate reaction was: How can I screw poor old Joseph? Not the other teams: me."

"But Marilyn . . ."

"She told me everything. Naturally, it's her job. You made life difficult for me."

"Is that what you've put on my assessment? That I'd be perfect for a job in the Mafia?"

"You'll see what I've put in due course. It's not over yet."

"I've got a question," Charriac said casually. "Is the whole of your procedure approved by De Wavre? Approved from A to Z? Are they familiar with your methods?"

He had made up his mind at last. Having left me to flounder, he'd sent in the 7th Cavalry at the last moment. Del Rieco sniggered.

"I *am* De Wavre. To be more precise, it's the name of my sister-in-law, if you really want to know. I handle the evaluation side and she deals with the employers. We're a family firm – only 30 on the payroll."

"And are the employers familiar with the details?"

"Of my methods? No. I don't know. It doesn't matter anyway. They're familiar with my results, that's good enough for them. I've placed over 400 people, and I've had only two dissatisfied clients. Two. Zero point five per cent wastage. Twenty times fewer duds than my leading competitors."

"You know what's going to happen? Someone will reveal what happens on these seminars."

"So what? You mean people will rehearse themselves? They do that anyway. I vary the scenario every time. I adapt it to fit the participants' profiles. I try to plumb every potential weakness that shows up in the course of the preliminary tests. It's never the same one. Everything is completely personalized. The seminar lasts a week, but I take ten days to set it up. There's no point in rehearsing a performance. It's like a written examination: boning up on last year's questions won't do you much good this time around."

"A little, all the same."

"Yes," Del Rieco conceded. "A little, but not enough to matter."

"What if a seminar goes really badly? Isn't that a problem?"

"For the participants, yes. They may as well carve out a new career in Turkestan; here, they're finished. We have a list of good ones, but we also have a blacklist. Firms can consult it free of charge. Anyway, what can really go wrong? What if someone *does* say I'm not doing my job? Who's going to be believed? An embittered reject, when I can explain in detail why I rejected him, or the best executive search consultant in Europe, who's never put a foot wrong?"

"Someone could write a booklet," I ventured. "'Behind the Scenes at De Wavre.'"

"Write it, yes, but sell it? How big would the market be? Two hundred copies a year? Why not an article? A journalist infiltrated us on one occasion. I had him tagged before the day was out. Stick around, I told him. Stay and watch, I've nothing to hide. He left the next morning. Who's interested? Know your problem, Jérôme? You're making a pathetic attempt to blackmail me because you're beaten. You were beaten before you started. I can't win this game fair and square, you told yourself, so how can I cheat? It all stems from that."

He had just signed my death warrant. I now knew what he'd written on my assessment form. A fearsome abyss was yawning beneath my feet. Not only had I been rejected; he was going to put me on his blacklist. I glanced at Charriac. The swine was enjoying every minute of it.

Our initiative wasn't a joint venture after all. Charriac had done me as much of a favour as treachery permitted. Being acquainted with the contents of my assessment form, he had let me dig my own grave. He had known from the first that we were doomed to fail. Without seeming to, he had launched me on a collision course that reinforced Del Rieco's opinion of me. It was positively Machiavellian.

I took only a moment to grasp the full extent of the debacle. For the past two days, ever since Marilyn had pleaded nicotine addiction and hurried off to submit her first report, Del Rieco had been privy to all my ploys.

He had turned away and was switching on his computers. All I could see of him was his broad back. I felt like sinking a knife in it.

"So that's that," I said despondently, addressing the nape of his neck. "I suppose there's no point in my going on."

He swung round, abruptly cordial once more.

"What? But of course! You have your shortcomings, Jérôme, but who doesn't? Even I do. What interests me is how you overcome them. You have a tendency to go off the rails. Correct it, and all will be well. Emmanuel is another kettle of fish. He tries to build in umpteen parameters – he engages in such complicated tactical calculations, he inevitably ends by getting lost. You aren't abnormal, either of you. We all possess certain characteristics. Making the most of them, that's the secret."

He sat down heavily, knitting his brow in thought. On a screen behind him, lines of incomprehensible instructions were scrolling down at a dizzy speed.

"I'll try to explain what I mean ... Each of us has a genetic predisposition to one thing or another. Everything depends on what we make of it throughout our lives. If you know something hurts you, you avoid it. If you think you lack stamina, you try to pace yourself. Ignore your capabilities, and the situation becomes pathological: you overtax yourself and start malfunctioning. Results are what an employer wants. It doesn't much matter how you set about achieving them, or how much of an effort it costs you: the salary's the same. What was that football match which made such an impression on our friend Morin? Marseille-Montpellier? Four-nil at half-time, five-four at the final whistle. What matters is what you can produce at the last minute. We aren't there yet. If you drop out now, the responsibility will be yours. I still don't know what I'll write about you on Saturday, after you've gone. I've taken some notes, it's true, but they aren't definitive. There are plenty of people who lead drab, anonymous lives until, one fine day, they die a hero's death. That's all one remembers about them: the few seconds in which they crossed their Rubicon. I want to see if you're capable of doing that. That'll wipe the slate clean. Adversity discloses a person's full potential. You can't tell if a beam is sound or worm-eaten until it's been subjected to stress. At the moment, all I know is the colour of the paint."

"In a previous life," Charriac said lightly, "you must have been a lion tamer."

The crow's-feet of a complacent smile sprouted from the corners of Del Rieco's eyes.

"Maybe, who knows?"

He had deftly reintroduced us into the game. Brushing aside our pathetic manoeuvres, he had reestablished his central authority, scared us, and then, having trampled around on us, set us on our feet again. He was a formidably strong player, a prince among manipulators, the more so since all he'd said had sounded so plausible. We could only concur.

"I see," said Charriac. "If I've understood you correctly, my friend Carceville and I are to resume our days-long attempts to wipe each other out."

"That's one option," Del Rieco said mockingly. "Not the only one, perhaps, but it's certainly an option. You're an interesting group, you know. I haven't been bored."

"Nor have we," I said in a glum voice.

Del Rieco gave me a friendly dig in the ribs.

"And now, gentlemen, back to work. Fond of your company as I am, I've got a job to do."

We passed the inevitable Jean-Claude as we emerged from the chalet. He ducked his head so as not to have to say hello. His bald head gleamed in the sunlight.

It took me a minute or two to recover my spirits. I guessed from Charriac's heavy tread that he was also shaken. Ten paces away from the hotel entrance, I expelled a deep breath.

"Well, that wasn't a great success, was it? Even those famous assessment forms of yours weren't worth a bean. Right now, Morin is probably telling Del Rieco how you blackmailed him. I doubt if he'll be pleased."

Charriac raised an admonitory forefinger.

"Results, Jérôme, results. I understood that: anything goes as long as it produces results. That's his theory, isn't it?"

I looked doubtful. Charriac remained unruffled. The man was a robot.

"He wants as faithful a simulation as possible," he went on. "All right, in business people try to turn people every day. Like me to give you a list of all the executives who have quit a firm, taking its client data bank with them, and set up on their own – *and* made a big success of it? Technically, that's prohibited. It's against the rules, sure, but some people are above the rules. Morin doesn't count – he's just a sidekick. No problem there, really not. It's the bottom line that counts. Money is the measure of all things, that's what Del Rieco was reminding us of. The day you go to heaven, St Peter will open his ledger and ask, 'How much are you worth, buddy?'"

He had lapsed into English. "You mean St Peter's an American?" I said.

"Of course. These days, God is an American."

Charriac's absurd, disjointed remarks were the only symptom of his mental turmoil. Outwardly, he hadn't turned a hair. I glanced at the lake, which threatened to engulf all my hopes.

"The question remains," I said. "What do we do now, tear each other limb from limb?"

"What else?"

"Here's a suggestion for you: we get everyone together, put them in the picture, and come to a collective decision."

"A soviet, eh? It's rather out of fashion, you know."

"No, just a general briefing. We start again from scratch. Otherwise, everyone'll go off at a tangent. We'll lose control altogether."

He hesitated. "Yes, perhaps . . ."

"Ten o'clock in the workroom?"

He grudgingly agreed. I was almost sure he wouldn't come.

I rejoined my team and gave them a rundown on the situation, holding nothing back. Marilyn wasn't there. Brigitte Aubert called her a snake in the grass and a lot of other unpleasant things.

"You see," said Mastroni, "we went wrong from the start. I was dead against it. We should have played by the rules."

"Don't worry," I told him, "Marilyn will have made a note of your objection. She isn't here any more, no need to pile it on. Your assessment form will read: 'Good doggie.'"

"It's pointless going for Mastroni," said Hirsch. "You're under pressure, I realize that, but think of the team."

He was right: I was starting to crack. I had to pull myself together. I slapped Mastroni's palm like a suburban adolescent.

"I'm sorry. No hard feelings?"

"No, it was my fault," he replied magnanimously.

"Great. How's the CD-ROM going?"

"It's ready," said Hirsch. "I had to get a translation made. It was funny, the guy who holds the copyright wanted to handle that himself – he was afraid we'd mess things up. That's what often happens with commercial translations: you find yourself landed with some appalling errors, so nobody understands the instructions. If a word doesn't mean exactly the same in both languages, you run the risk of legal problems. Anyway, I had the translation notarized by an expert. We've just put the disk on sale, and Brigitte has launched an advertising campaign. It had better work, because fish-hooks are a disaster waiting to happen."

"I've had an idea," Mastroni interjected. "Why not open a kind of aquapark where people come to fish during the close season? I'll have to see if it would be legal. We could throw in a restaurant, a hotel, and so on."

Hirsch chuckled. "An angler's Disneyland, huh? Not bad. Wouldn't it overstretch us financially, though?"

"Not if we brought in an outside investor like the CD-ROM guy. I'm sure there's a market."

"It's a bit risky. The secret of all these theme parks is the family. I mean, you've got the kids at home half the year. You don't know what to do with them during the school holidays, so you have to take them somewhere. It's no earthly use unless the kids like it. Go by what the kids like, and you clean up. Otherwise you're dead."

"I was thinking mainly of retired folk," said Mastroni. "They don't have any young kids, but there are more and more of them, and they get bored. Retired folk like to fish, don't they? It doesn't take much physical stamina."

"We'll have to provide something for the wives," I said. "They aren't too keen on fishing as a rule. Get working on it. Incidentally," I added, "who's going to bring us our coffee now Marilyn isn't here any more?"

Brigitte Aubert gave me a dirty look.

"Count me out. The sex object who waits on her lord and master really isn't my scene."

"Sex object?" Hirsch protested. "Jesus, you're well on the way to taking over the world, three-quarters of all the money in the States belongs to women, and you have the gall to talk about sex objects?"

"Hey!" I yelled. "This isn't a bar-room discussion. You're in class now. Argue the point another day."

We set off for the first floor at a few minutes to ten. Laurence's team members were already there, clustered around the window. El Fatawi chuckled and stepped aside to give me a view of the landing stage. Marilyn was standing beside the Italian boatman with a suit-case in her hand. Other items of baggage were stacked in the motorboat. Leroy came trotting up. We couldn't hear what was said. The scene resembled a clip from a silent film, jerky and grotesque.

"They didn't take long to make themselves scarce," Laurence remarked.

Today she was wearing a bright, cheerful trouser suit in yellow and blue. The pants were very baggy and fell to the ankles. It struck me that I had never seen her in a short skirt. If she concealed them so carefully, her calves were probably on the full side. She seemed to have recovered from last night, or perhaps she'd taken extra trouble with her make-up. Not a wrinkle marred her slightly tanned complexion.

The lakeside scene drew triumphant smiles from all present. Having watched it with relish for a while, I consulted my watch.

"Ten past ten. Charriac isn't coming."

"In that case," Laurence said with a sniff, "we'll do without him."

Below us, Morin was dragging a huge basket down the gravel path. The Italian, who had started the engine, helped him aboard and cast off. El Fatawi waved the trio a sardonic farewell, but they didn't see him.

"Anyway," said Brigitte, jerking her thumb at the window, "that's three fewer to contend with."

"They don't count," I said quietly. "There never were 16 of us in the first place."

She retracted her upper lip and bared her teeth like a squirrel nibbling a nut – a childish trick that must have charmed some grown-up when she was ten.

"You're right. Thirteen. That's unlucky, huh?"

Without replying, I whistled to indicate that playtime was over and invited everyone to sit down. The meeting that followed was utterly pointless, like the ones that used to exasperate me in my firm when verbal diarrhoea took hold. Everyone knew what everyone else would say, every phrase was predictable. The speakers obediently recited their lines like actors in rehearsal. Brigitte, true to her self-caricature, was sarcastic, Mastroni punctilious, Hirsch laconic, El Fatawi emotional, Chalamont hidebound. None of them diverged from their well-worn grooves and none contributed any new information or productive ideas. Laurence scarcely opened her mouth, she was so preoccupied. At the end of a totally wasted hour we agreed unanimously that the only thing to do was to carry on as if nothing had happened. Del Rieco held all the trumps; we had no leverage at all. Our extravagant illusions of the night before had burst like soap bubbles, leaving us drained with disappointment.

We returned to our offices with heavy tread. Hirsch checked his e-mail. The news wasn't good.

Charriac had discovered a new angle of attack and was now deployed on three fronts. For one thing, he had offered the supermarket chain a bigger discount provided he could benefit from special promotions, so the price war had been resumed. For another, he was continuing his attack on our share capital. He had made a public offer for our shares, claiming that a single group would increase profits. It seemed that some of our shareholders were susceptible to this argument to the tune of ten or twelve per cent of our authorized share capital – not enough, as yet, to pose a genuine threat. Finally and most importantly, he was taking up his position on legal terrain. Doubtless at his instigation, the parents of a little girl who had allegedly been injured by one of our hooks was suing us for a colossal sum in damages and calling on other victims to launch a class action.

"Oh, sure," said Hirsch, "as soon as someone sprains his ankle he wonders who he can sue. There are a million such cases a year. These days, if you manufacture brooms, you have to print a notice on them – 'Caution, do not shove this up your ass!' – or some guy will call the police and claim he wasn't warned of the risk."

"It won't wash!" Mastroni thundered. "A fish-hook is designed to catch fish by the lip. If you hook a little girl by mistake, it'll do to her what it does to a trout. How can you avoid it?"

"Yes," Hirsch replied, "but the case will be tried by a judge who has never seen a fish-hook in his life. He'll be shown photos of the little girl's disfigured face, expert witnesses will describe her injuries in horrific detail, and he'll find against you. It's law *à l'américaine* these days: fart, and you find yourself in court. There are lawyers who fill their pockets by dangling the prospect of a jackpot in front of their clients. This guy could cost us a fortune. He could take us to the cleaners."

"You can say that again."

"Hang on, that's not the end of it, I've got another e-mail here . . . Now he's contesting our articles of association. He says they don't conform to company law – he's demanding that we be wound up."

So that was what Charriac had been studying when I went to see him and he casually concealed his papers. He was a lawyer, I wasn't. There mightn't be anything in these legal arguments he was bombarding us with, but they were costing us valuable time. If the press weighed in too, which was a logical certainty, it would worry our customers. Or our shareholders.

"He really is firing off all his ammunition at once," I said. "A price war, an attack on our capital, legal manoeuvres . . ."

"Sure," said Hirsch, "the three traditional ways of driving a firm to the wall. He's after our hide, but that's no surprise. We'll defend ourselves."

"No," I said, "we'll counterattack. Saleswise, Mastroni, match his offer exactly. On the shareholder front, it's a shame we've lost Marilyn – she concocted great letters. Brigitte, do your best – I want something reassuring. Shareholders are timid creatures, they take fright at the least little thing. Hey, bring the American into play. If an American takes a slice of our equity, it'll mean there's money to be made. Charriac mustn't be allowed to know that. Ask the Yank if he'd be interested in taking 20 per cent, that would make a good impression. And you, Hirsch, instruct a really top-notch law firm. Hard men, unscrupulous crooks – the kind that defend drug dealers. Two objectives: one, to gain time and get the case bogged down – for the next ten years, preferably. Charriac thinks he's mighty smart, but he must have slipped up on a couple of formalities, and that's all the courts are interested in. Two, pay him back in his own coin. Go through his balance sheet with a fine-tooth comb and report him to the inland revenue. Call for a thorough audit, that should keep him busy. And put some ecological association on his track. Get them to denounce him."

"For what?"

"It doesn't matter what. Polluting our rivers, selling fish-hooks that contain dioxins, ozone, anything you like."

Hirsch emitted a sudden, hollow laugh that made us all jump.

"That's impossible! Titanium, perhaps, but not dioxins or ozone."

"Who cares? Nobody understands these things anyway. Take these demonstrators who parade through the streets with banners. Ask them precisely what effect dioxins are supposed to have, and ten to one they won't know. They've been told dioxins are shit, so they're scared of them, that's enough. Simply issue a statement to the effect that fish caught with Charriac's hooks are currently being analysed. We're still awaiting the results, but it seems there's some kind of problem."

"We'll dish ourselves as well," Hirsch objected.

"Look, we're on the edge of a precipice and he's just given us a push. What do we do? We grab him by the sleeve. Either he'll haul us back or we'll go down together. I want total war on all fronts. No quarter, no prisoners. It's out with the flame-thrower. I won't stop till we've burned him to a crisp."

We were too busy to go to lunch. Mastroni went off on a foraging expedition and came back laden with sausages, French fries, and cans of beer. He reported that Charriac wasn't in the dining-room either. Only Laurence's team had come downstairs.

"Their morale is low. They were looking bored."

"They're waiting to see who wins, not that it'll make a scrap of difference where they're concerned. Put yourself in their place."

"No thanks, I prefer my own."

We sent off e-mail after e-mail. Hirsch's printer kept chattering away, its activities punctuated by those agonizing moans common to all printers. The supermarket chain vacillated until the middle of the afternoon, when it reserved its position without accepting either offer. Our bewildered shareholders kept quiet, but they did not, at least for the moment, follow up our enemies' proposals. They, too, were awaiting the end of the contest before coming down on the winner's side. As for our legal operations, the lawyers exchanged totally incomprehensible memoranda containing spurious assurances of good faith and crammed with allusions to precedents of which we knew nothing. No clear-cut outcome seemed to be taking shape, and the case was sinking into a morass under its own weight.

My team members were gradually regaining their spirits. I could tell that from their relaxed faces and the humorous remarks they uttered out of the corners of their mouths without ever stopping work. Faces are like the sky: you can tell at a glance if it's fine or overcast, if the atmosphere is fraught with humidity, if there's a storm approaching or the clouds are receding. Ours conveyed that spring was in the air.

At three o'clock, Hirsch swung round.

"Hey, that's it: he's sending us our assessments!"

Mastroni and Brigitte dropped what they were doing and gathered round the screen.

"Really?"

"Yep, here they come."

I grabbed Brigitte by the arm. "Don't look, it's brainwashing. Who's to say he won't change a few little unimportant details, like substituting 'Useless' for 'Brilliant'? He's trying to impress us. It's a good sign. If he's resorted to that . . ."

"No, wait." She released herself. "I want to see, just for interest's sake."

I bent forward and switched off the printer.

"No, we're wasting time, it's just a trick. Read your horoscope, it'd come to the same thing. Those aren't our assessments. Charriac wants us to think they are, but they aren't. He's panicking – trying anything. It's a very good sign. You'll see your assessments, the real ones, on Friday night. This is nothing."

"We could take a look all the same. Are you scared, or what?"

"Or what. I could write you an assessment any day of the week. Think for a moment. What's he after? He wants us to spend the remaining three hours navel-gazing and saying to ourselves: heavens, is that what they think of us? It's Charriac who's sending them, not Del Rieco, don't you see? Hey, that gives me an idea. Hirsch, forward them to Del Rieco. Let him see the kind of methods they're using against us." I turned to Brigitte. "You really want to know?"

I tore off the few lines the printer had spewed out before I switched it off and pretended to read them aloud:

"Brigitte Aubert. Pretty but sexually frustrated . . ."

"You're right, it's bullshit – he's got it the wrong way round," she retorted with a deadpan expression that provoked general hilarity.

I smiled approvingly. I like people who know how to laugh at themselves. Five minutes later we received an e-mail from Del Rieco: "I don't understand why you sent me those forms. JDR."

"He thinks we made them up for fun. Tell him Charriac sent them to us, and we don't understand why either. Then cut the cackle, we've got better things to do. We can have a laugh about it on Saturday."

Around four-thirty, alas, we received the *coup de grâce*: our American changed sides and joined forces with Charriac. His contributions to their joint venture comprised his CD-ROM, his own financial resources, and the 20 per cent of our shares he had bought a quarter of an hour before. Charriac struck while the iron was hot by hastily setting up a holding company to manage the whole conglomerate. The companies interlocked like the pieces of a Chinese puzzle: the holding company owned some of the shares of Team A, which in its turn controlled 50 per cent of the shares of the holding company, which controlled one-third of Laurence's firm, 20 per cent of ours, and, through that 20 per cent, one-fifth of the second third of Team B's firm. It was enough to make one's head spin.

Hirsch tried to draw a diagram illustrating the complexity of these financial entanglements. It was almost indecipherable. Arrows adorned with percentages ran in all directions.

"It would take an hour to work out who owns what," he said. "The only certainty is, we don't have much left. With a bit of luck, he'll base his holding company in the Bahamas. Once he's there, we may as well give up: he'll be out of reach of the law and the tax people."

He wasn't far wrong: the holding company set up shop in Luxembourg, then sold its shares to a new holding company based in the Cayman Islands and disappeared before our very eyes. Like a conjurer extracting rabbits from his hat, Charriac produced a cascade of articles of association that enjoyed a brief existence before vanishing into thin air. He was dancing on a tightrope suspended above chasms of international law and switching shares around with the dexterity of a three-card trickster. He had shown us what he was made of and taught us a lesson that left us dumbfounded, almost admiring.

"I sensed this coming," said Mastroni. "He never intended to manufacture fish-hooks at all. He's surfing the money market. We've been screwed."

One thing bothered me. "How did he know about the American?" I said. "Did one of you open your mouth too wide? That's what started it all."

"Laurence," suggested Brigitte.

"I don't think so. She can't stand Charriac, so why should she help him? Besides, she's not the sort to try to shine by telling tales out of school. Who else?"

"We've never talked shop with the others," said Mastroni. "What are you getting at? You think there's another traitor in our midst? There are only four of us."

"Sometimes one careless remark can be enough."

"No. We're not crazy."

"Then there's only one answer: Del Rieco must have told him. I'm going to have it out with him."

I rose and made my way back to the chalet. Suddenly, all the fatigue of the last three days descended on my shoulders. I felt exhausted, crushed. I now knew how Laurence must have felt when she was drowning and saw me equivocating at the water's edge, searching around for pretexts not to throw her a lifebelt.

Del Rieco didn't want to let me in at first.

"Tonight," he called to me through the door. "Tonight after dinner."

"No, right now."

Childishly, I gave the door a shove with my shoulder. I was about to do so again when he condescended to show his face. He looked annoyed.

"What's the matter, Jérôme? Cracking up?"

"It wouldn't be surprising. Who told Charriac we were negotiating with the American?"

"I did, of course. A few lines in a newspaper article. You couldn't expect it to remain a secret."

"Why not?"

He stood motionless in the doorway, blocking it with his bulk.

"Because nothing remains a secret for long. I didn't draw his attention to it specially. It was buried in a lot of other crap, but he was smart: he caught on. Have you been taking the trouble to read the press digest I send you every day? He has."

It was true that Del Rieco had sent us a whole heap of e-mails every morning, digests of articles in trade journals. It was also true that we hadn't paid them much attention. The first day's batch had yielded nothing of interest, just technical articles on fly-fishing and fish farming. After that we'd stopped looking at them. Hirsch didn't even bother to print them out.

"He got in touch with all the relevant American firms before he found the right one," Del Rieco went on. "Then he started negotiating. How could I have forbidden him to? If I had, I'd have compromised my neutrality. He was operating within the rules in a wholly legitimate manner."

"All right, but why did the American negotiate with *him*?"

"Because his offer was an interesting one. To the Americans, we're just a bunch of identical Frogs. They negotiate with the fattest. If it's sentimentality you're after, go to Hollywood, not Wall Street. Did you make an in-depth study of the American's own position?"

I hesitated. "No, not really."

"You should have. Suppose you'd asked me the same question. I'd have told you that the majority shareholder of the American's firm is a pension fund, as it is in the case of many US corporations. The average yield on industrial capital is less than three per cent. The shareholders want five times as much. How do you quintuple your yield?"

I said nothing. He eyed me in a demeaningly indulgent way.

"Well," he went on, "you juggle. You buy and sell, it doesn't matter what. I'm not too sure you understand how a modern economy works. It's like a mine: you go wherever the seam takes you. When the seam is exhausted, you dig somewhere else. You have to eat, so you employ a few yokels to grow tomatoes and potatoes – or manufacture fish-hooks. But that's not where the real money is. I'm impressed by Emmanuel Charriac's performance, I must admit. You're not doing too badly yourself, but you aren't in the same league."

Every word was an arrow, every phrase a wound. I had irritated the man by trying to flush him out in advance, and he was getting his own back.

"It's too bad," he said pityingly, "Charriac set too a high a standard, that's all. You really aren't a normal intake. We usually get people who have made professional blunders, people who are very good but have slipped up in some way. They follow instructions nicely, we spot their weak points and recycle them into the right niches. But this time it's like a Balkan war. Very stimulating intellectually. With the possible exception of Madame Carré, none of you actually tried to make the grade. Instead, you were intent on mutual destruction from the outset. You transcended my logic and overstepped the mark right away. Talk about Chicago in the days of Al Capone! But it was you that started it, Jérôme. Perhaps you were overmotivated. Paradoxically, you know, that can be a handicap."

"It's your logic that doesn't add up," I hazarded pathetically.

"It isn't *my* logic!" he exclaimed. "It's the logic inherent in the system – it's the way of the world, not *my* way in particular. He who toughs it out wins. I can't help that. There are times – this is just between the two of us, but there are times when it makes me feel pessimistic. By the end of this century, not that anyone will notice the difference, this planet will be dominated by crime syndicates – by people with instincts like Attila the Hun, but wearing three-piece suits instead of animal skins. I won't be there to see it, fortunately, but that's where we're headed. Seems to me it's since they stopped teaching ethics in school."

"You're a fine one to talk about ethics."

"All right, forget about ethics. I'm talking about logic. Causes and effects are inextricably linked. Everything is pre-programmed, and no one can break the sequence of events. It's like a chain reaction: there comes a time when it's uncontrollable. It destroys everything, yet every detail remains precisely predictable. All that has happened here is merely a logical consequence of the attitudes you've chosen to adopt, you and the others. I don't believe in fate – that's just a loser's cop-out – but I do profoundly believe in logic. We can't foresee the future because we don't possess all the parameters. Every time we master one of them, however, we reduce the scope of our uncertainty. That's what I'm here for: to discover more about you and thus reduce my uncertainty about your future conduct. You, too, are subject to logic."

"But it's *your* logic," I repeated stupidly. "It doesn't work like that."

"Read the newspapers," he said with a shrug. "All right, Jérôme, that's enough, I've things to do. The game stops at dinner. We can resume this conversation tomorrow evening, when I interview you like the rest."

I was well on the way to losing every scrap of dignity and self-assurance. I tensed all my muscles, or my knees might have buckled.

"I came here in search of a job, Joseph, nothing else," I said, striving to keep my voice steady.

"So act accordingly," he replied curtly.

That was his parting shot – or rather, his final challenge. If he had left it unsaid, if he had confined himself to a cybernetico-philosophical sermon, things might have turned out differently. As it was, his fine words impelled me to carry them to extremes. He'd wanted to see how far we could go and prompt us to cross one more frontier. I had already ventured too far to retrace my steps.

My team, or what was left of it, forbore to ask me how the interview had gone. It was written all over my face. They looked at me and looked away.

"I've been in touch with Charriac's trade unions," said Mastroni. "I'm trying to land him with a strike. That could put the American off."

"You think so?" I said without conviction.

"Yes. I hinted to them that Charriac plans to fire 20 per cent of his workforce when the merger comes off. They're busy preparing posters and banners. If they cut up rough the American will get scared."

Not a bad idea, I thought. It wouldn't be the first time the unions had functioned as pawns on the financial chessboard. But the manoeuvre failed miserably. Charriac promised, swore, and testified in writing that he wouldn't fire a single employee. All he had to do was gain a couple of hours. Would he have kept his undertaking if the game had continued? No one could say. Probably not, but it didn't matter.

Our shareholders, seeing that the scales had tilted, were selling one after another. There came a stage when Charriac didn't even bother to buy them out. He now owned more than a third of our shares. Having obtained a relative majority just before drinks time, he announced that our two companies had merged without even convening a board meeting.

"No dinner for me," said Brigitte. "I couldn't bear to set eyes on his lousy face."

Hirsch sat down heavily in front of his screen.

"I may as well wipe the lot," he grunted. "It's no use any more, not now . . ."

Mastroni was the only one who tried to put a good face on things.

"We went down fighting," he said consolingly. "We made the final, after all. They'll take that into account."

"Just a minute," I said. "What did you say just now?"

"That we went down – "

"No, not you. Hirsch."

"I said I may as well wipe the lot," said Hirsch.

I clapped my hands. Everyone jumped.

"That's it, by God! That's the answer!"

They looked at me the way people look at a drunk, with a mixture of commiseration and vague distaste.

"What have you dreamt up this time?"

"Nothing, nothing, I need to give it some more thought. Where are you going to be later on tonight?"

Brigitte raised her eyebrows.

"Where do you think? At the opera, of course, then on for a late dinner at the Tour d'Argent."

"I must be able to get together with you. I'll manage it somehow. Come on, let's go and eat."

"Not me," Brigitte insisted. "Not hungry. The sight of that man would ruin my appetite."

"No, you've got to. We must keep up appearances to the end. And the end may not be where he thinks."

"Jérôme's right," said Hirsch. It won't be very pleasant, but let's save face. Anyway, it's been nice working with you all. We did our best. A pity we were up against a crook like Charriac."

"There may still be a chance of doing him down," I said in a low voice.

They didn't believe it. The game was lost and they were rubbing their bruises.

Charriac was even more insufferable at dinner than any of us could have foreseen. We lay in wait for him in our trenches, ready to repel his charge with shafts of derision, barrages of sarcasm, machine-gun bursts of irony. Our guns remained silent. Charriac described a weekend he had spent in Venice with some indeterminate young woman, itemized the bridges and backstreets of the city of the Doges, computed the annual turnover of the Hotel Danieli, and went on from there to conduct an examination of the Vatican's finances. To hear him, the historic battle between Christianity and Islam was just a fight for a share of the market – a minor matter compared to the Microsoft trial. He was on brilliant form, juggling paradoxes with a remote, unchanging smile on his lips. It seemed to convey that, although he toyed with various ideas, he himself did not believe in them and was merely showing off his talents. That smile was the only token of his extreme satisfaction. One sensed that he was relaxing, his mind already on other things. Furious at having been defeated, I had expected him to be arrogantly triumphalist. His feigned indifference to what had happened was doubly wounding. Its unmistakable message was: "You see? It was all so easy – just a preliminary workout. I've already dismissed the subject from my mind." His manner was even more humiliating than the brutal – or, worse, suave – arrogance we'd been prepared for.

Laurence, who seemed to know Venice better than he did, entered into his game and tried to trip him up. She made obscure allusions designed to brand him a philistine, an ignorant barbarian. He willingly reverted to the subject, quoted Casanova's *Mémoires*, discoursed on the genesis of the ghetto concept, and recounted an anecdote connected with colour theory and Harry's Bar. Preserving a pleasant, airy demeanour, he listened to Laurence with genuine attention when she brought the conversation round to painting. In short, he was the ideal table companion – exasperatingly courteous.

My team members were inwardly seething, I could tell, but they were smart enough to restrain themselves. Del Rieco did not, of course, put in an appearance.

Outside, the weather had turned stormy again. We could hear the wind whistling in the trees, and it was not long before a few heavy raindrops exploded against the window panes.

The end of dinner left us rather at a loss. Morin was no longer there to enliven the bar. Besides, Charriac's team disappeared immediately after coffee for a private debriefing session. I supposed they were getting ready to celebrate their success in champagne, savouring every episode and recalling how much better they had done than the rest of us.

And, above all, how much Del Rieco had helped them. For that was the fact of the matter, I felt convinced. From the start, the game had been rigged in such a way as to rule out fair competition. For some reason unknown to me, Del Rieco had decided to favour Charriac and do his utmost to help him, drawing his attention to relevant items of information, dictating the reactions of shareholders, suppliers and customers, disrupting our plans at will, smoothing Charriac's path and laying innumerable traps for us. What I still failed to discern was the mysterious bond that united the two men, but bond there had to be. All the machinery that looked so complicated and so realistic was just an illusion, a means of obscuring the plain truth: Charriac had to win. They had never meant to assess us fairly; their sole intention had been to justify a choice made well before our arrival.

I broached the subject to Laurence and Hirsch over a cup of coffee in the bar. Laurence, who had been the first to suspect that Charriac and Del Rieco were in league, had now changed her mind. According to her, they had placed us in an extreme situation, and we had all got our just deserts. In real life, she argued, there was no fair contest between a graduate of the École Nationale d'Administration and some poor sod from the suburbs. Here the odds had been better balanced and we had all had our chance. Excessive scruples and insufficient mistrust, a trace of naïvety and old-fashioned reflexes – those were what had underlain our defeat. Charriac, by contrast, was the image of what he aspired to be: brutal, underhand, merciless, icy. Laurence's eyes betrayed resigned admiration – ruefully admiring resignation, to be more precise.

"I've been eliminated," she said, "because, in the final analysis, I'm not sufficiently like them. Fundamentally, they're right: I don't belong on the staff of a major multinational. I'm not prepared enough to trample on everyone. Perhaps I never will be. They showed me the destination and I realized I wasn't too keen to get here."

"You mean they've done you a favour?"

"In a way. It's the same everywhere, you know. University, civil service, big firms, the arts – they all have a culture of their own, and if you don't fit in they don't want you. All that remains for me is to find my proper place. It isn't here. They don't like me because I don't like them. I don't want to be like them. They sensed that, and they made me feel it. I'd never be capable of doing what Charriac does, of becoming like him. It's rather brilliant, what they've done. They haven't wasted three years trying to mould me; they've summed me up in four days flat. I'm quite impressed: very little outlay, and far more effective than all the contact forms the big firms send their applicants."

"Contact forms?" said Hirsch.

She turned to him.

"Well, when you apply for a job with a major company, they send you an interminable questionnaire. The object is to make sure you're compatible with what you'll find if you join them. Not only that you're what they need, but, above all, that you won't be a nuisance to them, that you'll fit in perfectly, that you're in tune with the ethos of the firm, the in-house mentality. A computer processes your questionnaire and comes up with a profile of you. Del Rieco goes one better: he conducts the process live. At least you know where you are with him."

"In other words," I said irritably, "they kick you in the pants and you say thanks."

"More or less," she replied with the ghost of a smile. "I feel like a budding priest who's lost his faith and quit the seminary. I still want a job – I want one badly, but maybe not exactly their type of job. I haven't been happy these last three days. I've come to the conclusion I'm not made for this line of work. I'm going to see if I can find one that suits me better."

"There isn't one, Laurence. The civil service is closed to people of our age – well, perhaps not to you, but to me. I won't see forty again, I don't have any medical or legal qualifications, I can't repair a TV set or change a washer – I don't even have the wherewithal to buy a cabby's licence. What am *I* going to do?"

"No idea. Sell flowers at the Gare du Nord, maybe."

"Or play the squeeze-box in the bars of St-Germain-des-Prés. Sorry, Laurence, but that's not my line either. We're missing out on a marvellous love affair, you know."

This time she laughed aloud. "I'm glad you got that straight," she retorted. "I wouldn't have contemplated it anyway. Been there, done that."

"Well," Hirsch said drily, "I'm for bed. I'll leave you two lovebirds to bill and coo on your own."

But it was Laurence who said goodnight and made her exit, not only from the room but from my preoccupations. She wasn't in the running any more, and I doubt if she would have convinced me had she stayed. Neither of us desired the other, that much was certain. We were simply two ships that had passed in the night.

I continued the conversation with Hirsch. Although we put it differently, we were both on the same wavelength, both furious at having been duped. He shared my view that the game was rigged, and we kept unearthing details which confirmed that supposition.

"Those observers!" Hirsch exclaimed. "And De Wavre had the cheek to pass them off as psychologists! If Morin's a psychologist, I'm the archbishop of Paris!"

"But the worst thing was the American," I added. "We invented him, but as soon as we started depending on him they pulled the rug out from under us and we fell flat on our faces. In real life I'd have caught a flight to Los Angeles and gone and talked to the guy. Then it would have been a different story. You don't clinch deals by fax, you go to see people and talk turkey, eyeball to eyeball. The Internet is crap: nothing will ever replace human contact, but that's just what they denied us."

"As for those goddamned fish-hooks!" Hirsch chimed in. "Who came up with that idiotic suggestion? Pinetti, wasn't it?"

"I know. That figures. He was in on it too."

Vainly stirring our empty coffee cups, we worked each other up into a lather. At last, when I sensed that Hirsch was ripe, I put all my cards on the table.

"We're cooked, you agree?"

"Not only cooked but burnt."

"So we've nothing to lose?"

"Not with these people, no."

"All right, listen: we're going to screw them up."

He didn't ask why, only how, which was what I'd been hoping.

"We're going to smash their toy to smithereens. Clausewitz: War is the continuation of politics by other means. That's their favourite formula. They cite it every time they clobber someone, they talk of nothing else, they think it's brilliant – the ultimate philosophical truth. Plato was in vogue for 2,000 years; now it's Clausewitz. Okay, we'll show them. No holds barred, is it? Fair enough, but that goes for us too."

Hirsch didn't argue. "In practical terms?" he said.

"In practical terms, we pretend to retire for the night, then meet up at two in the morning and go to work on their computers. Are you in?"

If he'd said no I'd have stopped right there – I needed reinforcing in my fury – but he nodded fiercely.

We decided not to include anyone else in our commando operation. Laurence had already disappeared into another dream, Mastroni was too timid, Brigitte Aubert too inflexible, and the rest weren't worth a damn.

On the way to my room I passed the members of Charriac's team emerging from their meeting. Pinetti winked at me in an almost friendly fashion.

At 2 a.m. precisely I joined Hirsch in the lobby, which was dim and deserted. A small light near the entrance cast a yellowish glow over the stairs, but that was the only form of illumination. Nothing was stirring anywhere.

Hirsch had sat down to wait for me in one of the armchairs, wearing a pair of jeans and a black sweater. All he needed to complete his impersonation of an international terrorist was a balaclava and a sub-machine gun.

"Shall we go?" I whispered.

He rose to his feet in one lithe movement. His expression was inscrutable, but he seemed more determined than ever. Like me, he must have brooded on his resentment for hours, lying fully dressed on his bed.

Outside, the wind and the rain were fighting a duel. We were sodden and dishevelled by the time we reached the door of the chalet. Once there, Hirsch produced a sliver of metal from his pocket. I looked at him inquiringly.

"Comes of a misspent youth," he whispered, inserting it in the lock.

He must have lost some of his touch, because he took a minute or two to open it. At last there was a click, almost inaudible above the gusts of wind, and I saw his teeth glint in the gloom.

"It's not the Banque de France," he muttered. "They must feel pretty sure of themselves."

He pushed the door open and we slipped inside, quickly shutting it behind us.

"No lights," I ordained.

As soon as our eyes were accustomed to the darkness, Hirsch made for the computers and switched them on. Obediently, they purred into life and proceeded to fill two screens with cabalistic formulas.

Hirsch knit his brow, looking intent rather than apprehensive. Then, drawing up a chair, he sat down and started tapping away at the keyboard. I'm no computer expert but, like most people, I do have a few vague, basic ideas of how they work. I realized that he was trying to explore the contents of the memory.

Meanwhile, I opened various drawers. All they contained were floppies, but Del Rieco must have kept some written records of his activities, if only for legal reasons. I recalled a lecture I'd attended as a student. The speaker had categorically prophesied that paper would have disappeared by the year 2000, and that people would be communicating freely and exclusively by computer. Twenty-five years later, firms were using more paper than ever before. Never had official forms been so abundant or daily life so overburdened with legal procedures.

Next, I tackled the steel filing cabinets. Two of them were locked. The other two were full of files neatly suspended on rails. I extracted one and opened it on the central work table. It was too dark to read the documents it contained, so I removed a sheet and took it over to the window in the hope of deciphering a few words.

Hirsch turned his head.

"You won't get anywhere like that. Don't ruin your eyesight, we'll take it with us."

"First I must see what it is. A laundry bill won't get us very far."

The window wasn't much use, so I opened the door a crack. The cardboard cover bore an inscription in felt-tip pen.

"It's a previous seminar. January this year."

"Take it anyway."

"Found anything?"

He left the keyboard and knelt down, peering at the cables on the floor.

"Oh, there are seven or eight files, but they're all protected. I'll have a go on the other machine. They aren't hooked up, from the look of the cables, so it could be an easier proposition. I wouldn't bet on it, though."

I turned my attention to the cabinets again. All the files were identical in appearance. I examined another of them in the dim light from the door. It referred to another, even earlier seminar. I replaced it. We were both making as little noise as possible.

"Shit," whispered Hirsch. "Password required."

"Could you crack it?"

"Sure, but it would take me the rest of the night. An hour or two at least, if I was lucky."

"Some hacker, you are," I joked.

"You're welcome to have a go yourself," he growled.

"I'd sooner you tried to open this cabinet with that burglar's picklock of yours."

He nudged me in the ribs.

"It's not a burglar's picklock, it's for forcing car doors. A present from my nephew."

"The one who's doing time in Fresnes?"

"Yes, that one . . ."

Bending down, he inserted his tool in the crack and rotated his wrist. There was another click.

"Damn, I've broken it."

"The picklock?"

"No, the lock. They'll notice."

I shrugged. "At this stage . . ."

In the cabinet we found a bottle of whisky, another of Perrier, a couple of glasses, and a cloth. Hirsch rubbed his chin thoughtfully.

"Typical of people to stash their booze more carefully than their records. Maybe there's some ice in the other cabinet. How about a drink? My treat."

"I don't think this is the time."

He half turned and looked at the glowing screens.

"It's all there in that computer. What shall I do, take it away?"

I thought for a moment. "No, leave it there. First we'll see what there is in this folder. When a seminar is over they'd normally put everything down on paper to close the file. We'll get an idea of what to look for."

He was gracious enough to agree.

"Okay, and we'll try to dig out a flashlight before we come back. The passwords aren't all the same length, which means they'll have a different one for each file. When there are more than one or two, the usual practice is to jot them down on bits of paper and keep them not too far from the computer. You know how it is: you want to do some work and – hell, you can't remember the password, so you have to hunt for it. It's the same with PIN numbers: you note them down somewhere. Nobody's immune to mental aberrations. Our memories aren't like hard disks. The human element is the weak point in any system, always has been."

This seemed an unsuitable moment to engage in an ontological debate. I gestured to him to be quiet.

Tucked away in my well-lit bedroom with the door securely locked, we examined our haul, the file on last January's seminar. It opened with a list of the participants, 14 in all. Their names meant nothing to me.

Each candidate had an assessment form of his or her own, a large grid extending over two sheets of A4 stuck together with Scotch tape. Heading the columns were cryptic abbreviations: FA, PL, C, IP, and so forth, each box being occupied by a numeral or a letter. There was no grand total. From this I brilliantly deduced that the data did not add up and must differ in kind.

Then came some notes in Del Rieco's handwriting. I learned that a certain Monsieur Marceau suffered from a speech impediment, that Madame Montceny was a prude, and that Monsieur Halmer reminded him of Donald Duck.

Like us, the unfortunate victims had been divided into three teams. This was the seminar devoted to the wholesale meat trade, the one to which Del Rieco had referred with such amusement. Struck down by mad cow disease, the teams had reacted as best they could. One had contested the lab results and launched a campaign designed to discredit the qualifications of those who had come up with them, another had entered into negotiations with the authorities in the hope of obtaining compensation, and the third had turned to the producers of ducks and geese. Severe losses notwithstanding, all three had just about survived (the first less well than the others, the second distinctly better). They had never clashed head-on at any stage. Pointless to wonder if we should also have reached a preliminary agreement: no one would have observed it.

None of this was spelled out, of course. I managed to reconstruct the simulation only by guessing the significance of all the abbreviations.

The final sheets referred to some new series of tests, doubtless the ones that awaited us in the morning. There were more grids, some of the numerals being ringed in red.

The last sheet of all bore another list of the candidates' names, this time followed by a series of letters and numerals. Marceau was classified as "ACDBArs2114BZ", and the other assessments were similar. It was all Greek to me.

Hirsch was equally mystified. He gave a forced laugh and pointed to one of the boxes. "This letter A," he said. "We can't even be sure it's better than a 'D'. If that's all they've got in the computer, there's really no point in beating our brains. A coded message is indecipherable without the relevant key. We'd be just as stumped if we'd found our own assessment forms."

"Still," I said, drumming on the bedside table, "they must write it down in clear somewhere."

"Or they fax it to Paris, and that's where they do their sums. If so, we've had it."

I came to a decision.

"This changes nothing. We don't want to know exactly what they've cooked up for us, we want to wreck the joint. It's obvious they haven't put down anything on paper yet. Do you know how to make a mess of a computer?"

"Sure I do. So do you: you take a hammer and smash it."

"How about something more subtle?"

"You have to reformat the hard disk – four times. Do it only once, and you can still retrieve some of the data."

"Could you make it look like a straightforward accident?"

He hesitated. "Straightforward? Not really. Only a sector crash could do that. A nice little virus, on the other hand ... Yes, it's possible to introduce a virus that'll mess everything up, and no one will ever know who planted it. It happens all the time – half the Web is infected. And there are some that'll reformat your hard disk. Not four times, but once. That does an impressive amount of damage in itself."

"Got something handy?"

"No," he said with a laugh. "You think I walk around with a virus disk in my pocket?"

"Could you concoct one?"

He spread his arms.

"It's not worth it. Okay, we go back there, I reformat both machines, and goodnight. Who did it? they'll ask. Not me, I was in bed asleep. They'll see that someone has scrambled their computers, but who? If they ask, all you say is: what, *me*? It'd be another matter if they started bashing you on the head with a telephone directory, but do you think they would?"

No, I didn't. But not even that would have impressed me. I had encountered firms that taught their executives how to withstand interrogation and what attitude to adopt when raided by the Fraud Squad or questioned by an examining magistrate. The trick was to faze a policeman sufficiently for him to forget to inform you of your rights in good time, thereby invalidating the whole procedure.

"All right," I said, "that's what we'll do. Is it possible to drop a time bomb – one that won't go off till tomorrow, for instance?"

"With a virus, yes, but not with reformating – not without writing a special programme."

"Never mind, let's go."

We tiptoed downstairs and out into the darkness once more. The weather was still in two minds, alternating between gusts of wind and hatfuls of raindrops. A light mounted beneath the eaves had been left on in the yard. I hadn't paid it any attention during our first excursion. This time I felt I was escaping from a prison camp – having to cross open ground under fire from the watch-towers. Strange how some details become effaced, only to spring to the eye. The light served no purpose: no window overlooked the yard. Perhaps it was simply there to scare off the wild animals that must haunt the woods.

With Hirsch at my heels, I skirted the row of trees, then leapt on to the steps of the chalet. Just as I pushed the door open, the light went on inside.

Charriac was sitting in Del Rieco's armchair with a shotgun across his knees. Pinetti shut the door behind us and planted his back against it. We must have looked like a couple of students caught burgling the bursar's office. Charriac chuckled.

"*Les Visiteurs du soir*," he sneered. "Excellent film, but a trifle dated. Would you mind showing the butler your invitation card? I'm not sure you were on the guest list."

We stood there transfixed. I was the first to react.

"What the hell are you doing here, Charriac?"

He swayed idly back and forth as if the armchair were a rocking chair.

"I could ask you the same thing. Speaking for ourselves, we thought we might make up a foursome at bridge. That's why you came, I imagine. By the way, pass me that folder you're hiding under your arm."

Casually, he pointed the muzzle of the gun at me.

"Stop fooling around, Charriac. Where did you get that popgun?"

He glanced at it abstractedly.

"Oh, that? There's a rack in the barn. No, kindly keep your distance!"

I'd started to move. I stopped.

"Don't make me laugh. It's not even loaded."

"I wouldn't bank on it," he said slowly. "Russian roulette, they call it. Loaded or not loaded? Personally, I'm inclined to think it's loaded. Care to find out?"

"You're out of your mind! Come on, don't pretend you'd shoot me. I mean, why would you do such a thing?"

"For fun?" he suggested. "I don't find the idea unappealing. It's because of the assessment forms. I was wrong to send you those phoney files, but it was really odious of you to forward them to Del Rieco. He came to see me, and he was thoroughly disagreeable. We could do anything we liked, he said, but we mustn't mess around with his files, not even for fun. He was genuinely irritated – he said I was just as out of order as you. One mustn't break the rules, it seems. You tried to bring me down with you, you see, and that really wasn't nice of you. I tried to tell him I hadn't done anything at all – that you'd invented the whole thing – but he didn't believe me. He wants to arrange a confrontation between us, like something out of a detective yarn. I'm sure, knowing you, that you'll tell him the truth if he does. You were going to end up with nothing in any case, but now I'm not sure I won't end the same way." He paused. "All right, here's how I see things . . ."

He wedged the butt of the gun against his stomach.

"Pinetti and I were going for a quiet stroll," he went on in a jaunty voice, "when we heard a noise coming from inside here. Suspecting the presence of a burglar, I went to fetch a gun from the barn – purely for self-defence. As I approached, I was threatened by a shadowy figure. He was armed . . ."

He jerked his chin at a meat cleaver lying on the desk.

"A burglar on an island in the middle of a lake?" scoffed Hirsch, who had recovered his wits. "Armed with a cleaver? The man's off his rocker!"

Charriac ignored him.

"And do you know who it was? Poor Carceville, who, completely demoralized by his failure, had gone mad. It all happened so quickly: he lunged at me and I instinctively pulled the trigger. Coroner's finding: death by misadventure. Who would have thought it? I'll be badly traumatized, of course. I'll take months to recover. No, not months, just until I take up my nice new job. Jérôme, give me that folder!"

Moving slowly, I placed it on the edge of the desk.

"It won't do you any good, it isn't ours."

"I know: an additional sign of your mental derangement. Poor, mad Carceville took a folder at random and snitched a cleaver from the kitchen. Then he proceeded to attack the world at large like those sickos in America – the ones who snap and massacre an entire school. Undue stress. A vulnerable, overly motivated personality, but above all, undue stress. How sad!"

"And Hirsch? How will you explain *him* away?"

"Hirsch won't present any problem, you'll have murdered him already. With the cleaver. When I think . . . I only just escaped the same fate!"

I felt a pang of uneasiness for the first time. He seemed quite serious. The more he talked, the more he was beginning to believe in his imaginary scenario. The man was raving mad. I tried to exploit whatever was left of his reason.

"It won't work, Emmanuel. They don't just take statements when someone dies a violent death. They carry out ballistic analyses and look for fingerprints. You've left them all over the place. Even on the cleaver."

"Oh no, that was Pinetti, not me. He touched it when he went to Hirsch's assistance."

I felt goose pimples prickling my forearms.

"And if I write you a statement admitting everything?"

"Statements, pooh! They aren't worth a damn. Everyone retracts them."

I very gently raised my hands, taking care not to provoke him.

"It isn't worth it, Emmanuel, not just for the sake of a job. People don't kill for that."

He adjusted his glasses.

"Of course they do. There are places where they'll murder you for 50 francs. For your wristwatch. Your jacket. Your shoes. Even for no reason at all, just because you looked them in the eye. Human life is remarkably cheap, you know . . ."

What to do when confronted by an armed psychopath? By someone who has spent the whole week talking of killing, and who, no longer content with metaphorical turns of phrase, resorts to the real thing? We had indeed crossed the divide, all four of us. I tried to reason with him.

"There are other solutions, Emmanuel. Far less expensive ones."

"From your point of view, no doubt."

"No, from yours as well. Two dead men leave a mark. There'll be a thorough investigation, suspicions, articles in the press. Not good for your CV, that . . . I don't see what good it'll do you to kill me."

A dreamy expression came over his face.

"Nor do I, to be honest. All that blood . . . So crude, so vulgar! There's a much better solution. We'll all go and wake Del Rieco, and you'll tell him what you were doing in his headquarters. You haven't completely dished yourself, you know. Oh, they naturally don't intend to offer you as interesting a job as they've earmarked for me, but still, something that'll keep your family in groceries as long as your children aren't too demanding."

"And you'll tell him what you were doing in his armchair with that ridiculous gun on your lap?"

"Of course. I was defending his possessions and the social order at one and the same time. I heard a noise, I came running."

He lowered his eyes for a moment and pursed his lips.

"On second thoughts, that wouldn't gain me much. He'd believe me, but he might have his doubts. I'd sooner revert to my original plan."

I stepped back and leant against a filing cabinet.

"Emmanuel, you're in the shit. You aren't going to kill two people, even supposing you're physically and mentally capable of it. Let's call it a night, go back to our rooms, and forget the whole thing. Any other scenario is futile."

"Yes," he sighed, "but I've no idea what you did to these computers earlier on. I don't have Delval with me. Our friend Hirsch here could sell me any old story, and I couldn't verify it. If we could revert to the situation before your first visit, fine – except that we can't. You've been up to something, I don't exactly know what. It's very tiresome . . ."

"We haven't done a thing," said Hirsch. "We couldn't access the programs. They're protected."

"Not from the likes of you! You're lying! You didn't come here just to snaffle an obsolete file."

"You have my word," said Hirsch.

"Screw your word!" Charriac said angrily. "This is civil war. You give your word, and as soon as someone turns on his heel you shoot him in the back."

"In that case," I put in, "I don't see any way out."

Charriac adjusted his aim an inch or two.

"When someone says there's no solution, it's simply because the solution doesn't appeal to him. There's always a solution. Or several relatively unpleasant ones. Ah, I think I've hit on one . . . Pinetti, take that folder and put it in Carceville's room. Hide it there, but not too carefully. Then come back here."

I was relieved to note that he seemed to have abandoned his murderous designs.

"This solution of yours," I said, "what does it entail?"

"Nothing. You watch too much TV. In the end, the baddy tells all and the goody escapes and fouls him up completely. Except that *I'm* the goody, so I don't have anything to tell. We stop the clock, press the rewind button, and revert to the situation as it was half an hour ago: you're back in your room with the folder you pinched, and nothing has happened."

He would go and inform Del Rieco at once, of course, and I would have to justify the document's presence in my room. No one would believe my tall tale of a shotgun and a frame-up, not for one moment. Charriac was right: nothing would have happened apart from the disclosure of fraudulent manoeuvres on my part – manoeuvres that would promptly get me booed off the stage and blacklisted for ever.

This was something to be avoided. I had to encourage Charriac to talk himself into a state of exhaustion. He loved the sound of his own voice, loved preening himself in the mirror. Feeling thoroughly in control of the situation, he would want to savour it for as long as possible. There lay my opportunity.

"How do you plan to go about it?" I asked.

He looked saddened, but his urge to show off prevailed. He gave way, negating his infinitely more sensible statement of only a few moments ago.

"You disappoint me, Jérôme. How? You must have a pretty good idea. Pinetti will go and hide the folder while the three of us wait here. Then I'll call Del Rieco and tell him the truth: that you stole some documents and came back to look for some more. Oh, by the way, I found the details of tomorrow's tests – or rather, *you* found them and I caught you with them. The schedule is there on the desk."

He indicated an orange folder with the muzzle of his gun.

"It's amusing. Among other absurd things, they want us to play each other at mah-jong, God knows why. In my opinion, chess would be more to the point. No one who plays chess can be all bad. At least he knows he must anticipate his opponent's moves – and, more importantly, never underestimate him. You know how champions resign when they see their opponent has a winning move, even if he's incapable of seeing it himself and is getting ready to do something quite different? Great, isn't it? They credit him with their own intellectual ability. I admire that."

He had surrendered yet again to his love of digression, and his verbal diarrhoea began to flow once more. Waiting for the moment when his arm muscles would almost imperceptibly relax, I tried to distract him still further.

"But we aren't playing chess, Emmanuel. You've got a gun. You've just passed the point of no return. There's no comparison."

"Oh, come on! It's all the same whether you bump someone off with writs, smear stories in the press, or a 7.65. The only difference is, he commits suicide and saves you the price of a bullet. They shot Nixon down like a rabbit. They didn't even have to pay someone to kill him like Kennedy. We've made a lot of progress since then."

I was still covertly watching the expression in his eyes when events overtook me and everything went haywire. Pinetti, who had doubt-less grown weary of his boss's ravings, decided to make his exit. Just as he reached the door, Hirsch pounced on him.

There was a moment's confusion. Locked together and lurching this way and that, the two men seemed to fill the entire, cramped premises. Then, with a great commotion, they disappeared through the open door. Charriac sprang to his feet. I kicked him hard, just below the knee, and he doubled up with pain, forgetting about his gun. I seized it by the barrel. Abruptly wrenching the weapon away, he reversed it and dealt me a violent blow in the chest with the butt. The impact deposited me in a sitting position on the floor. A second blow, this time on the right cheekbone, sent a crimson wave washing over my eyeballs. I got up, clutching my bruised, lacerated cheek, and winced as a shaft of lightning pierced my chest. One of my ribs was broken, if not more.

Charriac had already limped outside, hopping on one foot. I staggered to the door. He was at the bottom of the steps with the gun to his shoulder. Not far away on the edge of the wood, Hirsch and Pinetti were rolling around on the ground, trying to throttle one another.

"Stop!" Charriac shouted. "Stop or I fire!"

They didn't, so he did. The gun was loaded after all. The sound of the shot reverberated around the yard.

For a split second, I remained frozen. He'd done it. The madman had made the transition from words to deeds. By fighting, Hirsch and Pinetti had unleashed the violence Charriac had barely suppressed from the outset. He took a step forward, trying to detect what was happening beneath the trees.

Without waiting to find out, I stole away behind him. Half running, half hobbling, with one elbow clamped against my chest, I made for the barn on the left of the chalet.

Once there I crouched down in the shadowy doorway, groaning softly. My cheek was bleeding, and every movement of my upper body brought tears to my eyes.

All movement outside had ceased. Charriac had disappeared. Across the yard, half hidden by the trees, a body lay stretched out on the ground. Hirsch, no doubt.

The pain in my chest and my cheek was excruciating, but I was more dazed than anything else. Eroded by the stress to which we had been subjected, all the barriers patiently erected by a long education had just collapsed. These cool-headed, rational men had suddenly mutated into playground tearaways scuffling in the mud – into game-cocks armed with guns. I myself was in the grip of the primitive emotions I'd kept at bay all my life: fear, hatred, a thirst for revenge, blood lust. Once they take hold of us, we feel as powerless as we would before a tidal wave. Like it, they spring from the ultimate depths; like it, they're unstoppable.

Retreating a few feet, I strove to pierce the gloom. I was crouching in a narrow defile between a tractor and some shelves filled with cans of lubricant. A little further away, the partition wall was obscured by a rampart of bales of hay. I made for this with the intention of hiding behind it, half crawling because I hadn't the strength to stand up. I'd just got there when I heard a whisper.

"Jérôme? Are you okay?"

I gave a start. It was Hirsch's voice. A moment later he was crouching beside me.

"I'm a bit the worse for wear, but that's all . . . Didn't he hit you?"

"No. The swine fired at random and zapped Pinetti. He's had it. Where's the rack?"

"What?"

He shook me. I emitted a stifled, involuntary yelp of pain.

"The gun rack! He said he'd taken his gun from a rack in the barn. There must be others."

"Hang on, we can't . . ."

"Sure we can! The man has a gun and he's used it. He's got nothing to lose, not now. We must save our necks, Jérôme!"

He left me and proceeded to search the barn. Gingerly as an invalid, I struggled to my feet at last. I was becoming inured to the pain – not the only thing I would have to get used to. I took a couple of slow, laborious steps towards the doorway and peered out into the yard. It was still deserted, but I could detect the beginnings of a commotion inside the hotel. The shot must have roused some of our esteemed colleagues.

Behind me, Hirsch uttered a cry of triumph.

"Hey, there are still two left! Here . . ."

He thrust something into my hands. It was a rifle complete with telescopic sight.

"There are the cartridges. It's self-service around here."

Oddly enough, he seemed to be enjoying himself. Some blood was trickling from his lower lip where Pinetti had hit him. I tried to calm him down.

"No, wait, this is crazy! We'll get out of here and explain things."

Kneeling beside me with a shotgun like Charriac's under his arm, he surveyed the edge of the woods.

"No, he's still out there, waiting for us. He'll have to kill us, it's his only hope."

"We could . . ."

"No, we couldn't," he cut in. "Pinetti took the charge in the chest, he can't be a pretty sight. The blood on my shirt isn't mine!"

Events had completely overtaken me for the first time. Charriac had lost his marbles and Hirsch was close to doing so. Anyone would have thought he liked playing soldiers.

"You'll see," he whispered.

He snatched up a can of oil and tossed it out into the courtyard. There was another detonation, and a puff of dust exploded quite some way from the spot where it landed.

"He's a rotten shot, but we can't take the risk."

Several minutes went by. I saw two shadowy figures steal across the narrow gap between the hotel and the trees. As if stupefied by what they had witnessed, the wind dropped and the rain ceased simultaneously.

Suddenly, a powerful, authoritative voice made itself heard:

"Jérôme, Hirsch, give yourselves up! It's no use!"

Del Rieco. Hirsch and I stared at each other, baffled, but we didn't have time to comment.

"Come out of that barn with your hands up!" Del Rieco called again. "You've nothing to gain by staying in there!"

Hirsch cupped his hands around his mouth, his outsize Adam's apple bobbing beneath them as usual.

"Where's Charriac?"

"Here with us. Everything's okay. Come out of there."

Hirsch tossed a second can of oil. This time, no one fired. He wiped his bleeding lip on the back of his hand.

"What shall we do?" he muttered.

I was still hesitating when Del Rieco, hidden among the trees, tried another tack.

"Pinetti isn't dead. You only wounded him."

Hirsch gave a start, shaking his head like a weary horse.

"What does he mean, *you* only wounded him?" he whispered in my ear. "It was Charriac who shot him, not us."

"Yes," I said, wincing with pain, "but they're getting Charriac's version of what happened. Hard luck, isn't it? It should be him in here and us out there with them."

"But listen, we've got witnesses. You, me, Pinetti – if he survives, that is . . ."

"Quite, but I wouldn't like to be in my insurance agent's shoes. My life expectancy must be rather limited."

He smiled at my little joke. Personally, I couldn't. The shooting pains in my cheek had spread to my jaw like a raging toothache. It was a very long time – not since my athletic youth – since someone had hit me. I'd completely forgotten how much it hurt. Perhaps my cheekbone had been fractured as well as my ribs.

The no-man's-land of the yard was small enough for us to communicate with ease. We had only to aim our words at the wall and they bounced off it before reaching the other party.

At the end of ten minutes, however, the situation had not progressed to any noticeable extent. Come out. No, you come over here. Del Rieco's tone of voice conveyed that he was losing patience. By now there must have been a dozen people with him: the edge of the wood was alive with excited whispers. The whole cast had assembled.

"Right," whispered Hirsch, "I've had enough. We can't stay here all night. I'm going to straighten things out."

"Don't be a fool!"

But he wouldn't listen. Using his hands as a megaphone, he called, "I'm coming out! Unarmed!"

"All right, out you come!" Del Rieco called back. He sounded relieved.

It all seemed very unwise to me. Del Rieco was probably a well-balanced, intelligent man, true, but he had been temporarily taken advantage of by a psychopath in the grip of murderous impulses, and that spelled danger.

I put out my hand to restrain Hirsch, only to withdraw it and clutch my aching chest. I would have to learn to gauge my movements more carefully. Hirsch put his gun on the ground and straightened up. Gingerly, I stretched out on my stomach in the traditional firing position and vainly prepared to cover him.

With resolute steps, like Gary Cooper in the final scene of a Western, he strode out into the yard. Halfway across he turned as if to say, "You see? It's quite safe."

That was when the contents of the cartridge hit him. To my horror, I saw him stagger backwards and collapse with blood spurting from his stomach. The report reached my ears a split second later.

I heard a woman scream, then Del Rieco's thunderous voice.

"No, Charriac!"

There was a second shot, followed by a sound like a hunted deer crashing through the undergrowth, and, after a moment's silence, a solitary sob. Hirsch was lying sprawled on his back in the middle of the courtyard. His hand twitched once and then lay still.

My head throbbed madly as I tried to think. Charriac had killed Hirsch or, at best, badly wounded him. Then there must have been a scuffle. Perhaps he had also fired at Del Rieco, or perhaps the gun had gone off when they tried to wrest it away from him. At all events, Del Rieco and the others now knew that the blame did not lie all at one door – if there was anyone left alive after this blood-bath. My feelings were those of someone who sees a centuries-old forest uprooted by a hurricane: a mixture of horror and incredulity.

Of course, Charriac could still concoct some vague excuse: that he thought Hirsch had turned to draw a gun, or some other explanation of the kind favoured by police marksmen in trouble, but his position had become much more uncomfortable.

Mine, to be honest, was little better. He was out there waiting for me, one way or another, and I was caught like a rat in a trap. If I tried to cross the yard, which was illuminated by the light beneath the eaves, I wouldn't stand a chance.

Illuminated . . . That gave me an idea. Squinting through my telescopic sight, I deliberately aimed at the light and fired. It was a sitting duck at fifty feet, and I hit it first time. Someone in the trees – Charriac, without a doubt – uttered a cry of rage and loosed off a shot that spattered the wall not far from my head. The yard was now shrouded in gloom.

I picked up poor Hirsch's gun, crouched down, and slowly counted to ten. Then I made a dash for it.

Charriac fired in the direction of the sound, but I wasn't there any longer. For some seconds, strangely enough, my nerves had ceased to transmit any sensation of pain, enabling me to run to the chalet and, from there, to hurl myself into the bushes beside it. One gun in each hand, I sat down on the ground – and suddenly doubled up in agony. My broken ribs were making me pay in arrears. Breathing with difficulty, I forced myself to remain motionless. Charriac was still somewhere out there with death at his fingertips.

Much later I heard a noise in the undergrowth far away to my right. Not long afterwards the pale beam of a flashlight pierced the darkness. It had started to rain again, fat, slow, solemn drops that refreshed me. The light went out, then came on again as if sending a message in Morse. Perhaps it was – I'd never been a Boy Scout. More probably, they were hoping I'd fire, so as to locate the source of the shot. I didn't budge. I was beginning to behave like a marine commando on operations: professionally, even though it wasn't exactly my usual speciality.

My silence must have convinced them that I'd fled into the woods, because they grew bolder. They weren't to know that I was partly disabled.

Delval was holding the flashlight, with Charriac following a few feet behind. I could see and hear them perfectly from where I was.

Delval shone his beam over the barn's interior.

"He's gone."

"Of course he's gone," Charriac growled. "Take a look at the gun rack."

"Empty!"

Charriac muttered an obscenity. He was still limping, as I saw when Delval turned and briefly illuminated him. None of us had been trained to withstand physical violence. It was one of the gaps in De Wavre's questionnaires.

I couldn't quite understand what Delval was doing there. He hadn't, like Pinetti, witnessed the sequence of events that had led to this situation, and he didn't seem perturbed by the turn things had taken – or by Charriac's alarming mental state. Charriac had probably told him some fairy tale in which I played the role of Bluebeard. He must have thought that I was the madman. This was worrying: no one is more resolute than a man convinced that right is on his side.

While Delval and Charriac were exploring the barn, I performed an encircling movement, half-walking, half-crawling. My chest was hurting less, my cheek more, but it didn't prevent me from covering the ground.

Having reached my destination, I noted with bitter irony that our positions were now reversed: Charriac and Delval were in the barn and I was outside, on the edge of the trees. I couldn't resist playing a little practical joke on Delval when he switched on his flashlight again: I fired over his head. I had no intention of wounding the poor man, but he dropped the light and dived back into the barn. I heard a cry of pain: he must have blundered into the tractor and given himself a nice bruise. A stupid thing to do – it wouldn't help to get him on my side – but you reach a stage when you don't weigh the consequences of your actions. Charriac swore.

I would have ten minutes' respite while they wondered if I was still lying in wait for them. Hirsch's inert body was visible in the beam of the flashlight, which had not gone out and was lying on the ground. The sight of his motionless figure gave me a lump in the throat.

As quickly as possible, I hobbled towards the track that led down to the lake. One glance at the landing stage showed me that the boat wasn't there. Either the boatman had gone home for the night, or someone had crossed the lake to notify the authorities, transport a wounded man ashore, or beat it in a panic – the reason mattered little. Del Rieco was my bet. He must have fled at top speed on some pretext or other, putting as much distance as possible between the massacre and his precious person.

My line of retreat cut off, I slunk towards the hotel. The rain, which was growing heavier, lashed my face. Thunder was rumbling somewhere behind the hills, and the sky was periodically lit by a pale glow.

The hotel seemed as peaceful as it had been the first day. I ventured a glance into the lobby, which was silent and deserted, then stole inside. The bar was in darkness, the foot of the stairs faintly illuminated. Stealthily, I made my way into the dining-room.

Laurence was there, kneeling beside Pinetti's motionless body. She looked up, wide-eyed, and shrank away in terror, almost losing her balance. I lowered my rifle and put a finger to my lips.

She straightened up and stared at me in silence. I could detect fear and disbelief in her eyes, but also – yes, no doubt about it – curiosity.

"You're not in any danger," I whispered. "You aren't my enemy."

Only two wall lights were on. I could hardly make out her features in this subdued, romantic restaurant lighting, but my eyes never left her face. I still didn't know if she represented a threat.

I pointed to Pinetti's supine form, which covered with a tartan rug.

"Is he . . ."

"No, a lot of pellets in the shoulder, but he needs to get to a hospital as soon as possible. He's losing a lot of blood."

"Charriac shot Hirsch."

"I know, I saw him, I was there. He said Hirsch was drawing a gun. Why did you do it?"

All at once, an immense weight seemed to descend on my shoulders. I put the two guns on a table and slumped down on a chair.

"I didn't do a thing, Laurence. It's too long a story . . . I never wanted this to happen . . ."

"But it did," she said. "Are you badly hurt?"

I very gently felt my cheek.

"Badly enough. I think my cheekbone's fractured, and I took a blow in the ribs."

"Where's Charriac?"

"I don't know. Still in the barn, maybe."

I was finding it hard to speak. Every movement of my jaw hurt the right-hand side of my face. I economized on words.

"You're insane," Laurence said. "Psychiatric cases. What possessed you to try to kill each other?"

"It was pre-programmed from the start," I said with an effort. "If people refuse to lose, these are the lengths they'll go to. And none of us could afford to lose."

"There are limits," she protested. "I didn't go to those lengths."

"No, there aren't any limits, not any more, you'll realize that some day. There haven't been any for a long time. Hey, don't make me talk so much."

"Let's have a look at you."

She felt my chest – I emitted some agonized moans – and presented her diagnosis: "Three broken ribs – possibly one or two cracked as well. Your intercostal cartilage isn't up to much, either."

"You're a doctor?"

"I used to be a nurse," she replied, tackling my face.

This time she evoked a genuine grunt of pain.

"Steady, it may not even be fractured, but talk about a bruise! Remember to present your left profile when they take your mug shot. The right-hand side of your face looks a real mess."

My mug shot . . . That was a million miles from my thoughts. Here on this wind-lashed island, institutions became abstractions. I shook myself.

"Where's Del Rieco?"

She gestured evasively. "No idea. He was going to his chalet, but he didn't dare, not with your civil war in progress."

"Pooh, a Saturday night brawl in the suburbs, that's all . . ."

I was trying to speak between my teeth without moving my lower jaw. As long as I took it slowly, it worked quite well. Perhaps I should have considered a career as a ventriloquist.

I thought I heard a noise outside. Charriac must still be out there, prowling around. I'd forgotten him for a moment.

I got up and retrieved my guns. I was terribly tired, but I'd already found that, once you've started something that has to be clinched as soon as possible, you get past the stage of feeling tired and know you'll go for broke whatever it costs. A look of fear reappeared on Laurence's face.

"What are you going to do now?"

"Settle my unfinished business with Charriac. Did you think I planned to bed down with my head between your breasts?"

Laurence smiled faintly. She had read it in my eyes, the temptation to sit there and give up, to exchange the storm and the bloodshed for a little tenderness.

"You could do worse," she said. "If you stopped this nonsense . . ."

I hadn't the right. I couldn't be the loser yet again, couldn't admit defeat, not now. Hesitantly, I put out my hand and stroked her neck.

"I can't, Laurence. It's between him and me now. Del Rieco is skulking in his mouse hole – there's no referee any more."

"Charriac's team are all on his side, you know. They think you're a monster, a psychopath out of a horror film. They've closed ranks."

"There aren't many of them left."

Almost tenderly, she laid her hand on mine.

"Jérôme, please stop this. Why not sneak off into the woods and wait for the police to arrive? I'll go with you if you like. I can't do anything for Pinetti in any case."

I almost nodded but stopped myself in the nick of time.

"Listen, Laurence, for 20 years I've said yes, amen, okay. They cut off my balls and I've just found them again. Let me be a man for another hour or two."

"Killing someone isn't the best way of being a man," she protested. "We've made a bit of progress since John Wayne. This is a civilized country, Jérôme. There are laws, courts, a police force, not just cowboys and Indians."

She would never understand what the world had become. Or had become once more. Or had never stopped being under a veneer of conventions, legal remedies, and notarized contracts: a fight for supremacy between primates. I gave up. I hadn't the time or the energy to explain this to her.

"Where's Mastroni?" I asked.

She spread her arms helplessly, two tears trembling on the tips of her lashes. Suddenly I heard footsteps in the lobby. Someone was coming. I gestured to Laurence to hide under a table and took cover with my back against the wall and my rifle aimed at the door.

The footsteps paused outside, then receded. It could be anyone. Not Charriac, though; he would have come in.

I relaxed and unglued my back from the wall. At that moment the door burst open, crashing against the wall just beside me, and a figure shot past at waist level. The man must have tiptoed back and got ready to launch himself. I almost fired, but I was hampered by the two gun barrels intersecting below my navel. No doubt about it: I had no natural gift for commando warfare.

By the time I'd levelled my rifle, the intruder had finished skidding across the floor on his belly and collided with a table leg. He got up, massaging his scalp with a comical look of mingled surprise and disgust. It was Mastroni.

He flopped down on a chair, still rubbing his head.

"Oh, it's you," he said. "You made it, then?"

"I did, yes. Hirsch didn't."

"I know, I know. I jumped on Charriac when he shot him, but it was too late. I nearly stopped one myself. Del Rieco was winged, I think. It was odd, he was behind me, but he went off holding his arm. A ricochet, perhaps."

Fine, now I had an explanation for the second shot.

"Where is he now?"

"Del Rieco? I don't know."

"No, Charriac."

"I don't know that either. He'll be looking for us. Got a plan?"

No. For the first time, I had no plan – other than forging straight ahead and gunning down anyone in my path. I handed the shotgun to Mastroni and kept the rifle with telescopic sights for myself. He took it, stroked the stock, and squinted along the twin barrels. I watched him in surprise: he seemed to be at home with a gun.

"This is more like it," he said. "I was feeling a bit naked. What happened, did he go bananas from one minute to the next?"

"Things turned sour, let's say. We've made the transition to a higher plane, a more direct confrontation. More direct and more overt."

"Yes," he said slowly, "you could put it that way. There comes a moment when things get out of hand. You know, like when you hit a patch of black ice. All at once you come unstuck, and if you haven't been trained you instinctively do the wrong thing: you steer into the skid, fail to recover, and hit a wall, right?"

I didn't reply. I had neither the time nor the inclination to discuss driving techniques. He nodded thoughtfully and went on:

"Maybe things started to go haywire right at the outset. Maybe we were simply driving too fast on black ice. Still, that's water under the bridge. What do we do now?"

"What anyone does when attacked: we defend ourselves. Got a better idea?"

Laurence had been listening apprehensively. "Listen," she broke in, "stop this. You think they're crazy and they're planning to kill you, they think you're crazy and you're planning to kill them. There must be some scope for negotiation, mustn't there?"

"That's how all wars start, my dear," Mastroni said paternally. "It's too late to go back once the blood starts flowing. We don't trust anyone any more, get it?"

I suppressed a smile. Too right we didn't trust anyone. To be honest, we never had. Mastroni's solid, serene presence was a comfort to me. Strangely enough, my injuries weren't hurting as much.

Laurence made a last attempt to restrain us. "Stay here. Barricade the doors and wait for daylight. The police will turn up sooner or later."

I swallowed a couple of times and sniffed. What with the rain and everything, I must have caught a cold on top of everything else.

"Oh, the police," I said slowly. "They'll simply fire first and ask questions afterwards. As for due process, I'm like most people in this country: I've no faith in our legal system. No, I'm going to wipe the slate clean. Then there'll only be one version: mine. Charriac has the same idea. He can't afford to let me live, he's got to silence me – it's his sole objective. He's a logical being, which means he's predictable."

Laurence was growing more and more agitated. "Alternatively," she said, "we could take the boat and go ashore. We'd be safe there."

"There isn't any boat. It's gone."

"I don't know what you're afraid of," she groaned. "There are witnesses: you two, me, Del Rieco . . . He can't kill us all!"

"He's already killed or wounded two people – he won't stop at that. I can't let Charriac bamboozle a judge. He's a lawyer, a good one. What do you expect us to do? Get bogged down in endless hearings and land ourselves with a year on remand while Charriac and his lawyers pull the code of procedure to pieces and hoodwink the judges? And then get sent down for five years, reduced to two with remission? And after that look for a job with a prison record? You're joking! Del Rieco has bolted. He can notify the police all he likes, you think that'll worry Charriac? Anyway, that's not the issue any more. Our necks are at stake now."

I'd said enough. I turned to Mastroni, thinking as I spoke.

"We must hold the lobby. Strategy isn't my forte, but if we bar the entrance we can cover the upper floors and the exterior at the same time. One of us . . ."

Laurence clung to my sleeve in a last, silent entreaty. I gently removed her hand and went on: "One of us will take up his position there and prevent anyone from getting past, the other will search the upper floors. Once we've secured the place, we'll see about the exterior."

"Sir, yessir!" cried Mastroni, snapping to attention and tucking his chin in like a US Marine.

He was only half joking. Like Hirsch, he seemed to be acquiring a taste for the situation.

"At ease, soldier. You, Laurence, will remain here. Your only job will be to set up a field hospital – a far more worthwhile occupation than your fish-hooks, I'm sure. Any wounded will be brought to you for first aid."

She gave up and resumed her place on the floor beside Pinetti.

"What's going on upstairs?" I asked Mastroni.

"They're closeted in their rooms, I think. I didn't see a soul when I came downstairs. They were all there one moment and gone the next. It's the same with birds. You start taking potshots, and suddenly there isn't another one to be seen. Our friends must be hiding under the covers, hoping the storm will blow over."

"What about the kitchen? Someone could get in from the rear of the building, couldn't they?"

"Yes," said Charriac, "they could."

He had crept in behind us by way of the service door. I'd seen the waiter use it a dozen times, of course, but because we never used it ourselves I'd overlooked it until too late. In my mind's eye, there was only one access to the dining-room. I momentarily cursed my lack of attention.

Charriac was aiming his gun at a point midway between me and Mastroni (a trifle more at me, perhaps). His glasses were askew and he'd lost his tie. His suit was crumpled and torn at the shoulder. Delval was standing warily behind him, poised to dive back into the kitchen at the slightest sign of danger.

Charriac was smiling. That was, without doubt, the most alarming aspect of the situation. Clothes apart, he seemed perfectly normal, just the way we'd always known him: alert, self-assured, faintly contemptuous.

"Greetings, all. Put down those guns like good boys, and no one will get hurt."

Laurence buried her face in her hands and started to sob. Personally, I felt more inclined to laugh at this scene from a cheap thriller. I wasn't scared in the least, strangely enough. I had the impression that the game was continuing – that a paintball would spatter my jacket at any moment.

"How about putting your own gun down?" I said. "It's two against one."

"Quite so, but I'd get at least one of you. The question is: which? Or I might get you both, who knows?"

Delval, scenting trouble, had prudently beat a retreat. Charriac gestured with the muzzle of his gun.

"Move, either of you, and I'll fire. Come on, we can't spend all night here. Carceville, you really are as stubborn as a mule. Why won't you admit you've lost? I never meant to hurt anyone, but they raised the stakes a little too high. Now, how do we get out of this impasse?"

If he launched into one of his long, didactic monologues, he might possibly lower his guard. I had to get him to talk, watching his eyes the whole time.

"Do you have a suggestion?" I asked.

Laurence ruined everything. Glimpsing the possibility of an armistice, she rose to her feet and started to say something I failed to catch.

Mastroni fired, Charriac too. I dived beneath a table. Seizing it by the legs, I tipped it on its side with a crash and cowered down behind it.

Several seconds went by. Contrary to what one reads in novels, they didn't seem an eternity but passed in a flash. A dense silence descended. The air smelt of powder, tangy and sulphurous. Very cautiously, I risked a look.

Mastroni was lying on the floor not far from Pinetti with Laurence stretched out beside him. There was no sign of Charriac. All that remained of him was a wisp of gunsmoke near the door.

I ducked under a table leg and emerged from my bunker. The movement must have snapped one of my cracked ribs, because the pain transfixed my entire chest. Half crawling, still clutching my rifle, I approached the two motionless forms.

Mastroni had been hit. He looked up at me with a pallid smile on his face.

"Buckshot," he mumbled. "The bastard loaded with buckshot. I took some in the leg. It could be worse, take care of the lady."

Little bloodstains were blossoming, one after another, on the expanse of riddled trouser leg between his ankle and his knee.

Still half kneeling, I turned to look at Laurence. If she had received the bulk of the charge she should be dead. But she opened her eyes, her face only inches from mine.

"All right?" I asked softly.

Her eyelashes fluttered. There wasn't a sign of a wound anywhere on her body.

"I was scared," she said. Then she started crying again.

I tapped her arm. "See what you can do for Mastroni," I told her.

He put out a hand towards us. "It's odd," he said in a puzzled voice, "I can hardly feel a thing, but I think it rules me out of the hundred metres. He was drawing a bead on you. I saw he was going to fire so I got in first. It must have deflected his aim, and I caught it instead. That'll teach me to save your life, won't it? Still, I think I hit him too."

He smiled bravely. I didn't. Anger surged over me. Hirsch, Pinetti, Mastroni . . . And for what? For some shitty job, 50 hours a week and 200,000 francs a month? I was almost as furious with Del Rieco, who had brought us to this pass. My temples throbbed, my blood pressure had to be at least 180. Somewhere deep inside me, a safety device must have given way. My one remaining idea was to finish the bastard off.

Heedless of the shooting pains that transfixed my chest, I made for the door to the kitchen. There were traces of blood on the tiled floor. I looked back at Mastroni and gave him the thumbs-up.

"Congratulations, you were right. You hit him!"

He smiled again, the strange rictus of someone seriously hurt. "It was par for the course. I'm a good shot, I couldn't have missed him at that range."

He broke off and bit his lip. He'd got over the initial shock, which has an anaesthetic effect, and the pain was breaking through. The balance sheet was really starting to add up: Hirsch dead or almost, Mastroni wounded, and, on the other side, Pinetti – and all to no one's benefit. Mastroni was lolling against Laurence's thigh like a big baby nestling against its mother. I gave him a final wave of encouragement and set off after Charriac.

I didn't have to be an Apache to track him down. All I had to do was follow the little drops of blood. Sooner or later he would notice he was leaving a trail, but by then I should be near enough. I was hurt, but so was he. We were on equal terms at last: strength and cunning versus strength and cunning.

I crossed a kitchen gleaming with cleanliness, then a larder filled with canned food. Two enormous cheeses reposed on a small table, and three cloth-wrapped hams hung from the ceiling above a capacious deep-freeze. The kitchen facilities were such as to reassure me about the quality of the food we'd been eating, but that was hardly my current concern.

To the left of the kitchen was a back door, open. Charriac had used it to enter the hotel and leave it again in a hurry. He might also be waiting for me just outside. I had left the shotgun with Mastroni, but the rifle was good enough. I got down on my stomach and risked a peep round the doorpost. A man lying in ambush aims his gun at chest level; he gets a big surprise if his prospective victim shows up six inches from the floor – I'd at least retained that much from the TV movies we were busy imitating.

But there was no one there. Dawn had broken, grey and dismal.

The rain seemed to have stopped, but dun-coloured clouds were lingering in the sky. I stood up, still half hidden by the doorpost. Facing me was a sort of passage, a miniature concrete canyon flanked by the larder wall and another, lower building without any windows. I quickly made my way along it, paused for a moment when it turned a bend, and repeated my TV trick.

All I could see was forest. As in the yard outside the barn, the branches of the first tree almost touched the wall. I scrutinized the ground, which was covered with brownish needles, but couldn't detect any spots of blood.

Charriac must have left by that route, there was no other way. He had either retired to the woods to lick his wounds, or, if not badly hurt, circled the hotel and made for the main entrance. What would I have done in his place? A moment's thought convinced me that, if he was inspired by the same malign urge to finish the job as I was, he would have chosen the second alternative.

Cautiously, I followed his likely route. The west side of the hotel was still in shadow. Hugging the wall, I stole along it. The scent of blood had filled me with a novel emotion, a keen excitement that set me trembling but robbed me of none of my lucidity. It was as if all my senses had become more acute. I had experienced something similar in the past when doing something reckless or subjected to a surprise attack – the rush of adrenaline, that chemical, secreted by the body itself, which renders life interesting – but in a far milder, more restrained form devoid of the savagery that now inhabited me.

I was halfway there when a shot rang out inside the building. I gave a jump. Charriac must have made much faster progress than I'd foreseen. I broke into a run.

I had almost reached the hotel entrance when I tripped and fell heavily. Just as I was scrambling to my feet, Laurence's panic-stricken figure shot out of the door.

I found the strength to grab her by the arm and drag her into the lee of one of the two troughs of alpine flowers that flanked the steps.

"Where is he?" I asked her eagerly.

She didn't reply. Her chin was trembling. Heedless of my broken ribs, she buried her face in my shirt.

Above us, a shot shattered the window and a tongue of flame briefly licked the sky. Fragments of glass rained down on us. Grabbing Laurence by the neck, I withdrew in disarray to the shelter of a fir tree and shoved her hard in the back. I still didn't grasp what was happening.

Laurence had ended up a few feet away. I joined her under cover, rifle at the ready. All at once I wondered if there were any rounds left in the magazine. Silly of me, but I hadn't had a chance to check. With some difficulty, I extracted the ammunition container from my pocket. It was an old round tin designed to hold cough pastilles, and it refused to open. I wrestled with it in a fury.

"It was Brigitte," sobbed Laurence.

"What about her?" I frowned. Brigitte was all we needed.

"She came to help me with the wounded, then Delval showed up. I don't know exactly what happened, but she picked up Mastroni's gun and fired at him. She was angry for Mastroni's sake."

I was flabbergasted. Even Brigitte Aubert had joined in this orgy of violence. The entire universe was subsiding into dementia.

Another tongue of flame flickered behind the window, hesitantly at first. Then it seized hold of the curtain and turned it into a blazing torch. The dining-room was on fire.

"Did she start that?"

"No. I don't know, I mean. It's quite possible, she's always been nuts. Oh, my God, the wounded!"

Distress revived her. She jumped up and blundered back into the hotel before I could lift a finger to stop her. Just then the tin deigned to open, scattering the cartridges on the ground. Laboriously, I picked them up one by one. I still wasn't up to scratch; Robocop had nothing to worry about.

My only memory of the following few seconds is one of total chaos. Everyone inside the hotel was shouting. I saw Laurence back out on to the terrace and down the steps, towing Pinetti by the legs. His head bounced on every step, which couldn't have done him much good. I heard El Fatawi calling for water and watched Natalie, De Wavre's only remaining representative, help Laurence to extricate Mastroni from the inferno and lay him down at the top of the track leading to the lake. Chalamont came tottering out in his pyjamas, dazedly scratching his buttocks. He had clearly just woken up and must have thought he was dreaming. I not only sympathized, I envied him.

I, too, could have gone to help, but I thought it better to lie low. The chief architect of the massacre must still be somewhere in the vicinity, trigger finger itching. I couldn't see him or Delval in the milling throng, still less Del Rieco, who must genuinely have high-tailed it for safety.

At long last, Brigitte Aubert appeared in the doorway. Her soot-smudged, smoke-enshrouded figure seemed to emerge from a pall of fog. She stood there very erect, Mastroni's shotgun ready to hand at her side, like a character in the final scene of a Western – Calamity Jane, perhaps. A pity Del Rieco wasn't there to see what she was really made of; he would have found it edifying. I could justly feel proud of my team. They had stuck with me to the bitter end, implicitly and unquestioningly, just like Charriac's associates. That's how you recognize a leader: by his followers' refusal to desert him. This may have been what De Wavre had wanted to discover all along.

Moving with lithe deliberation, Brigitte stepped over the supine bodies of the wounded. Calm, almost amused, she suddenly looked –

I can find no other words to describe it – radiantly beautiful. Without exposing myself too much, I called her name. Her face hardened. She levelled her gun, then caught sight of me. A moment later she was crouching at my side. All that betrayed her tension was a muscle twitching in her cheek.

"What happened?" I asked.

"Oh, I heard shots and went to look. Laurence put me in the picture. Poor old Mastroni tried to convince us he wasn't in any pain. He's badly hurt, you know. That really bugged me. Then Delval appeared. I didn't stop to think, I picked up Mastroni's gun and fired at him. Delval, Charriac, they're each as bad as the other. Simple justice, no? Besides, he might have been armed, how was I to know? I think I missed him, more's the pity."

Her tone was quite businesslike. She might have been describing the most commonplace course of events in the world.

"And the fire?"

The dining-room was a sea of roaring flames. Having consumed the curtains and upholstery, the fire was now marking time. Solid wood burns slowly and less easily than one would suspect, and the blaze did not seem to be spreading. A modern, plastic-sheathed hotel would already have gone up in smoke.

Brigitte shrugged. "No idea. Could have been accidental or deliberate, your guess is as good as mine."

"I must get Charriac," I whispered. "This madness will never stop while he's still alive."

She looked at me out of the corner of her eye.

"And I'd like to get Delval. After what they've done to us, it's a matter of principle. But there are plenty of Charriacs and Delvals in this world – it'll be hard to make a clean sweep of them. Hey, are you hurt too?"

Having been on my left till now, she hadn't had the pleasure of seeing my battered right profile. She laid an exploratory finger on my cheekbone.

"Ouch, don't do that, it hurts!"

"I can imagine," she said with a mixture of amusement and sympathy, like a mother addressing a child with a grazed knee.

Suddenly she froze and pointed down the hill.

"Charriac! Down there beside the lake!"

She was right: Charriac was making his way along the water's edge to the path I'd explored with Laurence. He was limping badly. Brigitte raised her gun. With an abrupt gesture, I thrust the barrel aside.

"No!"

She gave me a puzzled stare. "No? You disapprove of shooting murderers in the back?"

"You don't know much about shotguns, Brigitte. He's well out of range. Apart from that, he's mine."

"All right, go after him, you're the boss," she said, looking me in the eye. "Finish him off."

Would things have been different if she hadn't challenged me, if I hadn't been afraid of losing face in her presence? I don't think so. We'd all gone too far by now. In any case, I'd said it myself: Charriac was mine. I'd earned him. A duel to the death between leaders: that was the only possible ending.

I struggled to my feet with the aid of the tree. Brigitte remained where she was, propped on one knee with the shotgun across her thigh.

"I'll wait for Delval," she went on. "I've never liked him. If he's unlucky enough to come my way again . . . Hey, Carceville?"

"Yes?"

She bared her uneven teeth in a smile.

"Some seminar, wasn't it? If they don't find us a job after this . . ."

I smiled back with one corner of my mouth only – the left one.

"Yes, with Soldiers of Fortune, for instance. It's a good firm. Mercenaries are never out of work. We could always try . . ."

Brigitte's chuckle turned into a cough. She must have inhaled some smoke. Well, she'd asked for it. It wouldn't have been fair if she'd been the only one to emerge unscathed.

When I passed Laurence she neither turned her head nor tried to restrain me.

I got Charriac in the end. He's lying beside me, as dead as can be. He was crossing the clearing when I overhauled him. I'd made up ground on the ascent. You can climb a hill faster with broken ribs than a game leg.

I called his name. He turned and I fired. He could have fired too, but he didn't. I think he found it hard to see me: I was still on the edge of the trees and coming from the east with the sun behind me. He'd also lost his glasses. It was a fair fight for all that. He had his chance.

He toppled over backwards. I'm sitting beside him now, waiting. Although he's still warm, bluebottles are already buzzing around his open mouth.

Not long afterwards I heard the motorboat, then the distant shouts of policemen – or firemen. All is quiet at present. They brought the fire under control, I assume: the roof of the hotel, just visible through the trees below me, looks quite intact. They would certainly have ferried the wounded ashore first. I hope no one's dead – apart from Charriac. And I'd be sad if Hirsch had bought it. I liked him a lot.

I don't know if Brigitte got Delval. That's her problem. I hope, for her sake, that she managed to solve it. Satisfactions of that kind are rare.

I haven't given any thought to what is going to happen now. I could lay down my arms and meekly return to the lakeside, to civilization, to the world of international conglomerates, of muted but no less murderous competition – to the place where people kill symbolically and subject one another to every form of maltreatment short of physical violence.

I could, yes ... But maybe I won't. I don't envy the job of the examining magistrate they appoint. He's going to have to sort the murderers from their victims – a very tricky job these days. Unless, of course, we all plead insanity. But how to plead insanity in a world gone mad? We simply plumbed the uttermost depths of what lay inside us. Just as Del Rieco intended.

His goose is cooked. I don't think De Wavre International will withstand the banner headlines. I briefly toyed with the idea of killing him too – he was in charge, after all – but I don't know where he is. It would be pointless in any case. Whether or not he knows it yet, he's dead. Now it'll be his turn to sample closed doors, prospective employers who are always in conference when he calls them, frigid secretaries, restive creditors, sleepless nights, and the sympathetic but weary gaze of his nearest and dearest. The worst of punishments: an unending ordeal.

Not me, though. Never again. I still have a few rounds left. I could always circle the island and wade across the narrows in the north – the water can't be very deep – but my chest hurts so much, I don't know if I'd make it. What lies beyond? More miles of forest and mountain, and then the Italian frontier? But there are no frontiers these days. No frontiers, no places of refuge anywhere. The world is full of Charriacs and Del Riecos, people who want to know how much money you can make them and if you've got the right stuff inside you. Charriac now knows what he's got inside him: a bullet.

I'm genuinely glad I killed him. Even if it's futile – even if it'll take other people, lots of them, to finish the job.

I try to think back on all I've been through since the first day, but it's pointless. I made no mistake, not one. Things couldn't have turned out any other way. Now they'll come with their policemen, their magistrates, their journalists, and talk to me about my responsibility. What responsibility? My eyes smart in the light of the rising sun, my limbs are pervaded by a feeling of infinite lassitude. What could I tell them? That I never had a choice? That we're too much alike for them to judge me? I've nothing left that could inspire fear, the only thing they respect. I'd only make them laugh, and I doubt if I could endure that.

The motionless fir trees seem to be looking at me. I return their gaze. If I stay here for long enough without moving, like them, perhaps I'll turn to stone. A dialogue between vegetable and mineral – why not, when there's nothing human left?

But they won't give me time. The motorboat is coming back, I can hear its low hum reflected by the surface of the lake. I must make up my mind.